THE FINAL SUMMONS

THE NEW ENGLAND SPECULATIVE WRITERS

NE
S
W

CONTENTS

ISBN-13: **978-0-9600027-0-2**

ACKNOWLEDGEMENTS

Special Thanks our Kickstarter Supporters

Eric Mulder, Seth Holmes, Miranda Dal Zovo, Malinda Gibson, Susan Flagg, Phyllis Lowry, Sandra Budiansky, Nancy Tice, Derek Devereaux Smith, Sinead Walsh, Katrina Coll, Jenyfer Conaway, SZimmerman, Jenise Aminoff, Dustin Bragga, Denis LaFortune, Robert Isaacson, Scott Chisholm, Jacob W. Wall, Leland Morrison, Ken F Grant-author-The Wanderer, Justin Bell, Dana Cameron, Jaime M Garmendia III, Jon Pickering, Jorden K, Allosteric Grey, Haus, Dan Keohane, The Brown Family, Emma J. Gibbon, Kevin Cartwright, Mesona, Franny Jay, Brian D Lambert, Anders Cahill, AndrewO, in San Jose, Calif, Troy Osgood, A.J. Bohne

brief time each week on TV or within the cream pages of the latest pulp novels.

Today, we have the benefit of a connected world, something that was only tickling the outside all those years ago. Talent isn't constrained by a small group of publishers and the gatekeepers they employed to find the diamonds in the rough, but open for anyone who can spin a tale. We police ourselves in writing better stories and bringing them into the light of day. We cater to the readers and readers alone.

There was a time when we wrote, but didn't share our stories. We wanted validation without the risk of rejection. We have slipped those surly bonds and taken flight by giving these stories life! Right here, right now, a small group of authors have gotten together and shown what they are made of, that they stand side by side with those who have gone before.

Writing is as easy and as hard as stringing words together, one sentence after another until the tale is told. The masters weave the narrative into three dimensions, giving the characters depth, hooking us into the story, making us care.

And we do, shedding real tears and feeling empty after the story is told. The real world calls us back and our minds rebel.

Until the next story, the next champion, and the next vibrant world.

Fourteen talented authors have joined forces to bring you a collection of stories wrapped neatly within The Final Summons. Read on and lose yourselves, if only for a short while.

Peace, fellow humans.

Craig Martelle

FOREWORD

Good morning (or afternoon, or gleiblight or whatever your time measurement)!

Speculative fiction, science fiction, fantasy, and so much more are rooted in our desire to visit other places. Some are scary, some are hopeful. Some pull you in so fast you don't realize you've read the whole thing in one sitting.

All are unique. And they give us a chance to explore whole new worlds filled with exciting people and do things we wouldn't normally do. Unless you're a fae, or an alien attack bot, then maybe you will have been there before.

And done some of that. Maybe not.

The stories speak to us in ways that real life cannot on a palette limited only by the boundaries of our own imaginations.

Science fiction is my favorite. I was introduced to it at an early age and have been reading ever since. I was a child of the sixties, enjoying new Andre Norton stories when they were first published. I also watched the groundbreaking science fiction television series, Star Trek with each new episode. Such incredible tales in a time of national turmoil. But we could escape to fantastic places for that

1

THE MERITS OF THE CASE

CHRIS PHILBROOK

Part One: Why We're Here

"These rotations to off-world courthouses make what's left of my skin itch," Judge Emerson said to the security robot that escorted him down the space station's curving passageway toward his courtroom. "Though the low gravity sure helps my leg. And the air is fresher. Not any problem you have, eh?"

"No, sir," the mechanical bailiff replied with its voice-box synthesizer.

"They can put a colony on Mars and breach holes into parallel universes, but they can't give robots a decent, human sounding voice. Well...can't or won't? You know, when I fought in the first portal wars, we didn't have robots as advanced as you," the judge said as he switched his cane to his left hand—the prosthetic one. "Sure would've made fighting those goddamn ogres in Mississippi easier. And the elves...sneaky bastards."

"Yes, sir."

"Anti-magic shielding nearby might've saved these," he added, kicking his left leg and hand out. The metallic limbs didn't shine in the lights above. His augmentations weren't meant to be pretty. The federal governments didn't cover "pretty." "They been sitting long enough, you reckon?"

The robot paused at one of the doors in the ring and allowed the judge to come around. When the automaton seemed satisfied, a tiny pip of light blinked on its otherwise smooth faceplate, and the airlock door hissed open.

"Why do you suppose they put a badge on your chest?" Judge Emerson asked and walked into his chambers.

Two suit-wearing humans sat in the firm leather chairs in front of his obelisk of a wooden desk. Each wore a magic-jamming pin on their lapel. As he approached, they stood out of respect, and a tiny green light flashed on the strange metallic symbols they wore. He was safe.

"Thank you for responding to my curious summons, counselors," Judge Emerson grunted. "Sit, please."

"This better be good, Your Honor," replied the pale, taller, older lawyer.

"My pleasure," said the darker, shorter, younger lawyer. She tried not to stare at his replacement limbs and the augmented eye, but the judge could feel her gaze.

"You know what I like best about you, Thomas?" Judge Emerson asked the surly lawyer.

"I do not."

"Nothing. I don't like a goddamn thing about you. And maybe that's why you're a good prosecutor," the judge said to him. The three humans shared a chuckle as the robot stood idle in the corner where two walls covered in Earth-wood shelves, filled with a thousand books, met. The threatening machine didn't share in the laugh.

"Is this about tomorrow's case?" the defense attorney asked him.

"It is, isn't it? One more elf on trial deserves an in-chambers meeting?" Thomas quipped.

"Up here in space, we don't pay attention to the news like we might if we were back down on terra firma," the judge replied. "But after digging through some news, and some incarceration databases, I have discovered that we are discussing the fate of the last elf in human custody."

"Say what?" the younger woman asked. "If that's the truth, why isn't this space station crawling with journalists?"

The judge shrugged.

"So what's your point, Your Honor?" Thomas asked.

"I wanted to discuss the merits of this case prior to the kangaroo court we're going to hold tomorrow."

"I applaud your willingness to think outside the box," the Harriet said. "It's about time a judge took a moral stand in this genocide."

"Why are we even talking about this? You've sent a hundred elves to the airlock in these trials, Your Honor. Why you; why now? If anything but a death sentence happens in this," Thomas added with an inclined head, "it'll trigger an immediate appeal, and some other judge will sign off. The best you'll do is delay the inevitable. An elf is an elf is an elf. We don't even bury them on Earth anymore. Too many goddamn trees kept growing where they were buried."

"I didn't say my mind was made, Thomas. I shouldn't have to remind you that I fought against elves before I started presiding over their execution trials. Killed a whole lot of them during the reservation wars when I had two real hands to do it with. And thank you, Harriet. I pride myself on being a thinking man, when I'm able to think."

"So. We've moved the kangaroo court proceedings from the courtroom to chambers?" Thomas asked. "This crisis of confidence is a joke." The prosecutor snickered and looked out the porthole window as the immense, almost flat green and blue orb of Earth appeared. The window happened to show a peninsula of land that had been scorched smooth from nuclear bombs during the wars. Removing the worst monsters that pierced the portals took the worst weapons mankind had and left scars that would remain for all time.

"Call it what you will. Now I've asked you both to bring your briefcases or tablets or whatever gadgets—high tech or mundane—you're choosing to be professional with. Let's get them out, and start talking about the last elf in human custody."

The lawyers did as Judge Emerson said.

Part Two: The Merits of the Case

Harriet started. "Q'Lothien Andurel, best guess as age 33. Claims to be 278 years in his native dimension. Male elf. Brown hair, violet eyes, stands five feet, six inches. No tattoos or scars."

"Do we know where he breached?" Judge Emerson asked.

"He testified that his parents brought him through a portal somewhere in the American Midwest. Investigators didn't put a lot of effort into it, but the best guess is the Oklahoma portal right before we shut the collider down and started to lock the portals it poked in the universe off."

"Thank God for that," Thomas said with a cluck of his tongue.

"I don't think anyone would argue that shutting the portals and keeping the nightmares from the other side and the aggressive demi-humans out was a bad thing, Tommy," Harriet said after she rolled her eyes. "But it's what we're doing now with the people who came through and are stuck that defines us."

"No arguing, children," the judge said. "Merits of the case."

"Dammit, Judge," Thomas said, "the merits are this: He's an elf. An illegal inter-dimensional alien. End of story. Put him in the airlock and hit the switches."

"So no more trees grow?"

"Bingo," Thomas said.

"You're a bloodthirsty one, eh?" Harriet muttered.

"Look, I have nothing against elves or dwarves or orcs or ogres or anything that's from the other dimension," he said, leaning forward in his chair at her. "Barring manticores, and other things with too many limbs, but they don't belong here. Their magic doesn't belong here. They've screwed up our world for going-on forty years now. Time they get going back to the fairytale they came from."

"Does Mr. Andurel have any connections to our dimension?" Judge Emerson asked Harriet as he lifted his pipe with his manufactured hand. "Roots? Criminal record?"

"I don't like it when people smoke," Harriet said.

"I don't like it when counselors presume to persuade me from smoking this pipe. My chambers, my case, my rules."

"Right. Okay, um…." She checked her notes. "According to his own testimony, he traveled in the wilderness with family like elves tend to. Lived on the fringes. Parents worked as trappers and hunted in Canada for years. Did odd jobs for cash. There are three different police reports from about twenty years ago related to his parents helping hunt down some portal-hopping monsters in Washington State. Near the internment camps."

"Folk hero stuff?" the judge asked her and lit the now-packed pipe. He drew from it and exhaled. At least his lungs were still real. "Tug at the heartstrings stuff?"

"Basically," she said. "They helped the locals uproot some nasties and wound up getting ICE called in on them. Some people, man."

"You know, to a lot of folks, elves are just as scary as orcs," Thomas said. "Elves have a lengthy history of robbery, assault, murder, the list goes on and on."

"Not all elves are bad. Not all orcs are bad. Not all blacks were bad. Not all North Koreans were bad," Harriet said. "We have to judge people based on their individual merit, not the class of being they happened to have been born into."

"People," Thomas said with a wry smile.

"Does he have any criminal record?" the judge asked.

"Irrelevant, Judge," Thomas asked. "This trial isn't being conducted on the merits of any law beyond the Cross-Dimensional Being Act. I'll paraphrase it: Any person or persons born in a dimension not of our own has no right to life in this dimension and, henceforth, is declared as a threat to international security, to be removed at first opportunity that origin can be confirmed via due process. He's an elf; he gets airlocked."

"And all the passing of the act did was slow down the genocide," Harriet said. "Make it state-sponsored."

"Well we couldn't build a wall to protect us from the ones that already got through, could we?" Thomas offered. "We shut the portals down, but too many were already here. Already amongst the human populace."

"I'll ask again; does he have a criminal record?" the judge repeated. "Thomas?"

The prosecutor broke eye contact with the defense attorney and looked the judge in his human eye. He shook his head no, and the judge nodded in thanks.

"Your Honor, he has a family," Harriet added.

Thomas started to say something, but the judge stopped him.

"If you say irrelevant again, Thomas, I'll find you in contempt, and have my bailiff put you in an airlock. Remind me again how many elves I've sent to the stars over my career. Continue, Harriet."

"Married to a human woman, age twenty nine. Sarah Andurel.

Two children. Aidan and Kintarr. No criminal record, college educated."

"Half-elven kids?" the judge asked.

"Yeah. I have pictures." Harriet lifted her tablet and offered it to the smoking judge.

"You swipe. The Army didn't see fit to give me fingers on this hand that work on touch screens."

She held the tablet up, and as Thomas looked to the small circular window that now opened into the vast blackness of deep space, the judge looked at two bright eyed, beautiful children.

"Five, and nine," Harriet said.

"Handsome boys. Anytime they get both genes they are something to look at. Anything to indicate he's a bad father?"

"Nothing."

"Gainfully employed?"

"As much as an elf can be. He couldn't attend anything beyond public education as able, so he learned a trade via apprenticeship."

"Let me guess," Thomas started, "he played the mandolin on Broadway. Or worked in a greenhouse. Or at a petting zoo."

"No…" Harriet answered. "He worked with tile. Did breathtaking floors. Mosaics. Made his own tiles in a kiln, and working elven wood he grew on his wife's family farm in Oregon. Some of his stuff is museum quality."

"A craftsman. That's quite fine. Did he pay his taxes?" The judge asked her.

"No, in fact, he didn't." Thomas sat forward again, clutching a manila folder like it was a holy icon of his church. "Didn't pay a dime or an elven piece of gold. He owes big."

"Because he can't work legally," Harriet said. "Can we talk about how he donated money to several local charities? How he went to a black market chop-shop in the Detroit under hive to get his ears trimmed to try and blend in? How he worked part time as a paramedic?"

"Paramedic?" Judge Emerson asked. "I didn't see that. He's medically trained how?"

"Elven magic and herbalism. I have signed affidavits from his coworkers at the ambulance company saying he was exemplary."

"Now he's a hero." Thomas sighed. "And can we just talk about how there's no clause in the CDBA for conduct? For anything? Any entity from the other side of a portal is fruits of the poisonous tree. An infectious disease that has to be burned from the Earth. We've seen what they do when they're left here, unchecked."

"Make beautiful kids? Lay tile?" Harriet offered. "Most of the people our government is running down are refugees from the wars on the other side. People who refuse to live in the internments camps. Do I need to remind you that their entire world has been subjugated by demi-human alliances? Genuine genocide? Here is the only place they have for a chance at a decent life."

"No, here is not," Thomas said with sadness. "They don't belong here, and we risk losing our own reality because they've left theirs."

Part Three: To Airlock, or Not to Airlock?

"When you say, 'losing our reality,' Thomas, what do you mean?" Judge Emerson asked. "Like, 'Losing My Religion?'"

"We're giving up our way of life," Thomas said, risking a slip of frustration. "We're losing jobs to elves and dwarves; we're fighting more wars against races and species that shouldn't even be here. We had enough trouble with the Middle East and Southeast Asia before the portals opened. Now we're fighting against the Icewind Troll nation in Siberia, and the goblin hordes in Argentina. Baja California is goddamn wasteland. Ten more wildfires threaten to burn out of control at any given moment. Do you know how fast goblins can make babies?"

"I do, in fact. I fought in Buenos Aires. I saw it firsthand," the judge said and puffed his pipe. He chuckled and held up his prosthetic. "Firsthand."

"Then you know what we stand to lose." The lawyer pointed at the judge's good limb.

"How does it make sense to execute elves and pixies and all the other people that aren't expansionistic? If you have cancer of the toe, you don't start fixing it by chopping off the whole leg," Harriet said.

"Cancer isn't an issue anymore," Thomas said.

"Boy, you're right about that. Elven magic mixed with human pharmaceutical knowledge cured it," Harriet snapped. "But that's irrelevant, isn't it?"

"I'll have you be civil." Judge Emerson tilted away from his desk in his high-backed leather chair and exhaled a thick cloud of tobacco smoke. He looked at the pipe with something approaching love. Harriet coughed. "I summoned you both here to discuss the merits of the case."

"Again, Your Honor, no merits need to be discussed. The defendant's genetic identity has been proven beyond the shadow of a doubt, and that's all we require. He's an elf. End of story. Tomorrow isn't a trial. It's a legal proceeding to satisfy our collective consciences," Thomas said.

"Funny word, that. Conscience." Judge Emerson exhaled another thick plume of tobacco smoke. He coughed. "I almost thought I had one, once. Kinda forgot about it for a time. Did my job. Starting to remember it again lately."

"Sir, please," Thomas said. "The last elf in human custody. This is historic. You'll be the judge that shut the door on the elf problem."

Harriet snorted. "There are still ten thousand elves in the camps and in the wilds. Mr. Andurel isn't the last by any real means."

"Irrele—" Thomas stopped himself, and looked to the wide statue of the robot in the corner. "Look, I know he's your client, you were assigned to him, tough draw. But Judge Emerson and I… this could make our careers. Slam dunk case, big headlines on the news, we'll be famous."

Harriet just looked at him.

"At what point does a person turn the lens on themselves?" Judge Emerson said.

"Say again," Harriet said.

"At what point, does a person—a society, actually—turn the lens on themselves? When do we stop, take a breath, and think about the way we've done things? The way we've treated people, animals, or the environment? When does that happen?"

"There's no set time for that, I don't think," Harriet said.

"No, I Imagine there's not," the judge said. "But I sit here, looking at all these old, outdated books on my old, wooden shelves, and I think. We don't even make paper books anymore. Which means we don't need bookshelves anymore. One more thing we did for a very long time that doesn't make sense to do anymore."

"Judge, are you… okay?" Thomas asked.

"I'm not sure," he said with a puff of his pipe and a chuckle. "But maybe that's good. You know I fought against them all when I was drafted. I would've enlisted, but they drafted me first. Funny. I killed 'em all. I was scared. They were different. Pointy ears, weird eyes. Magic. We had to get that land back from them. We had to keep them from planting invasive species, right? Couldn't risk interbreeding. All the bad they did."

"All for good reason," Thomas said.

"At the time, it sure seemed like a good reason. But over the years, death warrant after death warrant, a man, starts to wonder. I can't just sign off, you see. I have to know them. Recognize them. Weigh their sins."

"Like Osiris," Harriet said.

"Just like Osiris," the judge agreed. "And when the war raged, the scales were set aside, but now, as the world calms, I find a great deal of imbalance, and I wonder whether or not the law I have upheld without question is right or not."

"Sir, your legacy is at risk," Thomas said. "Your entire career will be thrown in the bin over your waffling in the eleventh hour."

"Is that such a bad thing, counselor? Is it now?" The judge pondered. "Is a career valued so highly by a society such as ours worth the life of a single person? Will my fame wash away the memories of what I've done?"

"Are you going to throw away everything to make a political statement?" Thomas asked. "Because that's lunacy."

"Or courage," Harriet said. "When sane, reasonable men and women do the insane, we have to stop and take that breather. Can we live with ourselves?"

"Or will I be the judge that pried the door open again?" Judge Emerson said. "If I refuse to sign off on the execution of Q'Lothien Andurel, am I tearing open a wound that has just now begun to mend? Will my gesture of change cost us societal unity? Will it throw our courts into disarray?"

"I don't think you can afford the risk." Thomas leaned back in the chair. "You'll be branded a criminal."

"So was Rosa Parks. Martin Luther King. Gandhi. The list goes on," Harriet said. "Nothing is won without risk."

"So what matters more?" the judge posed to the counselors and the looming, faceless robot in the corner. "Avoiding the risk my potential statement makes or making a statement and standing by it. Do I defy the law?"

"Why? Jesus, why? Why are you even thinking about sparing one pointy-eared elf? Do you have a connection to him? He a son of an old war buddy or something? Help me understand why a judge with the nickname 'Execution Emerson' is getting cold feet at this point in his career," Thomas said.

Judge Emerson shrugged and took his pipe from his mouth with his mechanical hand. "I wonder if all we've done was for fear and not love."

The two lawyers sat in the judge's chambers, waiting for him to continue, but he didn't.

"What're you going to do?" Harriet asked him.

"Sleep on it. Hopefully by morning I'll decide how much courage I have left in me and whether or not that courage outweighs my sense of duty to the law as its written."

"I want you to do the right thing. The legally correct thing." Thomas leaned toward the judge and made eye contact before speaking again. "The thing we voted into law."

"But not the moral thing?" Judge Emerson posed.

"One in the same to me," Thomas replied.

"And maybe that's the problem. Maybe we made decisions—laws—not from morality, but from fear. Or greed. Maybe. You know I tell you what; y'all head back to your quarters for the night. I've seen and heard enough."

Thomas and Harriet gathered their things and stood to leave. The robot bailiff stepped from the corner and moved to the airlock door. They walked to it, and the robot awaited the judge's command.

"Bailiff, please escort these two fine counselors back to their quarters. Remand them there and gag all of their communications until further notice."

"But I have a vidchat with my son tonight," Harriet pleaded.

"We all make sacrifices, don't we?" the judge said. "I apologize and will get word that you are indisposed to your son for you. Have a nice evening, counselors." The judge nodded at the faceless machine, and the light in its face blinked. The door hissed open.

After the robot and two lawyers huffed and shuffled out into the corridor, the judge relit his pipe and smoked it.

He thought and smoked and thought some more until his bailiff returned in the morning.

One way or another, it was time to pass judgment.

"Bailiff, please have the defendant and counselors brought to the courtroom. Let me get my robe."

2

THE REDEMPTION OF GRE-334B

D.A. D'AMICO

G RE-334b observed the girl creeping down from the spidery tangle of plastic Christmas trees making up the bulk of the slope behind him, her improvised rubber shoes slapping against broken marble gravestones and the bridge he'd made of ornate wooden crosses. She'd come from the direction of the small settlement on the hill. Fifteen dwellings, all fashioned from slabs of discarded plastic sheeting and shorn with twisted tailings of aluminum and brass, but the one she shared was set apart from the others. GRE couldn't tell if it were by choice or a reflection of some kind of taboo.

"Gree!" She skirted a grove of stunted Chilean palms and Hau brush that struggled in vain to hold the shore. Their roots were awash with crushed plastic toys in faded shades of blue, green, and red. Styrofoam particles swirled like snow drifts through the landscape. Gulls wheeled overhead, their raucous cries competing with the waves' roar and the tumbling groan of rubbish to subdue the girl's thin voice.

GRE tracked her through sensors on his outer shell, remaining motionless except for his lower manipulator arms. Those arms were busy folding the stiff brown paper, creating triangles to form the hollow origami boat. Its importance hummed like a plucked wire in his mind, an urgent ache he was unable to ignore. The compulsion to understand the unknowable drove him as surely as the power cells integrated into his carapace.

"Unit 334b!" She passed the immense stone Moai, its gaze searching the ocean, its expression forlorn, as if waiting for redemption. GRE-334b spoke to that stone god often. He told it lies, whispering the untruths he could never tell the human population of Rapa Nui, uttering forgeries in a voice programmed never to deceive. It was an indulgence and a release. It was a *choice*, and he relished in his ability to exercise even that much control over his world.

"Gree." She approached him with the timidity of a feral creature. She'd never learned to trust mechanicals. He was still merely part of the landscape, part of the larger world she'd never understand. "Gree, I need your help."

Nina had come to his grotto once or twice a week, and along with her partner, she'd become a fixture in his life. He welcomed their intrusions into his routine. He'd become accustomed to the distraction. The women had become his pets as much as he'd become theirs, and he'd developed a level of fondness for them he wasn't ready to fully admit to himself.

"You appear well today, Nina. Where is Delfina?" he asked without turning, the origami boat nearly complete.

He studied the ragged planes of the girl's face, the deep valleys of burned flesh and scar tissue. Her left eye sagged, pupil milky white. Her nose appeared crushed and inexpertly repaired. The corner of her lip trembled as if she were about to cry, but it had done this intermittently since they'd first met several months back.

She'd been in a fire. Flames had ripped through the dunes of shredded paper up on the ridge where the power transmitting pilons sat. It flowed like lava across the volatile landscape, enveloping the small human settlement, eating deeply into the strata of heaped detritus and covering nearly a third of the island before mechanicals had been sent in from the mainland to contain it, GRE-334b among them.

In the international outrage following the catastrophe, hundreds of lesser mechanicals had been deployed. These were unfeeling robots, machines in the true sense of the word. They were trash collectors, recycling devices, and decontamination units. GRE had been given authority over them. He'd gone from first responder to watchdog, overseeing a mission to clean up a mess a century in the making, to repair the damage done in the time since the first multi-national garbage scows had landed on the Isla de Pascua to disgorge their filthy cargos.

The sentiment was admirable, but it quickly took on the cloak of futility, swamping the collectors and challenging the views of humanity with which GRE had been programmed. Seeing the desolation, the utter destruction coupled with abject despair, had shaken his faith, forcing him to rethink humanity, and his place among them. He'd abandoned his original purpose after only a few months, and it had warped his mind.

"I am at your service. You know that," he said, and with the final fold, he transferred the origami craft to his large construction arm. The arm swiveled, placing the boat gently on the dirty water. It swayed in the thin waves that managed to top the breakers of tumbled garbage.

"It's Delfina," Nina whispered. "Something bad's happened to her. Something's taken her soul."

GRE turned for the first time since sensing Nina, rotating the curved plastic housing that served as his face, while at the same time lifting on his torso ring and swiveling his lower manipulators out from the tight girdle of packed appendages to pull a pinch of coarse salt from the tiny denim bag on his right tread.

He sprinkled it over her.

She shrieked, scrambling backward. Her body tumbled over stacked heaps of Ouija boards that scattered like playing cards beneath her. With wild eyes and between heaving breaths, she asked, "What did you do that for?"

"Salt is a ward against evil." He brought the remainder of his chassis around. A humming squeal erupted from his lower servos. It was accompanied by the chemical signature he'd learned to interpret as the smell of ozone, and he estimated the wear capacity of his lower assembly had reached a critical point.

He wondered what would happen once his treads gave out and he was unable to move. Would a technician be sent to service him? Would they discover his flaw? If so, would they recycle him as callously as if he were just another piece of trash heaped on the lonely shores of this isolated island? Part of him welcomed it, a release from the lie his life had become, but something even deeper trembled. There was a Heaven for humanity, but not for him, not for his kind.

Nina shook her head, her wild black hair flapping in the stiff breezes coming from the ocean, tiny flecks of salt raining onto GRE's origami boat.

GRE tilted his cranial assembly in a gesture he'd learned from humans that signified confusion. "I assure you, the tradition is very old."

She wiped a droplet of saliva from the corner of her mouth, her shocked expression fading. GRE sensed her heartrate and respiration return to normal. He would try not to startle her again.

"You've learned something new," she panted, perching on a solid shelf of religious books, mostly bibles, stacked in complex, interlaced patterns that formed the outer wall of GRE's den. Behind her, the pale blue luminescence of the power pilons lanced into the churning sky. Their kilometer-high antennas greedily drank in power beamed from geostationary satellites and parsed it out to the civilized sectors of the planet.

"I have. Yes." He rotated back, although his direction had nothing to do with his sensor functions, and gestured with a fine motor arm toward the origami boat. "The ocean has been important to humanity for all of its history. 'From cradle to grave,' as they say. Many cultures practiced funerary customs where the deceased would be placed on a craft of some kind. They felt death was a journey...."

"Come to the house with me," Nina said abruptly. She stood erect. Her voice indicated command, but her body language displayed nervousness. She didn't trust him, but she sought to control him. "I need you to help me. I need you to do what I say."

GRE stacked his frame, gears churning, assembly rings rotating and locking as he pulled himself up to his full three-meter height. Rage threatened to tear his chassis apart.

Nina whimpered, but held her ground. "I *command* you to accompany me," she ordered.

The world seemed to quiet. Waves no longer slapped angrily at the corroding metal breakers. Gulls stood expectantly, their black eyes fixed on GRE as if awaiting his reaction. Time seemed to slow, as if it were itself afraid for the young woman. Then, like a human heart skipping a single beat, the world relaxed.

GRE compacted his frame once more, the hissing of hydraulics like a sigh as he swiveled toward a corrugated metal slope leading into the subterranean pit he'd constructed to protect himself from the frequent storms that pummeled these bleak shores. He *would* obey her. The choice had never really been his. "Before we go, tell me more about Delfina."

She didn't follow him, but her reedy little voice echoed in the damp blackness, audio waves rippling over his chassis as he fought to countermand her authority. Bestowed by genetic happenstance, but hardwired into his psyche nonetheless, her power over him was absolute. A clear command from a human was impossible to ignore. GRE had tried before. He *was* trying now, but the pull of programming was a fetish. Deep inside, he *wanted* to obey, and anger made him fling his belongings across the cramped, unlit interior.

His treads growled. He swivled, crushing a tree-shaped frame of barbed wire. Found jewelry hit the ground, a collection of gold crosses, pendants in the shape of saints and angels, scattered like pebbles across the compressed rubbish, their sonar echoes clear in the darkness. He surged. Indignation drove him against the rear wall. Platforms fashioned from ancient gravestones collapsed. The basket of fruit, apples from the stunted tree he tended near the valley of the Moai, clattered up the ramp, lost back into daylight.

"Are you coming, Gree?" Nina's small voice echoed through his sanctum with the power of a commandment.

"In a moment," he said struggling to construct a reply that would not violate his inability to lie. "I am preparing myself."

He jerked one last time, the tantrum toppling lead curse tablets retrieved from cargo containers originally destined for a museum outside of Rome, but somehow ending up among the planet's garbage here at Rapa Nui. They fell like dominos away from the deadly weapon they'd shielded, exposing his darkest secret, and revealing the deepest depths of his despair.

He stared at the miniscule block of exotic matter, a dark glob of swirling fury, inscrutable behind the hazy energy of its containment sphere. It had come to him as if in a dream, washing onto the shore, tantalizing in its implied freedom. It had felt like a gift, a validation of the disappointment that had been building inside him. What would it be like to touch such a thing? What would it be like to feel its energy annihilating every atom of his being, releasing him from his programming, his compulsion, and his servitude?

It was a sign, and it had been the first step in his descent into insanity.

"Delfina just started acting strange," Nina said as GRE emerged into the dim light of afternoon. "Ever since she got back from Rano Kau, from near the old settlement closer to the pilons, and I'm afraid the volcano got into her."

High clouds tore in churning eddies overhead, hinting at rain. The acidity would further degrade his chassis, but compulsion kept him moving forward. He *would* obey her, he had no choice, but it had placed a dent in the tenuous friendship they'd shared.

"There are *no* demons on this island," GRE said. He took a pinch of salt from his bag, and tossed it in Nina's direction, the large grains falling like scattered raindrops onto the corroded surface of a brass sundial.

"She's evil now, possessed or something. Crazy."

"Crazy, maybe," GRE said. "But I doubt evil, not in the sense you're implying."

Delfina was the happy one, the chatty one. She'd been the first to come down into the grotto, the first to seek him out and try to understand him. He felt an odd sensation at the thought of harm coming to her.

"I need you to fix her." Nina bent and retrieved the empty fruit basket. It had ended up against the flank of a barnacle-encrusted, wooden unicorn, once part of a merry-go-round ride, but now a washed-up relic like everything else on the island.

"I'm a shepherd. My sole task is to guide recycling units, to coordinate sorting and containment, and to repair the ruin humanity has wrecked on this island. I don't *fix* anything, certainly not people."

She looked up as she collected scattered apples from the loose rubble, her gaze traveling from GRE to the fluorescent orange box a dozen yards distant, and to the yellow drones around it, scattered like spilled popcorn among the heaps and drifts of waste. The drones had been stationary for months, bright statues, ornaments surrounding the maw of their intended purpose.

The hopper had sat there untouched since GRE had deserted his purpose. It had been intended as a refillable recycling container to be continuously loaded and compressed for pickup, but the imperative driving GRE to guide and manage the drones in their endless task had crumbled, superseded by a lesser subroutine.

"And how's that going for you?" She lifted an apple to her lips.

"Those apples are poisoned." GRE spun. Bearings squealed. He plucked the fruit from her grasp before she had time to scream.

"Why?" She gasped, the burns crossing the left side of her face taut and bone-white in the diffuse sunlight. Clutching at her tattered clothing, she as if she were about to flee.

"Mythology," he said softly, trying to ease her racing heart. "Fairytales. The poisoned apple is a popular contrivance for the delivery of toxins. I tend a tree in the valley and bring these apples to my dwelling as a reminder of how bad things sometimes come in pretty packages."

He thought of the sliver of swirling, exotic material not far away. There were entire days he would do nothing but study its shifting facets, lose himself in that exquisite perfection. He longed to caress it. He yearned for the oblivion it promised, the ballet of subatomic annihilation it could unleash if teased from its containment.

"Why would you do that?" She glanced at the apples and then at GRE. "Food is scarce here. People are hungry all the time, little babies dying, but you're ruining something you're incapable of eating? That's just cruel."

"There was no intended malice," he said. If he were human, shame would have colored his cheeks.

He wanted to explain real cruelty. If she only knew the anguish he felt, his sense of utter emptiness every time the compulsion took him, every time he felt an addict's craving to *understand*, but she couldn't comprehend. To her, GRE-334b was only a mechanical.

Nina stared at the growing clouds, her frown a grimace on her damaged face. She knew what rain would mean to her tender flesh. "Delfina needs you. Follow me. Now, okay?"

"I understand." He compacted, rearranging manipulator clusters for travel. "Go. I won't be far behind."

"I can hear her inside," Nina whispered. "She's growling or something. I'm not going in. You go."

GRE approached the metal sheeting serving as the dwelling's door. Nina scuttled back as he compacted to fit through the enclosure, his chassis pinging, and gears ratcheting his torso into place before he tugged on the looped rope holding the structure shut.

"Skree!" Delfina lunged through the door. A sliver of dull metal flashed from her hand. Her momentum knocked GRE back. She plunged the blade repeatedly against GRE's carapace as they tumbled, her voice a shrill, keening scream. GRE grabbed her with the fine manipulator arms located above his hips. He held her firmly, rolling onto the spade-like plates of his greater digging appendages to keep her from injury.

"Delfina, no!" Nina cried, tears staining the ruined landscape of her face. "Don't hurt him."

GRE paused to contemplate while the woman continued to stab at his torso. Nina cared about his safety, cared about *him*. It was a first. GRE had no friends. As a mechanical, the concept of family was alien to him, but something in his dynamic with these two women had changed. He'd become something more than a machine in their eyes.

He gently folded Delfina's arms behind her, removing the broken blade and subduing her as he rearranged his structure to bring them both upright. Delfina kicked and screamed. A torrent of foul language spewed from her parched and broken lips like sewage from an outflow pipe. She spat on him, the chemical makeup of her saliva giving him an indication that her enraged state was something other than demonic possession.

He lifted her slowly and rotated as he entered her dwelling.

"For your own good," he said as he deposited her gently onto the foam-covered wooden pallet that served as a bed. "You must be restrained. Do you understand?"

She swore. She yelled. She shrieked like a trapped animal as GRE ripped swatches of cloth from a pile of nearby clothing. He fashioned restraints, trying her appendages to the corners of the pallet just firmly enough to keep her still until she realized she could not break free. If she ordered him, GRE would be compelled to release her, but Delfina didn't appear to be in a state to think that clearly.

Nina entered the dwelling. Her face seemed to sag sideways, the wreckage of her features sliding disconcertingly out of sync with the bones beneath. Tears ran deep trails down her cheeks as if etched by an acid stronger than the rain falling lightly outside. "Will she be okay?"

"Release me!" Delfina screamed and swore. Then, in softer tones, she whispered, "Tell this thing to let me go, Nina, my heart. Set me free, and I'll show you true love."

"I just want you back. I want things the way they were before," Nina said sitting on the edge of the bed.

Delfina growled, twisting to reach the smaller woman, straining to claw at her. Nina hopped up, her distress clear even to GRE.

"What has happened to you, Delfina?" he asked.

"Delfina is no more. I am *tapu*, and my eyes are open. I see the shame of my people. I feel the disgrace of my world."

Nina sobbed. GRE compacted to move a little closer to the restrained woman. Sweat beaded her brow. Her heart raced alarmingly, blood pressure visible as a throbbing in her temple. Without thinking, he tossed a pinch of salt over her.

"You're sick. There is a chemical basis for your psychosis.

Nothing unnatural is going on here," GRE said. "And you are *not* possessed."

Delfina cackled, her broad features churning in a grimace GRE was sure implied mirth. "But you're not sure, are you, *machine man*? You throw superstition at me, but you don't know why. If you were human, you'd fear me."

She drew the words out with relish, sensing something in him he'd already felt in himself. His obsession made him question his own reasoning. It compelled him to wonder *what if*, and he fought against it. This was *not* real.

"Please, Delfina...." Nina reached out.

Delfina jerked. The strap holding her right arm snapped. She grabbed the smaller woman by the hair, pulling Nina against her face with a force far stronger than GRE would have thought possible.

"Save me," Delfina whispered, her tone soft, the rage in her eyes extinguished.

Then she twisted. Her gaze ignited, the demon returning to rip long strands of hair from Nina's scalp. Nina screamed. Delfina flailed, her nails raking the girl's face. GRE pulled the two women apart and once again subdued Delfina's arm. He held her still, rotating the digits in his left manipulator to reveal his smallest syringe, and gently dipped the needle into the vein in her right forearm. The puncture seemed to deflate the woman. She relaxed. Her wide features softened, and for a moment, GRE saw the woman he remembered.

"An analysis of your blood will be quick," he said. "And I'm sure it will expose the true culprit behind your current actions."

"Or maybe it will reveal my *tapu*, and you'll cut these binds."

"You are *not* possessed," he said firmly. "There is no basis to believe in such a thing. Demons aren't real."

Delfina laughed, rage replaced by a calmer but more disturbing posture. "And you're the expert, right, mechanical man? You *know*, because it eats at you to know. They *made* you to know."

"How can you know what drives me?" Could she have somehow divined the nature of his obsession? His meetings with her had always been superficial. They'd spoken briefly and informally when they'd bumped into one another as each crisscrossed the island or when she'd come to sit at the edge of his domain and ask for instructions on how to rebuild household components or small trinkets to amuse Nina. He'd never mentioned his addiction. He would never speak of his mad fixation to understand the unexplainable.

"I see things beyond your senses," she chuckled. "Yes, even you, mechanical man. I see through you into other realms, deeper wells of possibility."

"You can't." But she'd cracked his assurance. Could she see the things he'd hidden even from himself?

She stared directly at him, and an unpleasant sensation touched his core. "I know more than you dream, mechanical man. I hear the whisper of Rano Kau. I feel the breath of the island, and it's fetid, polluted, and crawling with creatures like you—no, not exactly *like* you, huh, mechanical man? None of the others have given themselves to addiction. None of the others stare into the void at night, caressing a sliver of hell and fantasizing of oblivion."

He jerked, a random surge of electricity arcing through his carapace like friction lightning. She couldn't possibly have deduced the presence of the antimatter. *Nobody* knew. Just as his innermost urge to end his existence was his alone to contemplate.

"How—?" he started, but the analysis of her blood had completed. She'd been poisoned.

He led Nina from the dwelling. Delfina had resumed her screaming tirade, all traces of the eerily rational being vanished. GRE had given up hope of answers. He couldn't understand how Delfina had known of the antimatter or about his craving for extinction, but there had to be a rational explanation.

"Is she going to be okay?" Nina stood timidly beside a heap of empty aluminum barrels, their dented covers slick from the rain now heading out to sea. She stared at the twisted plastic sheeting of her house, wincing each time Delfina screamed for her freedom.

"No. She's dying. There are traces of heavy metals, as well as fatal doses of exotic isotopes in her blood." He said it bluntly.

Nina began to sob. GRE slid his torso back, rotating his appendages to form a small cubby. Nina climbed against him. She hugged him, and she cried.

"Is there something you can do?" Her chin rested against one of his external speakers. He rerouted his responses to an output near his right shoulder.

"No," he said. "She *will* die. It is inevitable."

He held her that way for a long time. He couldn't understand why, but her presence comforted him. He felt something had changed between them, and it was unsettling. They'd become somehow closer, but at the same time he felt Delfina's death would drive the younger girl away. He would miss both women and the frequent visits they'd made to his grotto. He would miss the distraction.

"What did she mean when she said you fantasized about killing yourself?" Nina pulled away. Her good eye was rimmed in red, her cheeks sallow.

He wanted to tell her it was a mistake; Delfina's insanity had caused the other woman to make things up, but lying was beyond his subset of choices.

"It enters my mind from time to time," he admitted.

"But you're...."

"A mechanical? Yes. I may not be human, but I'm as alive as you are. And subject to the same failures of conscience." He did not continue, although the burden of his own insanity weighed heavily on his mind. She was better not knowing.

Let her believe mechanicals were nothing more than machines, devoid of hopes and desires, capable only of executing commands and performing manual tasks. It would be beyond him to explain the similarities between them. Simply thinking about it made him long for the dark matter's embrace.

"I must return to my station," he said.

Her eyes widened, a dollop of puss forming in the ruins of her burned socket. She started to speak, but he stopped her.

"I will return."

GRE gazed into the Moai's eyes. The stone monolith stared past him, expression filled with dismay or concern as it surveyed a landscape of rubble and ruin. Trash in undulating dunes stretched to the sea. Heaped plastics and metals jutted from the amorphic mass, interspaced with overflowing barrels of oily effluent that shimmered with heat, rippling with the chemical signatures of methane, salt, and decay.

In the distance, the human habitations seemed to teeter over a platform of ragged stone pebbles. Their squat dwellings were reminiscent of igloos, but colored with discarded logos in a dozen different languages. In infrared, he could see movement, bodies performing the mundane and mechanical functions of life. He wondered if Nina were among them. He couldn't tell at this resolution, but he hoped she would resume her normal functions.

An emptiness had taken root inside him, like mold on an already rotting carcass. He felt the absence of the two women like an ache, and something even more undefinable when his thoughts turned to Delfina. Her death would change his life, he was sure of it, and it was an unfamiliar sensation. Was it possible for him to *miss* somebody?

He swiveled his base. Thorax rings shifted down, internal cabling stretching as he pushed his appendages upward, rotating the spade-like diggers into a sunflower configuration. His internal gyroscope tilted, and he did something he hadn't done since abandoning his primary programming. He pinged the globalsat network.

A hurricane of information inundated his senses. Thousands of access commands per second shredded his bandwidth, but he ignored them, threading his way through the network until he reached what he sought.

Scans of the power pilons located at the edge of the dormant volcano showed high levels of the toxins he'd identified in Delfina's blood. Surface density analysis confirmed pollutants in the cooling lake adjacent to the receiving antennas, and deep radar overlays showed it had leeched into the surrounding ground water. The poison was already killing Delfina, but it would spread.

He disengaged, compacting into his standard configuration. This wouldn't have concerned him only a short time ago. He was immune to heavy metals and resistant to radiation, but the poison would consume Nina as it had already destroyed Delfina. He couldn't let that happen.

The churning clouds cleared. He swiveled, sensors locating the far-off power pilons. He knew what he had to do, and he knew he'd be doing it for Delfina and for Nina.

"Beautiful, isn't it?" GRE stopped to address the Moai as he left his grotto for the last time. He couldn't lie to a human, but found it refreshing in the presence of this ancestral construct. The gods of Rapa Nui didn't seem to mind. "See you soon, old friend."

Delfina was dead when he returned to the dwelling to say goodbye.

Nina sat on the small bed, her back to the corpse. She'd been crying, but her eyes were dry when GRE entered. A thin sliver of saliva trickled from the corner of her deformed mouth. Her hands trembled, and she could not look in his direction.

"I'd already put one in my clothes," she said. "I never intended to give it to her, but she *knew* I had it. She knew what it was."

The half-eaten apple rested in Delfina's lap, its flesh already brown, its once glossy-red skin dull and sinister looking.

GRE felt the familiar emptiness like a missing subroutine, an instruction set with no conclusion. For once in his existence, he didn't know how to react.

"She knew she was dying. She told me so. She also said she could answer the question that drove you, but you'd never be capable of believing her." Nina stood, stepping out of the small dwelling without glancing back. GRE followed.

"What question was that? Did she say?" GRE knew the answer. Delfina had somehow understood his insanity. She'd comprehended the leap of faith that had shifted his focus from shepherd and overseer and had forced him to search madly for meaning in his life.

"She said there *is* another world, one deeper than ours. She's seen it, but you never will because of the way they made you. What did she mean?"

GRE compressed. He turned his curved faceplate toward Nina. She shivered in the light breeze coming off the ocean, and stumbled zombie-like back into the small shed. GRE followed.

"Mechanicals are all given a job when they're constructed. I have the capacity and ability to autonomously control hosts of other machines. My programming is fluid, giving me an advantage over many of my kind. I have the illusion of freedom, but it's not enough."

"I don't understand," she said. "What more could a machine want?"

"Mechanicals are *alive*," he said. "Without variety or interest, life is torture. Even to us. Most mechanicals are given a single purpose, requiring much less processing power. It removes the burden of self-awareness."

He didn't want to tell her he felt this implied a subtle form of slavery. It was a forced hobbling of intellect. Those mechanicals were condemned to a parody of existence, a purgatory of awareness that left them painfully incomplete. Even so, he sometimes fantasized about that simplicity of consciousness.

"But not you?" Nina wiped her moist lips, pushing a rag roughly against her twisted flesh. "You have freedom."

If he were human, he would have laughed. "Freedom eludes me, even now. I search for it in the icons of religion and in the props of mysticism, but it evades me. My existence is futile. Life has nothing to offer."

"You sound as crazy as Delfina." Fear colored Nina's features, her fingers trembling as she clutched the hem of her oversized shirt.

"I've been consumed by obsession." GRE shifted his torso to give Nina more room. "I will never find what I seek because I was not built to believe." He feared the idea he might not have a soul, but trembled at the thought he did.

Nina lowered her head. "Delfina said she could see beyond."

"She did, yes."

"Then this isn't the end. There's life after...."

"Delfina was sick," he said. "Toxins were destroying her, and she'd become unpredictable."

But she'd *known* things. She'd somehow seen beyond her normal understanding, and GRE couldn't explain that.

"She was right," Nina whispered. "You can't believe her, can you?"

GRE didn't reply.

They burned Delfina's body in the dry cistern at the base of the ledge. GRE constructed the pyre, fueling the flames with compressed methane from the outflow pipes beyond the settlement. It was Nina's idea. It was cleaner than interment in the jumbled detritus of the island, and it also satisfied GRE's obsession with ritual.

"What will you do now?" Nina asked. She leaned into the growing wind, her body tense as if she planned to run away. She faced the distant power pilons, and GRE wondered if it were by design.

"I'm going to the other side of the island," he said. "I have a plan to get... closure."

He'd almost used the word revenge. His thoughts were wild, unlike any he'd had before. The antimatter, secreted in a compartment in his chest, beat like a human heart, and he glanced at Nina to see if she could sense the phantom rhythm.

"Can I come?"

"I'd rather you did not," he said.

"I'm coming. It's not negotiable." Her words were like a command. He felt the deep compulsion to obey, and the mounting rage that accompanied it.

He began to stack his thorax, rising in height as his anger rose. Then he thought of their conversation, and paused. "Delfina told you."

"Yes. She said you wanted to kill yourself, and she told me you'd do it where the poison took hold of her." Nina didn't look at him, but he could tell she was waiting for a reaction.

His upper frame turned in a complete circle, as if he were searching for something he could not see. How had Delfina known about the motivation he'd only discovered after she'd already died? It didn't make sense.

"She didn't want you to do it."

"I...understand." But did he? The only possible explanation was impossible. He couldn't believe. Yet, he couldn't lie. Did he, on some level, really understand, or was he simply becoming unstable as Delfina had in her last hours?

The power pilons jutted into the sky like impossibly long fingers, like the hand of the Lady of the Lake from Arthurian legend. Their tips glowed eerie blue as they slurped power from satellites far overhead, distributing it in the form of tight energy beams to distant relay points. Water lapped at their bases—dirty water, deadly and toxic water.

GRE had given Nina protective boots and instructions not to touch anything as he began fashioning the origami boat from a large swatch of discarded billboard paper.

"It signifies a journey," she said, clutching at the small metal container holding a handful of Delfina's ashes.

"Good. You were paying attention."

She smiled, the ruined side of her mouth cracking. "It might even be a new beginning... if you're willing to believe."

He didn't reply. Instead, he swiveled, grasping the makeshift urn and deposited Delfina's remains into the paper boat. Then he removed the antimatter from its hiding place. The tiny sliver of exotic material swirled with iridescent fury within its magnetic bottle, hypnotic, overpowering.

"A new beginning," he said placing the antimatter into the boat opposite Delfina's ashes.

Then he took the bag of salt from his torso, and tore a hole in its side. Crystals dropped like tears into the water, but GRE carefully arranged the sack in the boat so it would continue to slowly seep out.

"And that will give us enough time?" Nina asked from behind him. GRE didn't move his frame as he used his delicate manipulators to rest the meter long craft on the still water, pushing it gently out into the center of the lake.

"It should." The boat floated in equilibrium. It would continue that way until enough salt was lost, and then it would capsize.

Ironically, some of the radioactive substances in the water were capable of destabilizing the containment field surrounding the exotic matter. When that happened, a good chunk of the island would be instantly annihilated. He'd have to get Nina far enough away before then.

"I believe in you," she said as she turned away from the lake.

He wasn't as sure. He thought of Delfina and her conviction he'd end himself. He could still prove her wrong. If they hurried.

3

SEVEN DAYS

RACHEL MENARD

Monday

"Trial two-hundred and fifty-six of the time portal. Goal...ten minutes into the future." I hold up my watch as the second hand slowly clicks its way to twelve. "At exactly nine-seventeen in the morning of Monday, October the eighth. Commence start-up."

Abraham nods. Even though it's been close to twenty years since he's spoken with a lisp, he still limits his words when I'm recording.

I set the camera down, wedging it between a stack of textbooks and my yellowing notepads. Abraham's brown fingers dance across the touchscreen until the hum courses through the large, silver ring standing in front of me.

I hold my breath, waiting for the smoke, the wisp of fire, the whine of bending aluminum.

The first prototype was steel and square with copper tubing. It cracked down the center forty-two seconds into the trial. We needed a more malleable structure, one that could bend with the force being pushed against it. The aluminum melted on its first trial. The cement floor is still warped from the burning metal.

The electricity pooled in the corners of the square structure, hence the new, round doorway, which survived the trials, but didn't create enough energy to bend time. After changing the wires from copper, to gold, to silver to a copper alloy doped with germanium...the math checks. This should give us the power we need to rip through time, to create our own black hole, to fulfill man's greatest wish—we will alter destiny.

A spark races from one side of the door to the other in a beam of light. I let out my breath and lean over Abraham's shoulder. He flinches when my hair falls across his neck. I push it behind my ear and point to the screen.

"Is it collapsing?" I can see the series of numbers filtering down on the screen, the fabric of space and time broken down into complex digits. One misplaced decimal point, one one-millionth of a mistake, and this could warp the cement floors again. Or worse.

"No, it looks stable."

Another light shoots across the door and another. It's like a spider web now, reaching from top to bottom, across the sides.

I stand back and watch like a new mother marveling at her mewling infant. The lines grow fatter and connect into a glowing pool of light in the center. There's a flash. I reach for my goggles and a red rubber ball marked with 256. I have two-hundred and fifty-five more of these balls, sealed in a plastic bin, untouched. We've never reached this point. We've never had an active portal.

"Is it ready?" I ask.

"I don't know," he says. "I've entered the parameters." That's the best he can give me, because at this moment, neither of us knows what will happen. We are standing at the edge of exploration, like God, creating life from darkness.

I throw the ball into the glowing light, more than half-expecting it to be spat back at me in a melting ball of flame. But it doesn't come. The light swallows it whole.

"Shut it down," I say.

Abraham drags his fingers down the screen, and the light disappears from the center of our portal. I take off my darkened goggles and blink away the spots in my vision. I hadn't realized how bright the light had been, like looking into the center of creation itself.

Abraham pushes his glasses up his nose and cocks his head toward the portal. It's warped in the center, slightly collapsed, and steam rises from the top. We'll have to find a way to strengthen that without compromising malleability. If this works...if this works...I have visions of a bigger lab, more resources, more staff, a Nobel Prize...but first, I need that ball back. My entire future, my entire career, rests on the fate of one rubber bouncy ball.

"What time is it?"

"Nine-fourteen," he says, glancing back at the blinking recorder.

My journey into time travel began long before now, twenty-eight years ago to be exact, when Dad gave me a book of short stories by H.G. Wells. After I read *The Time Machine*, I had nightmares for weeks about the Morlocks, but they were the kind of monsters who couldn't be stopped by ripping open a closet. They didn't exist yet. The only way to stop them was to know they were coming, to step into the future.

"Thirty seconds," Abraham says and holds up his watch. I position my goggles on my forehead in case I need to draw them down quickly. I still don't know how the ball will come back to us. If it will be another flash of light, or if it will appear from the wall and roll across the floor as if it's always been there.

Or, of course, it could not come at all. It could have been disintegrated.

"Ten, nine, eight, seven, six..."

It's like the countdown to New Year's Eve, except when the ball drops, there will be no one to kiss. No one except Dr. Jenkins, who I would gladly kiss if he weren't my employee and ten years my junior.

"One," he says, and I grind my teeth into my lower lip.

It's so quiet in the warehouse, I can hear the tick of my watch, but no trumpets, or flashing lights, or fireworks to announce that we've done it, we changed the fate of the universe.

"Holy…Catherine." Abraham points to the portal.

It's like a shadow at first, a clear film of something red. Then as the seconds tick by, it grows darker, more solid, round, red with three black characters on the surface.

It drops to the cement floor, in the melted divot, and bounces once, twice, three times before I snatch it from the air and twist it in my hand.

My fingers are shaking. I can barely move. It's my writing on the side—256. I clutch the ball in my fist, dizzy with possibility. Now that we know the portal works, we need to go farther. Bigger. I won't release the data until we have something worthwhile, a human trial, at least a week ahead of us. If I show our findings before then, someone else could recreate our portal and beat us to it.

"Start the portal again," I say.

"We should stabilize the structure first."

"It can last one more test." I reach into the bin of blank rubber balls and scrawl 257 on the side of one. Number 256 I tuck into my pocket. "Trial two-hundred and fifty-seven of the time portal. Goal…seven days into the future," I say for the benefit of the camera. "At exactly nine-twenty in the morning of Monday, October the fifteenth."

"Okay." Abraham wipes the sweat from his brow. Underneath it, though, is a smaller version of the same self-satisfied smile I have. He will get equal billing on the credit for this, and he's earned it. I plucked him myself from the Yale doctoral candidates. He was a welfare kid from the South Side of Chicago, born with a cleft palate and raised on food stamps. He stood against privileged white boys with private school educations and pulled himself into the graduating class of an Ivy League education. To me, that meant more than awards and accolades. He had tenacity. Dedication.

The light web forms across the portal again. I yank down my goggles, which even then, don't shield me from the strength of this light. It's like looking directly at the sun, a sun that I created. That *I* control.

The top of the portal bends slightly inward, and the light wavers like a golden puddle. I need to throw the ball now.

It flies from my fingers into the pool of light, except this time, the light doesn't swallow it, at least not as smoothly as it did before. It chokes, and the top of the portal finally bends enough to give way. I shield my face as it blasts outward, and something like a boulder strikes my chest. I'm flung backward against my table of piled textbooks. I'm buried in a paper tomb.

"Catherine!"

Abraham, my dutiful employee, frees me, while my ears ring with the sound of my failure. My ribs ache with the agony of being thrown across the room. Looking at the heap of burned metal in front of me, I start calculating what it will cost to rebuild, and I know we don't have it.

Tuesday

Writing grants is something I despise. It's another reason why I hired Dr. Abraham Jenkins. He started writing grant letters when he was seven and asked for help from Operation Smile to fix his cleft palate. His letter was answered, and he was posing for press photos with a wide, perfect smile within six months. He has a gift with words, with asking for money without sounding insecure or pathetic. It's something I can't do, and we'll have to do now that I've broken the portal.

I type in the code for the door to our lab and expect to find Abraham sweeping up yesterday's mess, but it's still there, the twisted remains of our portal and the fluttering pages of my notes. Dr. Jenkins is perched in front of his computer as enrapt as a twelve-year-old boy looking at porn.

"What is it?" I set down my coffee on an empty surface and make my way toward him. This time he doesn't flinch when my hair brushes his shoulder.

"Look at the data." He taps the screen. I follow the numbers on the screen, a secret language that only he and I and few others would be able to decipher. It's our timeline, broken down into manageable numbers. Something that makes sense. Something that can be decoded and pulled and twisted and bent to make our portal work.

And the numbers are counting perpetually down, decimal by decimal.

Wednesday

I set down my coffee cup, and it rolls to the floor, among the papers and debris of the time portal. It lands in good company, with five other empty Styrofoam containers stained with the remnants of coffee and sugar. My ex in college was an environmental science major. Always used to beg me to drink out of a reusable coffee mug.

"It's cups like these that are destroying the planet," he would say, which is why I kept using them—to annoy him. Oh how I would love to call him now and tell him how wrong he was. The cups didn't destroy the planet. I have...in a way. In actuality, the world will go on forever, exactly as it is now. Never changing. Never evolving.

It's twelve-oh-six a.m., October the tenth. My eyes burn from staring at the computer screen. Our figures, the timeline broken into fractions of fractions, and fractions of those fractions, are running in a perpetual loop. They run the length of seven days and repeat again from the top, from the second our portal broke.

Abraham flips back to the live feed, another series of scrolling numbers. We are exactly where we should be on the timeline, two days after my mistake, but it's not a line anymore. It's a count-down. The end of everything, or the beginning, however I want to look at it. We will reach October fifteenth, the destination I programmed for ball number 257, and then time will re-set itself, back seven days to my fateful, fantastical, flop.

I kick the pile of empty coffee cups. We didn't break through time and space. We tore it in two. We created another dimension, a seven day loop that we'll be stuck in for all eternity unless we can find a way to re-join the ongoing string of time.

Abraham picks up one of my loose coffee cups and examines it before he throws it in the trash. "We need to rebuild the portal," he says, as if it's that simple.

"With what?"

"It doesn't matter," he says. "We can steal the parts. The money. Call in favors. Beg for help."

"No," I say, still clinging to the hope that this will all be fixed. I'll get my time portal working, earn my Nobel Prize, and answer man's most desired wish. But not if my research goes public and someone else beats me to it. No one cares about the woman who sent a rubber ball ten minutes into the future. They care about living long enough to see flying cars. The day we encounter alien life. They want to find out if Styrofoam cups really will be the death of us. The person who bends time for that, that's whose name they'll remember.

"I'll get the money," I say.

"Catherine." He straightens his glasses and gathers his words. Abraham has the admirable and frustrating quality of never speaking unless he's thought about what he's going to say first. "This isn't a game. We don't get to keep what we have. We'll be starting from scratch, with nothing."

"I can read the numbers." Zero. It always reaches zero before it starts again. Nothing. A rebirth. Contrary to what Abraham said, this is like a game, a video game that has to restart from the beginning. The lead character doesn't get to bring his points and his weapons with him. He starts with nothing, which is exactly what Abraham and I will have. I could make the same mistake with the portal over and over again. It's likely I already have. Ten times, fifty times, two hundred and fifty-seven times. I don't know.

He picks up his phone. "I'm calling Dr. Svensson."

"No." I take the phone from him. Dr. Johan Svensson is the leading researcher in black holes. If anyone is going to use my research for his own gain, it will be him. "Abraham." I keep a tight hold on his phone. He doesn't understand that if we solve this, and in the process I give away my years of hard work, moving beyond these next seven days is meaningless to me. I'd rather repeat it over and over again until I get it right.

"You know the probabilities," I continue. "We have to assume we've done this before, and this isn't our first loop. The most logical solution would be to call Svensson, which means we already have, and he couldn't help." I drop Abraham's phone into my pocket and lean over his chair. "This is our work. We know it best. We can fix this, but I need you with me. Are you still with me?"

"Yes," he sighs. "But by your logic, we must have tried to fix this ourselves before too."

"Then let's get it right this time. I'll get the money."

I keep his phone with me when I go outside. He makes a valid point, one I'm going to overlook. There's only one chance to make the first mistake. There are endless numbers of making more than one mistake, infinite possibilities, which is why I can't assume this is our first. By my logic, we could have already tried every solution in our grasp and failed every time. Not this time, though. I am going to do something I would never do.

We've set up our operations in an old factory building in Pawtucket, Rhode Island. It used to be a textile mill. The remnants of a water wheel still sit in the dried up creek bed that runs along-side the building. It's a perfect autumn day with the leaves in mid-shift from green to yellow and orange. The sun is out, but there's a crispness in the air.

I stand beside the broken water wheel and take out my phone. Mom's number is in it even though I haven't called her in six years, and that was only to congratulate her on her third marriage. I didn't feel obligated to attend the third wedding. For the fourth, I might not even feel obligated to call.

"Hello," she says on the third ring as if she knew I would be the one to break our six year silence.

"Hello Mom," I say as coolly and professionally as I can.

"How are you?"

"Not well." I don't need to extend this conversation any longer than necessary. "We've reached an impasse in our research. I need to borrow money."

"I knew there had to be a reason for this call." She sighs. "How much do you need?"

"A hundred thousand."

There's a pause, as I expected. It's a lot of money, and the bare minimum to buy the wire and aluminum sheeting we will need to get in days to fix the portal and try to realign time. In that respect, it's very little money. It's also very little money to her. She earned millions from Dad's death, and millions more the moment her second husband, Paul, died of a heart attack on the ninth green.

"That's a lot of money," she says.

"I know."

"Your benefactors run out of checks?"

"I need it quickly," I say. No time for grant writing.

"Catie…is something wrong?"

For a split second, she sounds genuinely concerned, and I consider telling her everything, about what I've done, to urge her to spend a million dollars today because if I don't fix this, then the money will be right back in her account by Monday. But then she'll know she was right. I would have been better off marrying into my future than trying to build a door to reach it.

"There's a Swedish team on the verge of a breakthrough," I say. "I have to beat them to it. I will pay you back within six months, as soon as one of my benefactors writes a check."

"You spend half of your life on something, and now all of a sudden, it's a rush," she says with the relief that everything is how she likes it to be—with my research struggling and the validation that she made the right life choices. I made the wrong ones.

"I can get you the money this afternoon," she says. "I'll have Lou transfer it to your account."

"Thank you," I say and pause. "If you have time next week, we could meet for coffee."

"I do. That sounds lovely."

"How about Tuesday? The Westin?"

"I'll be there."

I end the call, not sure if I want Tuesday to come or not. There is something empowering about knowing the world could reset in five days.

Thursday

The sound of Abraham's voice bounces off the cement floors while he calls in every favor we have to get the parts we need to rebuild while I clear away the shards of the shattered portal and see what I can salvage.

"I understand you don't have a truck. I'll have one sent to pick it up," he says. "We need it today."

On the computer screen over Dr. Jenkins' shoulder, the numbers continue to wind down toward zero.

"Great," Abraham says. "I'll have the truck to you within the hour." He ends the call and makes a new one. "I'd like to rent a box truck," he says.

Friday

I decide to give myself an honorary degree in mechanical engineering. The aluminum sheets arrived uncut. Sparks fly from either side of the saw blade as I attempt to follow the thin pencil lines Abraham drew onto the surface. A piece snaps free with a jagged, crooked edge. The time portal already teetered on the edge of a knife, one, one-millionth of a digit from failure, and now it's going to be pieced together with crooked, raw metal.

It doesn't matter. If I fail this time, I'll have another chance. And another. And another. By law of infinite probability, one time we will get it right.

I shut down the saw and pick up the nearest cup of coffee. Empty. In the other room, I hear Abraham on the phone.

"I need it overnighted. I know tomorrow's Saturday. I'll pay."

These crooked cuts will mean nothing if we don't have the wire.

"Fine. Just get it here." Abraham ends the call and sets his phone on the desk. Bending over his lap, he rubs his fingers on his temples.

I pick up another coffee cup. This one feels heavier. I take a sip of cold coffee and make my way to him. Neither of us have left the factory since Tuesday apart from my coffee runs, and we each made a trip home for a toothbrush and change of clothes.

"The wire will be here by six a.m. tomorrow," he says. "That's the soonest I can get it."

"That's good," I say and tap the camera to make sure it's still recording. If we make it through to the other end of time, we will want this all documented for posterity, whether we choose to release it the scientific community or not.

"It's not good." He raises his head. He's not wearing his glasses, but there are two dents in either side of his nose to show where they should rest. He has dark eyes, almost black, and thick lashes. He's better looking than he knows. If he hadn't been born with the cleft lip, he would probably be someone else, somewhere else, and I am sure right now, he wishes he was.

"We can't re-build it in two days."

I lean against the table and take another sip of cold coffee. "This isn't starting from scratch. We have the plans. We just have to follow them."

"And then what?" he says. "It failed. It will fail again."

I wince at the mention of failure. The portal didn't fail. The red ball, number two-hundred and fifty-six, is still in my pocket. We bridged space and time. I'm the one who failed. I should have stabilized the structure before the second trial.

"We'll re-create the experiment," I say. "Set the portal back seven days. The structure will fail again as you say." With the warped metal, probabilities are high for that. "We'll have the same adverse reaction in reverse. We'll bend gravity back to the existing timeline where we will re-join it in progress. No one will even know we were gone."

"There are more than a million ways that can go wrong."

I close my fist around the empty coffee cup and throw it to the ground. "I know that," I snap, as tired and dirty and exhausted as he is. "We only have to get it right once."

The most likely outcome is the portal will fail before we want it to. Or we could push ourselves onto another seven-day loop by creating a tertiary dimension. Even if the fix works as I've described, we could rejoin the timeline on Monday morning and have to explain to the world why we all moved back in time. There are no guarantees. We are working with something less than a hypothesis now. It's barely a dream.

"I'm starting to think our efforts would be better spent working to get a message to ourselves to stop this from happening," he says.

"If that was a possibility, we wouldn't be here to send the message." I tap the screen on his computer. "Those numbers wouldn't be counting down our lives. We're here because the mistake was made, and it will always be made. We have to go back to the place after the break." The few seconds right after the portal collapsed. That's where we belong.

I return to the other room to cut through another piece of metal. Like Abraham, I have the feeling two days will not be enough time to get the portal rebuilt.

Saturday

The outer structure of the portal is complete. None of our proto-types have been very sleek or shiny. It was never about how it looked, only that it worked. But this one is especially raw-edged and rough. The center is already sagging. It might not survive the day, let alone the immense jolt of power we plan to send coursing through it.

Abraham is on the step ladder, grunting as he clips handfuls of copper wiring to the inside casing. Every few seconds, he looks back at the computer screen, to the diminishing timeline. I pick up a text book and set it in front of the screen to block it for myself as much as him. I can't stop looking at it either.

"We have to stay focused."

He nods and clips another handful of wire to the inside lip before he drops his hands and sighs. "We're going to die," he says. "This version of myself is going to die. Every bird, every tree, every man, woman and child out here will die when Monday comes."

If we fail, they won't die; they'll live forever. Even people who have died during this seven day loop will be re-born on Monday to die again, but I know he's only using the word in the metaphorical sense. On Monday, Dr. Catherine Spencer and Dr. Abraham Jenkins will show up to this lab at eight a.m. ready to make the final preparations on the time portal for the two-hundred and fifty-sixth test, and neither of them will know that before lunch, they will forever alter space and time.

"Why did you pick me?" he asks. "There were better candidates who applied."

"It depends on what you consider 'better'," I say. I interviewed one especially gifted young man who informed me how lucky I would be if he chose to work with me. "I needed someone with a good work ethic, who knew how to write grant proposals." Who wouldn't try to take my research for his own.

"I keep thinking about the things I should have done. The things I shouldn't have done," he says.

"Is taking this position one of them?"

"No," he says quickly, which is a relief. "But I should have spoken louder when you wanted to do the second test. I should have stopped you."

"You wouldn't have been able to do it. I'm pretty stubborn and arrogant when it comes to my research."

He bends down to pick up the bundle of wire. "I know that, Catherine. I've worked for you for two years now." He smiles at me when he grabs the wire with his perfect, surgically-altered mouth. I watch his tongue roll over his teeth and envy the doctors who made it. They gave the world a better gift with science than I have.

Sunday

Even with the textbook blocking the countdown screen, I can sense time slipping away. It slaps me with every tick of the second hand on my wrist, which is why I unlatch the annoying watch and throw it across the room. I don't need it.

"Catherine," Abraham says. "I need a hand."

I grab the other side of the aluminum sheet and hold it in place while he screws it to the main structure, hiding the tangle of chips and wires inside. It's almost to specifications. We didn't have enough of the specialty wire to complete the electrical map. We had to substitute plain copper wiring for the bottom quarter, a substitution I hope doesn't cost us too much.

Ever since I closed the cover on H.G. Wells' *The Time Machine*, I've spent a lifetime poring through the intricacies of time travel and the problems it could cause. This was one of those problems. I always knew it was a risk, and I ignored it in my quest to prove to everyone I could do it.

In my thirst for greatness, we broke the line. We made an infinitesimal split from the timeline, a hairline fracture, and from that fracture, we formed this loop. Somewhere else, there is a past and a future, but we will never reach it, not until we veer back to the main highway. Until then, we only exist now, here, on these seven days, and it's still hard not to feel like I've accomplished something. I successfully managed to alter the sequence of life. If I could tell the scientific community what I've done, they would curse me, and secretly applaud me. I've done something great. Something greatly awful and greatly amazing.

"I think it will hold," Abraham says and holsters the electric screwdriver like an old West pistol.

"We should test it." I take the book away from the computer screen. "Ten minutes."

He sits down in the chair. I check the camera before I lean over him. My hair doesn't fall to his arm. It's tied back into a bun at the base of my skull. I haven't washed it in days. I feel the ache of lost sleep in my bones and the slight thrum of a building headache from too much caffeine.

Abraham slides his fingers up the screen, and the hum races through our patched together portal. Already one of the aluminum panels is rattling. A screw drops to the floor and settles into the divot. I clutch my coffee cup and hold my breath. The first of the spider web strings of light reaches across the center. Abraham lets out a sigh.

Reaching into my pocket for the ball, number two-hundred and fifty-six, I feel the same excitement I did for the last trial, maybe more so. I cut the metal sheets for this portal. I twisted the wire. Every inch of this we made ourselves, and not just the calculations to make it function.

As soon as the pool of light is a foot wide, I throw the red ball through it, and Abraham shuts down the power. Our rattling portal comes to a rest with a gentle sag in the middle…just like before. But is it sagging more than before? Less? I've looked over the original recording forty times or more already, trying to find the push that sent us all over the knife's edge. It had very little to do with the equipment.

"It can survive one more test."

I'm the push. My unwillingness to give up or stand in second place, and I'm going to do it again now. It doesn't matter if the portal is sagging too much or too little or if we have copper wire in the base. We don't have time to build it again. We have to go on.

"Eight more minutes." Abraham stares at his watch while his foot taps on the floor.

I should be more nervous, and I'm not. Maybe my confidence is still too great to shatter. I believe we will fix this, if not on this loop, then the next one. We have infinite trials. Infinite mistakes.

"Three minutes," he says.

I pick up my coffee and take a sip. It's at the verge of being too cold now. I run my nails through the Styrofoam. If the ball returns, we'll move onto the next trial—seven days. I go back through my notes and research. If this works, we are almost guaranteed to land on the main timeline at the point we broke free. We *have* to set the portal for seven days. That's the only way we can assure that the same amount of power is being generated. Like water, time will go to the lowest point, the hole, the tear we made when we broke free. It wants to be whole again.

What I don't know is if that will be clear to anyone else but us when we arrive. If we go back to the split on Monday, October eighth with this extra loop of seven days' time on our phones and calendars and in our stars, will anyone know it's not actually October fifteenth?

"Ten, nine, eight…"

When Abraham reaches one, the faded image of a red ball appears in the center of the portal. It drops to the ground and bounces once, twice, and again I catch it, and read the numbers I wrote on the side.

"Two-hundred and fifty-six." I show it to Abraham.

"I'm setting it for seven days," he says and resets the portal. I tuck the ball into my pocket, and we both stand back as the hum courses through our handmade portal.

A piece of the aluminum inside falls free as soon as the first line of light crosses the center.

"It's not going to last." Abraham wraps an arm around me.

"It will hold," I say. I have to believe that, otherwise it would be pointless to try.

The pool of light forms in the center of the opening. Another piece of the siding falls to the floor. The top bends inward; a shower of sparks sprays from the bottom where we substituted the copper wire.

Abraham moves toward the fire extinguisher, and I hold him back. "Let it fail," I say, and it does. The same blast strikes me in the chest, only this time, Abraham falls with me, against the wall, under the pile of papers. He scrambles out from the mess and slams his hand on the screen to kill the power.

"No," he says, while I'm still climbing my way out of books. "It didn't work."

The numbers on the screen are still scrolling downward, moving ever closer to zero.

"It didn't work," I say, legitimately shocked. It was supposed to work. All the calculations checked.

I pull myself onto the scratched leather sofa I've been sleeping on these past few days. I had a cat once. Martin. He died while I was in grad school, and I kept the couch he loved to scratch. He's behind us somewhere, in the past. The new version of me will remember him, but I won't remember this.

Abraham sits down next to me with his hands folded. "We can repair the damage. We have time. What if we set it for seven days in the future? We can rejoin the timeline there."

"We could also create a new loop," I say quietly. I achieved my greatest wish. I made time travel possible, if not incorrect, and no one will ever know about it. "I need to think."

I reach behind the couch for a bottle of champagne I'd been saving to celebrate. From the floor, I pick up two of my empty coffee cups and fill them to the brim with the champagne. I hand one to Abraham and take a sip. It tastes faintly of stale coffee.

Abraham holds his cup in both hands. "What if we're wrong?" he asks. "What if those numbers mean nothing? They could be a glitch. We could be panicking over nothing."

I laugh and take another sip of coffee-flavored champagne. "I like your hypothesis, Dr. Jenkins. I suppose we won't be able to test it until tomorrow morning." The countdown isn't wrong, though. The portal, all of our research, the last ten years of my life are based on that readout…but there are always possibilities.

Abraham sits back against the couch, drinks his champagne, and runs his fingers over the bald spot on the sofa's arm. "We could also remember what happens. We'll have more time to think."

We have endless time now, and it's not enough. We're nothing without our memory, our previous notes, our mistakes. We're just copies of who we used to be.

"Do you have a cat?" he asks, picking at one of the holes in the couch.

"I used to. His name was Martin."

"I had a dog," he said. "Baxter." He smiles at me with those perfect teeth, and I take one more swig of my champagne before I set it down.

"I don't want to talk about your dog or my cat."

I lean across the couch and kiss him. If I only have a few hours left to be me, then I want to spend them like this.

Monday

I wake up in Abraham's arms, my chest pressed to his. Before I sit up, grab my shirt, and re-tie my unwashed hair into a new bun, I marvel at the small scar on his upper lip, the one imperfection I was never close enough to see before. Proof that no science is perfect, not even the one that appears to be.

It's eight twenty-five. I'm not wearing my watch, and my phone is on the other side of the room, but I can work backward from the countdown clock now. We have about fifty-two minutes before time re-sets. I'm not as anxious as I thought I would be, maybe because of Dr. Jenkins' help, but I feel at peace. How many times have I wished I could start over? And now I get my chance.

Abraham stirs on the couch. I don't look at him. I stare at the clock while he gets dressed and stands beside me.

"Any last options?" he asks, running his hand along the back of my neck.

"No." I pick up a random coffee cup and shake it—empty. "I suppose I don't have time to get more coffee."

"You'll have plenty of time." He nods to the screen where just below the zero, the sequence starts all over again.

"Next time, I'll call Dr. Svensson," I say.

"No, you won't," he says, and we both laugh, because he's right.

I try for another coffee cup, disappointingly empty. For a lack of anything else to do, I pick up one of the fallen aluminum panels and push it back into place. Abraham, without question, grabs his drill and drives the screws into the metal.

When it's secure, I reach into my pocket and take out the red ball, number two-hundred and fifty-six. "We did it, you realize. We had a successful time travel test. Ten minutes."

It seemed so small before, and now, ten minutes into the future is the difference between being in the loop...

I drop the ball, and it bounces over empty coffee cups.

"Set the portal to ten minutes," I say.

"Why?" he asks as I shove him into the chair.

"Because I'm going to go through it."

"You can't. We haven't done human trials yet."

I reach over him and slide my finger across the screen. Sparks spray from the singed edge of the portal as electricity pours through it. Our newly repaired panel starts to peel free again.

"I can cross the gap," I say. "I know our work, and I can keep working from the other side."

The first beams of light shoots through the portal, and the small pool of light gathers in the center. I'll need a large one to cross through. Another bolt drops from the portal, and my biggest worry is that it will collapse before I can make it.

"I'll go with you," Abraham says.

"No." I squeeze his arm. "This is for me to do. I'm the one who made this loop. I'm the one who needs to end it, and there's a chance this is our first trial." Albeit a small chance. "You could remember. You need to stay here and explain it to…" Me. If I can't fix the loop, he and the new version of me will have to do it. We can try from both ends of the spectrum.

"We will fix this. I'll find you on the other side." I kiss his almost perfect lips one last time, hoping that's true.

Behind me, the portal is just wide enough for me to step through. The countdown clock is seconds before zero. A small fire burns at the bottom of the portal. I have to go now. Closing my eyes, I walk toward it, and I feel like I'm being reborn. This is what I always wanted. Not to bridge the gap between space and time, but to walk it. I wanted to be the one riding in the time machine.

I fall forward and strike my chin on the hard cement floor. It's my floor, my lab. Another body is next to me. Another falls onto my shoulders.

"Who are you?" She scrambles off my back as soon as someone else falls from the wall. I recognize the jeans, the blouse, the hazel eyes and the unwashed hair.

"You're me," one of the other one says before I can.

Oh God, they're everywhere, littering the room like my empty coffee cups. They're all me, in various states of exhaustion and filth, and they keep coming. I was right, I had done this before, endless times.

I push myself against the wall, trying to keep from getting crushed. "Get out of my way," one of them says. My elbow smashes into another Catherine, and I do a quick head count. Forty, fifty…sixty? Two more spill through the wall. We keep coming as the seven day loop continues to spin. What have I done?

4

THE TERROR OF LONDON

STEVE VAN SAMSON

Part 1

The drawing room was still, and it was dark. Within lurked a near perfect silence, broken only by the steady machinations of a nearby clock.

The old man turned to regard the ticking thing which cared little for his solitude. But the face of the grandfather clock was obscured—swallowed by the darkness of the hour. Once again, nothing could be discerned beyond the obvious. The hour was late. Very late indeed.

What little light there was came from a brass candelabra. Unmolested by breath or by draft, its three candle-flames glowed like strange ethereal things, but they could not hold the old man's gaze. This slid down the flickering shaft, onto the surface of a most impressive desk. The Bureau Mazarin was a piece fit for a Duke—imported from France, long before its current owner was born. Like most things in Covington Manor, the red and gold desk was usually immaculate, pristine. Before tonight, it had never known the touch of blood. Absently, a wrinkled hand pushed something out of the light. Something curved and pale that might have been bone.

In the shadows, framed portraits and statuary from around the world stood on table, on shelf, and next to book-lined walls. The surroundings spoke of worldly travels and rare privilege, but to the room's only occupant, such bric-a-brac was worthless. John Arthur Covington was a man who yearned for one thing alone—to once again feel adrenaline coursing through those useless sticks that had once been his legs.

John's formative years provided little enough time for anything beyond the retracing of well-established footsteps. He was his father's son, after all. The heir to a long line of healers that stretched four generations into the city's past. Duty and family weighed quite a lot, but there was nothing to be done. John was a good son and had become a fine upstanding member of society— another stalwart Covington for queen and country.

And if the man were secretly dead inside, such crosses were his alone to bare.

A curious thing occurred on the day he first loomed over a living subject—the cold power of a scalpel in one hand. In that moment, John Covington had discovered his first taste of true thrill. Not the sort described on a written page, but the real thing. The sort one's heart pumps to every nerve and sinew.

Of course, a surgeon's work was nothing if not bloody, but its potential woke something deep inside the young man. Something primal. Whether it was the prospect of saving lives or of plunging steel into warm flesh, the yearning that had plagued him since boyhood seemed satisfied. A surgeon's life might be no proper adventure, but there were certainly worse fates.

Thinking of those days made the old man's lips curl into a mirthless smile.

Such times seemed impossibly distant—less memory and more half-forgotten dream. With a twitch, he slid his wrinkled hands to the tops of large wheels. One on each side. The chair was a rolling chaise—an Alderman No. 9. The latest in a long line of mobile prisons.

A single push set the device in motion. Its large wheels carried the current patriarch of the Covington line across the drawing room. Ambivalently, John glanced up to where the bottom edge of a frame could be discerned. He didn't need to see the painted eyes of his great grandfather to know they did not approve.

The Covington line had been an affluent one for at least five generations. Doctors, surgeons—men of science, working to better the lives of the miserable and afflicted. Except for the one Covington who, after passing his final exam, decided that racing his horse down the steepest hill in Sussex would be a cracking good way to celebrate.

The race itself had been a short, one sided affair. John's horse, a pale gray thoroughbred, hadn't taken more than four steps before snapping an ankle. The rider hadn't been thrown, but instead remained in his saddle the entire way down the hill. In fact, if class-mate Tom Rutherford had not been along to witness the stunt, John would surely have died. Bent, broken and pinned beneath ninety stone of demised thoroughbred.

The great Dr. Bernard Covington had insisted on performing all of his son's surgeries personally. Though if God himself had held the scalpel, the result would have been no different.

To the old man's recollection, it had been around that time that the Covington portraits had begun to glare. John looked into the darkness above, to the very spot he knew his great grandfather's eyes were. He would not suffer their faces for much longer. Very soon he would leave on one last grand adventure. One final jaunt before the bill came due. After that, his relatives could look down their noses at whoever the hell they liked.

The Alderman rolled to a stop before a very large window. The moon was of little help, but such limited visibility could not stop John from seeing the view. Most of his adult life had been spent absorbing that garden, that fence, that cobbled street. He could feel them even now, burning beneath his dead heels.

Lazily, John turned again to the south wall, where the grandfather clock ticked and ticked and told him nothing. With ease, thumb and forefinger found particular spots on a hairless scalp remembering ancient, long gone aches. The pain existed only in echoes now, but it was real. His thumbs traced tiny circles, feeling the ticks of the clock pulse beneath his paper skin.

Seventy-nine. God, how could he have gotten so old? With a weary sigh, John's eyes meandered to a small Bombay cabinet, just barely outlined in candlelight. All his concentration fixed upon a tiny keyhole he could not see, but knew to be set into the cabinet's only drawer.

From a pocket in John's robe, a sizable keyring was produced. There were more than two dozen keys, though most were fairly small. As it happened, in Covington manor, doors were not the only things which required their touch. There were too many secrets. Too many little things to hide from prying eyes.

With a subtle key-turn click, he slid the drawer open. Inside lay a stack of literature—though calling them such felt wrong. Something like honoring a crow by dressing it for Christmas dinner. Dreadfuls, the common folk called them—an affectation which made clever reference to both subject matter and overall quality. They were trash rags. Adventuresome drivel for young boys, nothing more.

Though the room remained much too dark to see them properly, as John ran fingers over the rough, wood-pulp paper, he thought of his father. The great Bernard Covington would have cast the things into the nearest fireplace without second thought. Such trash had never been intended for consumption by men such as the Covington. John knew this well. It was the very reason he was smiling.

Picking up a small stack, he turned them to catch as much of the distant candlelight as possible. After flipping past a number of *Varney the Vampire* and an incomplete run of *Black Bess*, John stopped. The publication he had been looking for wasn't as old as the rest. The headline had been printed with a bold, whimsical font typically employed by circus posters. Letter by letter, his eyes devoured the title.

Spring-Heeled Jack: The Terror of London

Both above and beneath the title were fanciful illustrations of Londoners in varying states of distress—all of them, recoiling from the titular antagonist. Spring-Heeled Jack, the very specter said to have haunted England's green and pleasant land these past fifty years, appeared in every panel. Skulking around corners, leaping overhead and overall, making a proper menace of himself. The artist had based the appearance of the fiend on eyewitness testimonies—depicting ole Jack with curved claws, a mouth full of fangs and two horns protruding from his forehead.

The sight of those horns caused a familiar itch to prickle once more atop the old man's skull.

Hungrily, John's eyes swept across the central and largest illustration. Below Jack was a horse drawn carriage. The driver, whip in hand, was gaping up at the spring-heeled terror soaring overhead. In the carriage's windows, two faces were drawn, as well as little hands pressed firmly against the glass. Passengers, John remembered, as a slanted grin grew on his lips.

After placing the remaining Dreadfuls back into their hiding place, he slid the drawer closed. With the dull click of a turned key came the urge to again check the grandfather clock. But this, like the old aches on his scalp, John Covington decided to ignore. The Terror of London felt warm upon his lap. The effect was strangely comforting. Inside, locked within badly penned drivel, adventure was waiting to live again.

The old man rolled up to the desk which had been his for a very long time—whether the portraits of his progenitors liked it or not. After setting down the magazine, he mused at the sudden juxtaposition. Obscuring a patch of hand-worked filigree was a scrap of worthless trash. A publication intended to entertain a class of people who would never know the term Bureau Mazarin.

Straightening his spectacles, John found that his eyes wanted to wander. To regard the strange tableau at his right. The arrangement of blood and bone was abominable—belonging even less than the magazine, but he pushed it from his thinking. Then, with a deep, cleansing breath, John turned the paper cover of *Spring-Heeled Jack: The Terror of London.*

As his eyes scanned the first few paragraphs, memories began to unblur. Out of the haze, appeared a small horse drawn carriage led by a heavy-eyed driver. The carriage rumbled as it moved down a winding dirt road with rolling moors on one side and a steep drop-off on the other. There was a city nearby, from whence the carriage had come. Canterbury, John recalled. A fact, oddly, never mentioned in the text.

Coming around the bend, the driver (a man called George Plott) caught sight of something that made his eyes go wide. Though he had passed the old church many times before, George was less inclined to do so at night. The thing was more corpse than former house of God. Its roof, as well as the south and eastern walls, were gone completely—returned to rubble and dust at some point in the previous century. Despite this, the structure yet supported a pair of windows, which had always looked like eyes to George Plott. Seeing them now, he licked his lips and swallowed hard.

Part of him wanted to snap the reins—to race his horse drawn carriage past the ruin as fast as possible. The other half wanted to turn around and try again in the morning. The mind of George Plott worked feverishly—weighing both options as well as his own threadbare courage. As it happened, many seconds passed before he noticed the moon was missing. In the dark, a panicked George Plott squinted to see, but the world was shrouded. His eyes would adjust, but for now all they could discern was the pale, box-like ruin on the road ahead. Even in the pitch black, the church glared with square, empty eyes.

The sound was sudden, jarring. Shattering the still of perfect night was a sound most terrible. Part cry, part howl, it rang and it soared—gripping the carriage driver's heart as if in the talons of some hellish raptor. If asked whether he were hearing the voice of man or beast, George Plott would not have been able to say.

As if on cue, the moon broke free of its cloud to shine a solitary beam upon the glaring ruin. There on the wall, directly above glassless windows, which now seemed more like screaming mouths than eyes... there stood a man. Or perhaps, not a man. The fiend lunged, belching forth a burst of blue phosphorescence. The display froze poor George Plott where he sat. His joints felt no more supple than those of a statue, but the carriage horse was moving plenty. It snorted, angrily shaking its head, as if to deny the very existence of the howling thing. The animal's panic was inadvertently forcing the carriage back—nearer and nearer to the edge of the road and the steep drop-off just beyond.

It was then, as he struggled for control of the beast, George Plott remembered his carriage held passengers. Emboldened, he pulled hard on one of the reins—desperate to turn his horse the other way round.

Behind, the night once again flashed blue. George turned to the church, needing to locate his enemy. But the howling fiend was no longer on the wall—it was in the road. And it was running! In the moonlight, a pallid face was visible, as well as a pair of inhuman eyes that burned like balls of cold fire. The fiend was shaped like a man. Tall, gaunt and dressed in a long black cloak over what might have been an oilskin. By God, the thing had horns.

In mid sprint, the creature who could be none other than the fabled Spring-Heeled Jack, leapt high into the air—ten feet, twenty—more!

With the cries of his passengers in his ears, George looked up just in time to see a final crack of blue flame. The world flashed into livid detail, before once again going dark.

GONNNG!

The grandfather clock rang loud and true—filling every nook of the drawing room. John flinched, discovered he was clutching at his chest. His heart raced—but from the excitement of the story or of the jarring nature of being pulled from it, he did not know. Unnoticed, the Dreadful fell from his hands, flopping limply upon the Bureau Mazarin.

GONNNG!

Again the clock thundered and John turned to the south wall. He stared into the darkness, directly upon a face he could not see. He stared like that for a long time. Every successive chime counted by the old man's bones.

Twelve. That was the final number. He had been right after all. The hour had indeed been late.

Once the echoes of the clock's declaration had faded, John turned in his Alderman No. 9. His spine was straighter than before. His ears more acutely aware of the suffocating silence. Extending a shaky hand, he slid the candelabra to the right—fully illuminating the abominable arrangement there. Most of the bones were thin and curved, though some were large enough to have once held eyes. The leavings of Covington manor's many cats had been easy enough to acquire. The animals had all been so trusting—unable to sense danger until it was too late. An unfortunate sacrifice, but unavoidable. The book had called for lives. For organs and bones and their connective strings.

Blood had been the final ingredient. The blood of the summoner.

Acutely aware of the space growing between himself and the final stroke of midnight, John leaned forward. Reaching out, he slid the candelabra closer to the grim menagerie—taking care not to disturb the design beneath. The five-pointed star had been difficult to render, what with the special ink being his own blood. Thinking of it, John felt a twinge of pain under the bandages on his left hand. It was a good pain. It meant that none had been harmed for the night's endeavor save for himself and a couple of cats.

With a shaky hand, John opened a pocket watch, then abruptly snapped it shut. Two minutes past midnight. Had he done something wrong?

John fingered at his collar, finding it difficult to breathe. He thrust a key into the desk's central and most shallow drawer, extracting a small book. Leather-bound and embossed with the image of a serpent, the book appeared far older than the man who held it. John stopped at a drawing which closely resembled his obscene work of art. The left page showed a detailed illustration of a goat-faced pentagram above a bit of text which read: "blood of the summoner." On the opposite page was scratched a list of ingredients—instructions on creating the very tableau that now besmirched his great-grandfather's precious desk. John's eyes narrowed, reading each item carefully before falling upon a phrase written below in a far shakier hand.

"He calls at midnight." John whispered the line. His voice sounded so small—so far away. A chill found the nape of his neck, stiffening the tiny white hairs there. John looked up, taking in his surroundings with hungry eyes. Though no breeze could have infiltrated his sanctum, the candle-glow danced upon every surface.

Moments later, a new sound boomed into existence. Not the brassy gong of a grandfather clock, but something like the first note of a thunderclap. Hearing this, John's heart galloped, fueled with the thrill of the moment and of moments still to come. Again the thunder boomed—and again and again.

For a brief moment, John worried the sounds would rouse the servants, but of course, such a thing was impossible.

This hellish knocking… It was only for him.

Part 2

John's eyes were firmly fixed upon the massive double doors. He, himself, had locked them hours ago, after Mayhew had taken his uneaten supper away. One second the doors appeared distant, the next they were close enough to touch. With a steadiness that would have surprised the old man on a different day, he pushed forward a key—closer and closer—toward a tiny hole he could not see.

"Probably best to keep that locked. Privacy and all that…"

The voice was winter breeze—a scalpel that slipped through air and darkness with gleeful abandon. As John turned, his body felt stiff. There, in front of the large window, peering out into the moonless night there stood a man. Or perhaps, not a man. Pale, smartly dressed, and skeleton thin.

"It's late, John," said Gideon Crux. "Shouldn't you be in bed?"

John Arthur Covington felt himself try to speak, but his throat had become so dry he nearly choked. He found himself needing water the way a man lying face down in the Sahara needs water.

"Mr. Crux," John sputtered at last. "You've come."

"Of course. Refusing a summons would be rude…and there is nothing I detest in this world more than discourtesy. Especially when such *pains* were taken." The thing by the window spoke in tones of polite conversation, but there was a storm brimming just beneath. "I wonder…will begging work half as well if you only use one hand?" A startling sound sliced through the still—like a deep draft taken in through the nose. "That cut smells deep."

"Begging..." Hissed the old man. "You'd like that, wouldn't you? Well, you should know... you'll hear no begging tonight. Not from me."

"Bold words... but ultimately impotent." Gideon Crux turned a shining black eye from the window—setting his gaze upon his host. Then he began to walk around the darkened room, admiring its decor as if for the first time. "Forgive me. I fear the long years in this business have filled me with the blood of a pessimist. Tell me, John—have you the date?"

John sighed, resignedly wheeling himself back to the Bureau Mazarin. "I know what you must be thinking...but you are wrong."

"Wrong am I?" Mock-outrage had entered the slithery voice. "Age has emboldened you, John. Though it seems to have done little for your sense of propriety. Wrong, indeed." The voice of Gideon Crux had become playful. "As of three minutes ago, the date is the seventh of August...in the year of your Lord, eighteen hundred and eighty eight. You, John Arthur Covington, latest in a long line of blah-blah-blah...have whiled away all the years in your contract, save five. My presence in this room, at this late hour, can mean but a single thing...you, nearing the end of said contract, wish to renegotiate the terms. It is not exactly a new story."

Scowling, John worked his jaw and said nothing.

"As I said..." continued Gideon Crux. "I have been in this business a very long time. And, if I were being *kind*, I might suggest that you save your mewling words. I have heard them all before and in every imaginable sequence. The letter of the contract is set— as is that which is owed for services rendered. Even a proper beg would do little to change that."

"I've already told you..." John's voice came out half a whisper. "You'll hear no begging from me. I have no delusions, Mr. Crux. From where I sit, I can see the door at the end of this journey, and I know what lies on the other side. Unfortunately, the thought of another five years—waiting—rotting away in this chair..." Vehemently, John shook his head. "I don't need time, Mr. Crux. What I need is to live. To feel something real—if only for a single night."

"Is that so?"

The old man in the chair averted his eyes and said nothing more.

"Interesting..." Gideon Crux uttered the word slowly, thoughtfully, as if savoring the unexpected spice. "How very interesting." His voice was distant at first and then, suddenly too loud, too close. *"Tell me John, what exactly would you like to feel? Escape? Release? The earth, once more, burning beneath your heels?"*

"Yes." John Covington had to fight off a shudder. "All of that. Dear God, yes." John's words seemed to explode out of him, but they felt weighted. Contorted by something like shame.

"God is not here, John," hissed the knife-like voice of Gideon Crux.

The moments that followed were long. Unbearably long. The only sounds were thoughtful footsteps, traveling from one side of the room to the other, and the incessant ticks of a clock that no longer mattered. Unable to bare the stagnancy, John unlocked another of the desk's seven drawers. From this, he extracted a glass center bowl—lidless and quite empty. Flickering light played within the many hand-cut facets, lending them an eldritch quality.

"Always liked that bowl," mused Gideon Crux. "Though... seeing it again, I can't help but wonder. Which is more empty? The bowl itself? Or the man who is unable to fill it?"

John snickered. "I'd say it were a draw." After a long, silent moment, he set the object down upon the Bureau Mazarin. "This bowl once belonged to my great aunt Helena. It has not held fruit in over ten years. Not since..." His eyes drifted to the Penny Dreadful. To the illustration of the carriage and to the devilish fiend who leapt and soared above. "Since that last trip to the country. On a long, winding road, just outside Canterbury."

"Ah yes. Canterbury." The voice of his guest rang with newfound indifference. "I remember Canterbury. Though, to tell you the truth, John...I much prefer the version described in that penny novel. If only it were life that imitated art and not the other way round, eh?"

"That book is a fiction. Trite nonsense."

"Oh I know it is, John. I *know*." Crux spoke as if to a wounded child. "That night outside Canterbury was wrought with more of your trickster nonsense and little else. Leaping upon that carriage and slapping the cheeks of its driver. One! Two!" Sounding dejected, Gideon Crux unleashed a long sigh. "At least you scared the hell out of him. I quite doubt the wretch was ever the same again...not to mention *the horse*."

"I didn't scare anyone!" said John, a quiet maelstrom beneath his words. "Not me. Never me. That was Jack."

Gideon Crux gave a shrug. "Your point is a moot one, John. Besides, whatever name you want to use, the real story wasn't exactly the sort of thing that sells trash novels, now is it?"

John Covington glared with a tremble upon his upper lip.

"What the public wants—nay, craves...is tragedy. Excitement. Ghastly piled on top of horrendous!" This Crux said with a dramatic flourish of one bone-thin arm. "Canterbury may have been a laugh, but as a final act I found it woefully lacking. You had been saving that last jaunt up for over nine years and the best you could come up with was a panicked horse and some rosy cheeks. If you ask me, John...your work peaked where it began."

No response.

"Oh come now... tell me you haven't forgotten the Blacksheath Fair! I can picture the two girls as if they were right beside us now. They could not have been more than fourteen. The papers said the assailant was no man, but a hideous, horned fiend that, without provocation, did fall upon these poor defenseless moppets. Correct me if I'm wrong, but I recall reading that both blouse and skin had been torn open by iron claws. Shredded, John...the way a lion will a gazelle, before licking off the skin. Sadly, before the fiend could be apprehended, it was said to have leapt a tall fence and bounded away—*all with maniacal laughter on its lips."*

As he gazed into the facets of the glass center bowl, the old man found himself wishing it would spontaneously shatter. When the voice of Gideon Crux resumed, it came in an ice cold whisper.

"But that isn't the full story, is it John? The papers didn't know about your eyes, but I do. I was there. Right by your side. I remember the wanton passions they held. Say whatever you will. Place the blame upon some alter ego if it helps you stomach another night, but I know the truth. You enjoyed hurting those girls, John. You relished their every shriek and you wanted more. Wanted to go deeper."

"No! That wasn't me! I never wanted to hurt anyone. Not ever!" John slammed an open hand down onto the hard Mahogany. "God damn you."

"Oh he does, John. Believe me he does. Perhaps you should have called him instead." A short series of steps carried Gideon Crux to the other side of the desk—the flickering flames lending him an aspect of the horrific. "But then, God could never fill your dear Auntie's bowl."

Gideon Crux—everything about the man was too narrow. Prominent bones jutted out above the hollows that were his cheeks. Crowning these were two of the bluest eyes that John had ever seen. They burned and they froze and by God, they did not blink. The man wore no hat, only an oily crop of pale hair which was slicked back—plastered to his scalp.

As John drank in his guest's countenance, he watched thin, tattered lips part to reveal a row of sliver-like teeth. These had the shimmer of pearls and were far too numerous for a human jaw. The offered expression both approximated and parodied a smile. The terrible grin turned John's bowels into ice—forcing him to face the sort of creature he had once again invited into his home.

"'Once more unto the breach, dear friends. Once more. Or close the wall up with our English dead.'" The fierce blue eyes stared and burned and did not blink. "'In peace there's nothing so becomes a man as modest stillness and humility. But when the blast of war blows in our ears, then imitate the action of the tiger... Stiffen the sinews, summon up the blood.'" As he spoke, the man-shaped thing stalked around the bend of the desk. The suit he wore was neat, if a handful of decades out of style. Absently, his sharp hand brushed some unseeable dust from an equally sharp shoulder. And when the foot of the Alderman No. 9 had been reached, Gideon Crux stopped to glare. "You pretend to regret. To possess no blame...yet I did not summon myself. Not tonight and not fifty years ago. You can lie to me but not to yourself. Never yourself. I know you, John. You wish to be the tiger. To feel claws sprout from your fingers. Even, for one last time, to leap and soar with the unfettered lusts of Spring-Heeled Jack burning in your chest. Admit it, John. Say it."

"Yes." John's voice came low but with an edge.

Long fingers wrapped around the armrests of the rolling chaise as Gideon Crux pushed so close to the old man, scarcely a centimeter separated their noses. John tried to wheel back, but the added weight of the thin man was incredible. Utterly dispropor-tionate to his slight, bony frame.

"Sorry. Didn't catch that."

"Yes!" Blurted John. "Yes, damn you!"

"Then give me a real ending!"

When the gash that was Crux's mouth opened again, John could almost see his reflection in those tightly packed slivers of pearl.

"No more of this fear-mongering, trickster nonsense. Screaming girls, toppled carriages, and slaps on the cheek might be good for a laugh, but I want a final act worthy of the immortal bard. A misadventure for all time. Deliver me this, John and we shall have betwixt us, an amended accord." With this, Gideon Crux straightened, gliding back a step. Then he extended a hand.

John had to fight just to hold onto consciousness—his face a mask of determination. Wordlessly, he reached out, seized the creature's hand, and shook. Then, pulling away, John set that hand upon the empty center bowl and shoved it forward.

Once again, an unsettling smile stretched the tattered lips of Gideon Crux. He swung a skeleton arm over the bowl. Then, with a flick of the wrist, he dropped numerous *somethings* that pinged into the bowl, thin and high—bell-like.

"You ask for one final jaunt... I give you five. One for every year I now reclaim."

When John could breathe normally again, he redirected his gaze. The center bowl now held five small berries. They looked like black currants, but on closer inspection, John saw that they weren't black at all, but red.

"These are different." He sputtered the words, unable to look away from the red currants that were somehow darker than black. "Crux...why do they look different?"

"Our contract has been altered—per your request, John. I suggest you not squabble over every letter." Gideon Crux smoothed out the lapels of his jacket. "Doing so at this stage would be most...*discourteous.*"

Heart pounding near out of his chest, John raised his eyes to the spot where his guest had been standing. Of Gideon Crux, there was no sign, but at the end of the Bureau Mazarin were objects he had never seen before. A rather fashionable top hat and long coat—the garb of a modern English gentleman. In the low light, the garments looked full black, but somehow John knew that was not their true color.

It was all too much. With a weak gasp, the old man slumped

deeper into his Alderman No. 9 and allowed consciousness to slip away.

Part 3

There might have been dreams. Of flying. Of air moving past his face. Of legs that could feel and carry and leap. But if such things did exist, they were obliterated by the clap of bottled thunder, which exploded in John's skull. The sound both jarring and terrible was followed by another, just as loud. And then again. The old man craned his head toward the doors of the drawing room. Someone was knocking.

"Sir?" called a distant voice. "Can you hear me? Are you alright?"

The panicked voice felt familiar. Slowly, John stirred, but every inch of him ached. Placing hands on the rails of his rolling chaise, he forced himself into a sitting position. The pain came from every-where, but dulled quickly. It was then that John realized he had been dreaming. Not of flying, but of darker things. Spells of blood and bone—and of a late night palaver with the devil. It was all perfectly ludicrous.

"Mr. Covington. If you can hear, me, please..."

"I'm here, Mayhew" John cried out at last.

"Sir!" The voice on the other side of the doors flared up with relief. "Thank heavens! We feared—that is... I have been knocking for quite some time."

The old man could hear the relieved voices of further staff alongside the shuffling of many feet. His vision proved slow to focus, but John could see the candelabra. The candles it had once held now existed only as pools of hardened wax besmirching the surface of his great grandfather's precious desk.

"I'm fine, Mayhew. Just...fell asleep in the memoirs again."

"Ah, the old memoirs," said Mayhew "Another ink well drained, I presume?"

"You know me too well." As John said this, a flash of pain kicked hard, causing his teeth to grind. When he opened his eyes again, they focused on something which laid upon the desk. Though he could not recall how it might have happened, the magazine had been torn utterly in two. As if by themselves, the old man's eyes flitted across an intact section of title.

—*Jack: The Terror of London*

"Well done, Sir." There came a pause. "Will you be taking your breakfast in the drawing room today?"

"No!" The word exploded past John's lips before he had thought to stop it. His eyes thrust forth like daggers. They were focused on what lay past the torn magazine and hardened pools of wax. Unlike the old Dreadful, the occultist tableau was quite untouched. "I believe that today, I shall breakfast in the parlor."

"Very good, Sir," chimed Mayhew—newfound mirth in his voice.

As footsteps padded away, John's eyes moved to the glass center bowl. As he stared, the heels of his dead feet began to throb hotly—pounding in time with his tired heart. Inside the bowl were what looked like small, dark berries. He counted them once and then again. Four. Why were there only four?

As if in a dream, John's head turned. Slowly, the Bombay table which held his guilty pleasures came into view. Strewn atop the rich wooden surface sat a stylish top hat and coat. By the look of things, they had been tossed there rather unceremoniously. Beneath these, poking out by only a few inches, was something which glinted in the morning sun. Something silver and very, very sharp. Seeing the tip of the knife had a profound effect on the man in the chair. And in that moment, John Arthur Covington remembered every detail of his dream. His ghastly, horrendous dream.

In retrospect, he had gotten his wish, as promised. The one thing he had yearned for ever since Canterbury. John had once more felt the earth burning beneath his heels. The red currant had twisted him into an entirely new terror for Londontown. One which had coursed over cobbled streets and around dark alleys— not with mischief in his heart, but with the cold power of a scalpel. The adventure had been a messy one, but such was to be expected.

A surgeon's work is nothing if not bloody.

5

THE OLD WORLDERS

EMMA LOWRY

The wind howled as it ripped past the sparse trees and sparser houses, picking at the leaves and the wooden shingles. Dust billowed up from its resting place and painted my boots a dull red. As I sat on my front porch, the sun fell to the orange horizon, a dying fire beneath the consuming night sky.

I pulled my handkerchief up over my mouth and nose, closing my eyes as the dirt blew by. The red dust smelled of rust and baked insects, burning my nostrils and throat. People who forgot their masks during dust storms stumbled out of the crimson clouds coughing up blood.

Horse hooves struck dirt down the road. Down the path, a man dropped down from the worn saddle while his pale horse swatted at flies with its tail. The deep grooves in his tired face made his distant gray eyes look even further away. His name was Louis Ford, or something near it. He returned to this dusty graveyard of a town once each week to bring a carefully wrapped letter to our mayor.

I stood from my weathered seat. The porch platform sat only a foot from the ground, its supports long sunken into the red earth.

The boards creaked with each step, my boots summoning thin spurts of dust that rested within the ancient wood.

I headed to the center of town and the mayor's house. Louis Ford waved to me, the bones of his thin hand visible as I neared him.

"Nicholas," he called. "How was the harvest?"

"It was alright," I told him. "Better than the last."

I tugged at my leather gloves as I walked, pulling the worn material from my hands. I tucked them under my belt beside a holster that had hung empty for several years. The wind tore at the length of my coat, whipping and licking at my calves as I strode over the packed road.

I reached Ford and shook his hand. He nodded his graying chin and worked up a thin smile. He held the letter under one arm and looked toward the mayor's house.

"So where'd you just come from, Louis?" I asked him.

"Stanleyville, down south thirty miles or so." A rough chuckle escaped his throat. "Compared t' them, I'd say you folks have it easy here in Devon Gorge."

"Really?" I inquired. "What's the news from Stanleyville?"

Ford looked down, his brow creased, and then turned his gaze to the mayor's building. "I, uh, I have t' get this to Hertz, Nicholas. Sorry t' be curt."

I nodded to him as he started up the steps of the mayor's porch. Louis knocked once and the door swung open.

A few minutes later, Louis Ford exited, pulled himself up onto his horse, and started off back down the dirt path, fading into the now purple horizon. His bobbing silhouette melted into the darkness.

The mayor emerged shortly after, his thick fingers scratching at his mottled goatee. He looked at me for a moment, questioning the reason behind my presence, and then went on his way walking. He fiddled with the letter in his hands nervously, opening it and closing it several times, as if hoping its message would change.

He stopped suddenly, his heel digging into the ground, and turned to face me. "Nicholas," he asked. "Has there been word around town recently about that house down on the north side?"

"No, Mayor Hertz, there hasn't. Why do you ask?"

He stared at me for a moment, his eyes dark under the shadow of his brimmed hat, his thumb tucked into the waistband of his jeans. He looked back down at the letter.

"No reason. Just wondering. No need to fuss." His lips made a straight, taut line.

"Does it have to do with that note, Mayor Hertz?" I inquired.

In a strange, aggressive tone he replied, "That ain't your concern, Nicholas."

He turned his back to me once more and started off again. I watched him, curious, as he disappeared back into his home.

The house he spoke of down at the end of town was abandoned. Its door faced the empty surrounding land. The people who had lived there a couple years ago were called "Old Worlders" by locals in town.

These previous occupants spoke maniacally of a society said to have once existed here. They spoke of incredible man-made creations that simply couldn't exist. They claimed that these fantastical things had been around long ago, and they insisted that the house was a part of it, that it had revealed something to them, but their words were meaningless gibberish.

Anyone with sense, I figured, went on their way without believing the Old Worlders' nonsense.

Over and over again, I thought of the mayor outside his house, looking down at the letter Louis had brought him. I wanted to know what had made him so anxious. So, as the blanket of night met the dying light of the horizon, I made my way down to the house once occupied by the Old Worlders. The house's blue paint chipped and peeled as if a thousand small hands had picked at it with dirty fingernails. The exposed wood was dotted with the decorations of rot. The vertical supports leaned inwards, exhausted and giving in. The lower roof of the porch sunk toward the center, and the front door looked like it sat in the mouth of a monster. The house smiled at me as I approached.

I wanted to know what the talk was about this house and why Mayor Hertz seemed concerned. Perhaps it had something to do with what was happening in Stanleyville? Did it have to do with us?

As I climbed the porch steps, they groaned. I approached the door, dark with a single glass pane level with my face. In it was my reflection, and I was reminded by my black-dusted cheeks that it had been several days since I last shaved. I noted to do so once back home.

The wind whispered by me while I stood at the entrance. I waited for sound, for any sign of movement or habitation, but the soft hum of the night's gentle breeze alone filled my ears.

I tried the clouded brass handle, then paused.

What was I doing here? Nothing good ever came from this house. But something was telling me to go on, something that I couldn't quite describe, so I tried the handle again. After some force, it turned suddenly. The door swung open with a cry.

Shadows cast by the pale moonlight crawled up the walls like the fingers of beasts. The foyer split off into two rooms on the left and right. A collapsed staircase climbed up the middle. The place was eerily empty, like its insides had been torn out, leaving behind a cold, lifeless shell. Instinct told me to leave, but I was drawn further inside.

I cautiously entered the room on my right. The air was still but the dust, once baked into the floor's woodgrains, jumped free beneath my footsteps. The room's only furnishing was a chair in the far corner. It waited, statue-like, having been ignored since its previous owners left.

The walls were covered with strange golden frameworks, each containing an image within their rectangular bodies—an image so perfectly real. It was like looking through a window into the life of another person. A chill ran down my spine.

I had seen images hung on walls, but never anything like this. They were never more than pencil and charcoal. My home was filled with drawings I'd done in my free time, but in all my years of practice, I had never created something like the images in this house. There was *more* to them, some indescribable dimension enclosed within their decorated frames.

The life that sparkled in these fabricated eyes was unsettling. They stared at me from behind their glass panes, their small worlds each so full of color. I had no idea what they were or where they came from.

One showed a single man with bright blue eyes and gray hair. He smiled, his teeth clean and white. He wore a bright yellow jacket of some foreign material. It looked crisp and almost shined in the sunlight. There was a mountain in the sky behind him, one that towered high over the lands around it. Something was raining down behind him—a swarm of small white specks that clung to his hair and clothing.

Outside, the insects sang an off-key melody to the moon.

I studied a new image, this one containing a metallic red shape. It had dark wheels that were coated in something black; the setting sun danced off the contraption's colored flanks as if they were wet with water. A man appeared to be sitting in it, shielded by a long glass window. Two round lamps sat across from each other, imbedded into the front of this strange carriage lit with a white, unnatural light.

The thing, painted with uncanny precision, matched the wild stories of the Old Worlders. I didn't know what to think. I was scared and amazed, and my mind was torn between what I knew and what the Old Worlders had told us. I searched for a place in between, but I was lost. If their stories about this red object were true, what else was?

The rest of the strange paintings depicted people. Lots of people, all in unfamiliar clothing. There was so little dust in the world in these frames. There were no storms of wind, no great crimson clouds closing in over the horizon. I glanced down at my own clothes and the red stains the earth left on them.

I wondered how the Old Worlders came across images such as these. How had they even come to exist?

A strange feeling crept up my spine. The air thickened, and the stench of red dust faded away. I began to panic as the atmosphere changed. I felt on the verge of suffocation, of passing out.

My toes went numb first. Then fingers. Suddenly my legs wouldn't move. I attempted to breathe; the air within my ribcage turned cold. It bit at my throat as I took in another breath. Tremors crossed my chest. My face ceased to feel, and I became lightheaded.

My eyes flicked back to the images mounted on the wall, but they were no longer alone. Around them, a thin paper blanketed the paneled wood. It was decorated in pink floral designs subtle enough to melt into the soft colored background.

The light in the room was bright and warm with the golden glow of late noon. Sun dust, white instead of crimson, floated in front of me.

The room now housed an assortment of furniture. Against the wall, a long bench with cushions, all coated in a soft red fabric unbleached by the sun, faced a glossy knee-high table.

My feet sank slightly into an ornate rug that hadn't been there moments ago. Designs ran along the edges of the rug, and larger, more intricate floral images sprouted from the center.

Voices called back and forth somewhere outside. They were high and cheerful and spoke joyous gibberish.

A woman walked into the room and smiled. She was beautiful, her skin smooth and eyes bright, and she wore a crisp, green shirt and jeans.

"Bradley," she said to me contently. "Glad you're home. The kids are outside playing baseball. They hoped you would pitch for them."

The words she spoke made no sense to me. Her accent was unfamiliar, certainly not from Devon Gorge. What was she talking about? Baseball? Pitching? Pitching what?

Despite my state of confusion, my mouth spoke words on its own: "Sure, hun. Did Harris finish his homework this time before going out?"

The voice that came from my throat was alien. I had no control over my mouth or the formation of my words. I felt like a passenger in an uncomfortably intimate vessel.

"Yes." She laughed. "I made sure he did it when I got home from the office."

My lips curved up in a smile, and I nodded. Again, I had not willed the gestures. My hands—which I realized were not my own—moved to take off my coat. It was made of a clean gray fabric, stiff in the shoulders. I laid it across the short table and started by the woman, through the doorway on the far end of the room and into the next.

This room was floored with a smooth white stone cut into small squares. The walls were lined with white cabinets, and at waist height stood a long marble-topped counter housing more cabinet doors. There was a wooden table and four chairs, all in pristine condition. To my left was a door leading out the back of the house. I could see outside through an open window beside it.

Two children played in grass so green it stung my eyes. They both wore bright shirts and shorts. The breeze nipped at their light hair. A tall tree full of life and leaves stood just behind them. Past it was a line of short houses similar to this one, all painted different colors and vibrant in the golden sunlight.

Outside that door, that grass, those houses—it couldn't be. Everything was impossible and defied the reality I knew.

I felt the gentle air as it flowed in through the window. It sent tingles down my arms and toyed with my hair. I closed my eyes for a moment, took a deep breath in, and looked out at the grass once more.

Something rose within me, a strange but comforting feeling, as I watched the two young children run back and forth in the yard.

The scene fell away, the colors faded, the stench of sun-baked earth returned. The world was once again dust and darkness.

I stood alone and empty in the room, looking at a solid wooden door with rusted hinges. The floor's smooth white stone had transformed back to rotting wood, and the thin air tasted of burnt rust. Longing to return to that other place filled my chest.

I walked back into the room with the pictures, the floorboards creaking under my feet. I looked at the decorated wall. My mind fought to retain the image I had seen, the life in which I had momentarily lived.

Questions raced through my head. Doubt told me that I had imagined it all in state of wonder. Something deep within me shouted back and defended the honesty of my eyes.

I knocked on the door of Mayor Hertz's house. I had to tell him. I knew he misunderstood the house of the Old Worlders, just as we had all misunderstood its owners. He had the power to tell the whole town the truth, but he needed to know it.

After a moment, the door swung open and I was met by a slender man with a short tuft of black hair and a matching mustache.

"I'd like to speak with the mayor," I told him.

"Name?"

I frowned. "You know who I am, Jameson."

"Name?" he repeated.

"Nicholas Payne," I answered.

Jameson nodded and then stepped back, closing the door.

"Wait," I insisted, "I need to talk to him now. It's important!"

The doorman paused and looked at me for a second, puzzled. "Mayor Hertz is having dinner with his wife and children, Mister Payne. You can speak to him afterwards."

I started again, but the door was closed before I could convince him otherwise.

I waited outside for some twenty minutes, pacing in the dust in front of the mayor's porch. Little pebbles bounced off of the toes of my boots and scattered like roaches under lamp light. What would I say to him? How would I say it? I began to walk frantically, trying to piece together what the house meant for everyone in this town.

The door opened once more, and Mayor Hertz took a step out onto his porch. He saw me and sighed, his shoulders sinking. He took slow, deliberate steps down the two short stairs, his arms crossed over his chest, and stopped beside me.

"What is it, Nicholas?" he requested.

"That house," I began. "I looked around in there, the one owned by the Old Worlders, and I..." My tongue had trouble explaining my visions. "I saw things. Very strange things."

"And so did those Old Worlders," Hertz replied. "They were always 'seein' things.' They were crazy. It's why we drove 'em out two years ago. You remember."

I nodded. "Yes, but it was strange. Have you ever been in there, Mister Hertz?"

"Nope, and I don't plan to ever set foot in that lunatic place."

"Yes, but…the things I saw, Mister Hertz. A world where everything was different. I was me, but not me, and I—he—had a wife. And kids. And they were playing outside. And the grass was so green, and there were so many houses…" The words stumbled from my mouth.

The mayor looked at me silently for some time. His jaw was moving, but his lips remained sealed. I could see him thinking. The wind howled in the distance. A scowl slowly formed across his face.

Finally, he replied in a low, harsh voice. "That place breeds insanity, Nicholas. Those Old Worlders breed insanity. I've been talkin' with some townsfolk, and we've decided that it's time that house be brought down."

"What?" I cried. "You can't destroy it! Maybe the Old Worlders were on to something, Mayor Hertz."

"What do you know, huh? Look at what that house has already done to you! Only a day, and it's driven you into lunacy. Everyone who's ever stepped foot in that house has come out speakin' nonsense. It's dangerous to all of us, and we're burnin' it down!"

"You don't understand," I pleaded. "You need to see for yourself; you need to feel what I felt!"

He strode past me, back up his porch stairs and into his house. He slammed the door. The noise cut through the hum of the night.

I couldn't stop thinking about that house. I turned over and over in my sleep, the images on the walls burned into my mind. In my dreams, they moved. They spoke in the accent that Bradley and his family had. They were trying to tell me something, something important, but the roaring sounds of fire drowned out their words. I had to know more. I needed to see more.

When I woke up the next morning, I returned to the house of the Old Worlders. As I approached, I spotted the silhouette of a person standing down the road. The person appeared to be gazing at the crumbling house.

When I got closer, I saw it was Louis Ford.

"Louis?" I asked.

He looked over and nodded to me, his thin hands tucked into his pockets.

"Nicholas," he said. "Good t' see you."

"What are you doing out here?"

He looked back to the house. "The next delivery wasn't so far off. I figured I'd stop by Devon Gorge on my way t' it."

I stopped to stand beside him, and his pale eyes flicked back to me.

"You know what this is, Nicholas?"

"I went inside yesterday," I told him. "I saw some odd things."

He nodded as if unsurprised. "'Course you did, Nicholas."

I held his gaze, hoping for further explanation. Louis rested back in his stance, leaning on his heels.

He commented, "It's amazing, isn't it?"

"Yeah," I answered, slightly frustrated. "But what, why?"

Louis Ford inhaled slowly, deliberately picking his words. "It's a bridge. Or hole, if that's how you see it."

"In what?"

"Time."

I gazed at the house. Finally, my thoughts pulled themselves together into a short question. "You're telling me what I saw was real?"

"Like the dust on your shoes, Nicholas," he replied.

"So the Old Worlders were on to something?"

Louis shook his head, his eyes focused on a point too distant to see. "More than that," he murmured. "They were right. They knew everything. This point here, right before you and I, this is the place where our existences meet. T' stand in that house is t' stand in a tear in space and time." Louis Ford's tone was flat, like this was all entirely ordinary to him.

A tear in space and time. The phrase circled in my reeling mind. "How do you know all of this?" I questioned.

After a pause, he answered, "I've traveled up and down this region for quite some time now. I've seen it over and over."

"Where are you from?"

"A different place. A lot of different places. I've lost track of them all."

He stepped away from the tear in time and turned toward the center of town.

I looked at the toothy smile of the collapsing porch roof and muttered, "So there was a world before? A different world?"

Ford nodded and then repositioned the brimmed hat on his head. A morning gust blew the thin red dirt of the landscape past our feet and ankles, painting our boots. He started on his way, walking with loose shoulders and a wandering gaze.

"Hertz wants to destroy it," I said.

His back straightened, his heels driven into the dusty ground. He didn't turn to face me.

"What will that do?" I asked.

Ford shrugged. "I don't know," he admitted. "I suppose it'll be gone."

"But people need to know," I pleaded. "People need to see."

He turned to face me, the grooves of his face dark and almost deeper. His brows pulled together, and his eyes were lost in the shadows of the ascending sun.

"Then save it, Nicholas."

———————

I hammered my fist on the mayor's door until my palm prickled with pain. Jameson opened the door, his face twisted in annoyance.

"What?"

"I need to speak with Hertz."

"*The mayor* is not available."

"Make him available."

Jameson stared, eyes wide and filled with disbelief, as if I had uttered something horrible. He slammed the door, the wood stopping only inches from my face.

I knocked again, furiously, but received no response. I jumped off the porch and yelled up at his windows, demanding he talk to me. My voice cracked several times during my wild shouting.

Daytime had brought more townspeople to the street. They stared. Men and women carried containers and water, children ran across the dusty roads, and the elderly rocked in chairs on porches. They continued with their chores, but they kept glancing at me, scurrying their children away.

"The Old Worlders were right!" I yelled, my throat growing sore. "You need to see, all of you! You need to know!"

My heel caught a rock, and I stumbled back a step. I caught myself and looked up at the townspeople. They stared at me like I was a rabid animal.

"Please," I begged. "Believe me!"

Red, burning dust blew into my eyes as they sped away from me.

I sprinted back down the road, my mind racing as fast as my feet. I wanted to know more. I needed to know more. Who were they? When was it? Where was it? What happened to those Old

Worlders? To that other world? If that house fell under the mayor's foot, I would never know.

I ascended the steps of my house's porch in a single flying bound. The heels of my boots struck the wood planks with a crack. I pulled open my front door, leaving it ajar as I made my way up the narrow flight of stairs and turned into my bedroom. The blotchy ceiling was slanted, forcing me to hunch over. The room was bare except for my bed against the back wall and a dresser by its side.

I opened the dresser's top drawer. Inside it was empty except for a coat of red dust and a single revolver. It slept on its side, its smooth metal clouded with time. Six shots waited quietly in its cylinder. I withdrew the gun and slid it into the holster on my right hip.

I hadn't felt its weight for a long time. I drew my revolver several times, trying to regain the speed I'd once had. I didn't want to use it, but I feared the Hertz wouldn't listen to reason and he'd try to destroy the Old Worlder's house.

How I wished that my walls could be decorated with images like the Old Worlders'. They were like windows into other lives. What was it like to be surrounded by the soft floral designs that had delicately colored the walls of that home?

Before the sun descended behind the horizon, I departed.

Down the road, people gathered at the mayor's house. I saw the stout form of a man with his thumbs tucked at his hips. The brim of a hat made the movements of his head clear. He spoke excitedly to those around him. Mayor Hertz rallied the people to begin their march.

He pointed north, toward the tear in time. I ducked between houses to a different street. What had begun as a walk became a run. My feet pulled my body against the power of the wind. The tail of my coat cracked as it ripped through the evening air.

When I arrived at the house of the Old Worlders, I paused

shortly before heading up the steps. I looked briefly toward the center of town. I could just make out dancing torch light and the writhing silhouette of a mob.

I climbed the stairs and entered, closing the door behind me.

My feet carried me back into the room with the framed images. My eyes flicked over each of them, drinking in the colors and preserving the detailed paintings in my memory. My hand came to rest on the stock of my revolver.

I let my head bow. I was disappointed to see the worn, dusty planks instead of floral carpeting. I wanted to live in that old world where the grass was green and the hearts were light. Where fathers returned home to find children in the yard playing. Where there was little dust and little worry. I wanted to exist in the time I had witnessed. It had been beautiful.

I closed my eyes.

I heard approaching commotion and the mayor's booming voice.

Then there was silence.

I looked up. The world was different—vivid, lively, breathtaking. The light pouring into the room was soft and golden. My feet sank into the carpet, and I heard the voices of the two boys and the wife in the other room. The warm scent of something cooking crossed my nostrils. It was sweet and smelled of caramel, a scent I had all but forgotten.

The gray coat with padded shoulders was hung up in the corner of the room. I removed a brimmed hat from my head and placed it on a hook beside the jacket. My hand lingered there for a moment. My fingers—the man's fingers—trembled.

I—he—looked out the window. A shape flew parallel to the horizon; it resembled a bird whose wings didn't flap. It left a soft trail in its wake, drawing a stripe across the yellow sky.

The man's wife had silenced the children. I heard another voice, one that was grainy and modified like someone speaking through a pipe. Its accent resembled that of Bradley and his wife, and I had a hard time understanding it.

The woman spoke with a wavering voice: "Bradley…"

"What is it?" my mouth answered. There was silence.

"No," she said. "No, no…"

A spark of terror ran through me. Bradley understood the meaning of this tone, this diction. I started backward, about to turn and move into the other room, but my feet stopped. My gaze was drawn back to the flying silhouette in the sky.

It moved slowly, leisurely, puffing out the thin line of smoke behind it. Something moved at its belly. It was a hatch opening.

Bradley's heart began to race. Why? I wondered. I wanted to move back, to follow the sound of the woman's distress, but I was powerless here. I was a bystander, an audience, witnessing the unmalleable past.

I watched the dark, moving object in the sky.

Something dropped from the open hatch. It was large and oblong. Square fins protruded from one end.

It fell slowly—so painfully slow. I could feel this man's hopelessness. He couldn't stop it. He couldn't escape it. He could only watch as the seconds crawled by and the dark object neared the earth. He tried to back away, toward his family, but fear cemented his feet to the floor.

My dust-filled world rushed back, and the cool night swept by my face. There was a new light outside. A fire crackled at the end of a torch.

I moved to the front door and opened it. The crowd of people standing before the porch of the house stared at me. Hertz was with them.

"What are you doing here?" I demanded.

"You know why we're here, Nicholas," the mayor replied. "This place has caused our town too much trouble, too much lunacy."

I shook my head. "You're wrong, Hertz. You have no idea how wrong you are."

"You do what's right and come on down from there," he growled.

I held his gaze. His eyes were illuminated by the torch in his hand, drops of light dancing across his pupils. He bared his teeth at me as he spoke.

"Nicholas, get out of that house."

The people gathered around the mayor watched in silence, unsure of what I might do next.

"We were all wrong," I told them. "We were all so wrong. The Old Worlders, they knew. They knew because they saw it all, the world before this one. Something happened to that world, just like those Old Worlders said. Something happened to them…

"I won't let you burn it, Hertz. I won't let you destroy the one hope we have of knowing the truth."

"This is your final warnin', Nicholas."

My hand wrapped around the handle of the revolver on my hip. I drew it, turning my shoulders and straightening my arm. The silver muzzle fell in line with the mayor.

"This is too important, Hertz," I told him.

He drew his own weapon and fired off a shot. Sloppily aimed, it punctured the front door's wooden frame. I ducked back into the house, slamming the door shut as other townspeople pulled firearms from their belts.

Bullets peppered the walls for a moment. Moonlight slipped into the house through the scattered circles the volley had left behind.

I backed away into the room with the framed images, facing the window. I watched Hertz raise his torch, his face twisted in fury.

His eyes locked with mine as he set the flame to the porch. The ravenous orange beast took quickly to the old wood.

I had to get out.

Then my legs were frozen, my hands and feet numb. My mind slipped away, and I gazed out the window.

Golden sunlight washed over my face. I watched the finned, black object descend. I heard terrified voices in the other room.

There was a faint whistling. The noise grew clear and loud. The object fell to the ground.

With an unbreakable grasp, terror held me at its mercy.

The object hit.

A cloud of dust and fire erupted from the ground, sprouting into the sky like an infernal tree. The light was blinding, the thunder deafening, and my bones trembled.

This cloud of fire raced across the earth, eating up the landscape. It swallowed the world and drove onward, a stampede of hellfire horses. The rising mushroom of orange light filled the sky and put the sun to shame.

My feet grew hot. The floor was burning. Air scorched my lungs. Heat ripped at my legs, then my torso, my hands, my shoulders. It climbed further and further.

I was consumed by a cloud of red dust.

6

FLY IN DANISH

DAVE PASQUANTONIO

F lit perched on a jade plant, watching the human, her contempt matched only by her hunger. There was nothing to eat in this house!

After all the effort it had taken to enter the house yesterday, Flit had assumed that she would find a bounty. Even the most fastidious of humans usually left a bonanza for the non-discriminating housefly.

But not this human.

The best Flit had done was to discover a stray piece of Nasty-Dog's kibble under the stove, but the morsel was so dry that she couldn't pry even a speck off of the nugget.

After a long night spent fruitlessly searching for fuel, Flit needed food—now—and then she needed to get out of this hideously-tidy house.

But then the human opened a paper bag—and Flit's world exploded. A wave of sugar, apple, cinnamon, and dough smells swept over her.

Her struggle to get into this house, her long night of futile searching—they were worth it. She needed that Danish. And she would have that Danish.

The human placed the pastry on a plate and turned toward the coffee maker on the counter. The intoxicating scent, coupled with intense hunger, made Flit uncharacteristically careless. Driven by food-lust and desperation, she flew straight at the treasure, ignoring the human, her compound eyes locked on the prize, the pastry looming—

Movement from the rear.

Flit dived up and to her right as the human's gigantic hand came down and past her, clumsily slapping the table instead of her fragile body.

She took an angry buzz around the kitchen, and then flew into the adjoining dining room and hung upside down from the ceiling, grooming herself as she planned her next move. Her empty crop throbbed in anticipation.

Perhaps the human would drop crumbs on the otherwise spotless floor. A single fleck of pastry outweighed a bowlful of Nasty-Dog's horrific food—and it would give her the energy she needed to escape.

But there were no crumbs. Besides, crumbs were not treasure. A pastry—now that was a prize worth fighting for!

Flit crawled across the ceiling, hung from the door frame, and peered into the kitchen.

The upside-down human was eating the Danish—and far too neatly! There were no crumbs—and half of the pastry was already gone!

Movement from behind.

Flit jump-pivoted to reverse direction. Nasty-Dog looked up at her. It wagged its tail.

It was mocking her.

She dismissed Nasty-Dog's effrontery and pivoted back to face the kitchen.

The human put the remaining Danish on the plate and drank its coffee. It was ignoring the pastry. Perfect.

The scent of the Danish washed over Flit. She analyzed and prioritized the odors. Dough—easier to eat when moist, she knew from experience, so the sooner, the better. Glazed sugar—perfect for quick bursts of energy, and needed now more than ever. Chunks of apple smothered in a cinnamon-infused gel—

Yes. The gel. *That* was the real prize. Flit's feeding tube twitched in anticipation.

But would the human leave any gel? Sugar slabs and pastry crumbs were worthy fare, and would certainly sustain her, but Flit was not a housefly who settled. She had been the biggest maggot in her clutch—and had successfully laid five clutches of healthy eggs herself—because she *did not settle*. In the world of houseflies, size went hand-in-hand-in-hand-in-hand-in-hand-in-hand with how well one fed. And to feed well, one never settled.

Flit craved that Danish—especially that gooey filling, rife with pectin and sucrose and preservatives—as much as she'd craved anything in her 32 days of life. It would be hers.

The human grabbed the Danish, took another bite, and plopped the remaining portion onto the plate as it again reached for its coffee.

The human was eating too quickly!

Decision time. Flit could wait for the human to finish. Perhaps it would leave a few dried particles, and she could feed decently, if not glamorously—

No. Scouring for crumbs was for *settlers*. Flit quivered in anger. She would not end this crusade.

She would not *settle*.

The human stood up, coffee cup in hand. It turned and walked to the sink.

Away from the table.

Away from the Danish.

Decision made. Flit slid a foreleg over her antennae, ensuring that they were grit-free and optimized for flight guidance. Then she jumped, performed a barrel roll to right herself, whisked to the table, and landed a cautious ten inches from her prize.

The human's back was still to her. It was adding something to its coffee—a different sugar, Flit sensed, one inferior to the pastry's sugar glaze; its scent momentarily tempted her. Perhaps she could abandon the Danish, wait for the human to leave, then scoop up a few spilt granules—

No. She would not be led astray by specks of inferior sweetness. Not when a Danish was in play!

She jump-hopped three inches closer. The human was still at the counter.

Flit shivered with joy. Success was close at wing!

She stepped closer still to the plate. The aroma was all-consuming. The hairs on her legs bristled in anticipation.

She was about to claim her prize.

Flit planned the next few seconds. She'd land on the center of whatever the human had left and stomp on any remaining apple filling with her feet. Since she tasted with her toes, she'd spend a few microseconds basking in the glow of success and sweetness. That is what one did when one achieved victory.

Then she'd lower her feeding tube into the cinnamon gel. The filling was most likely viscous enough so that she could draw it into her feeding tube without delay. If the slurry was too thick, she'd simply vomit a drop of stomach acid out of her tube onto the goo and break the mixture down enough so that she could slurp it up.

A solid plan for a delicious and well-earned—

Movement from above.

The human. Its back was no longer turned.

And its huge hand was coming down at her!

Humans foolishly swat directly at flies, so Flit did what all successful flies do—she jumped forward, then took off and veered, the air from the failed swat gently propelling her. The *thwack* of the human's meaty hand on the table startled Nasty-Dog into an insipid barking frenzy.

Flit landed on the ceiling and schemed as the human shook its fist at her.

So close to the prize—yet thwarted again!

The human stared, its hands on its hips, its huge upside-down face peering up at her, filling Flit's thousands of simple eyes with its single bland expression.

Flit scrubbed her two front legs together, and then preened, waiting for the human's next move. It was standing between Flit and the Danish. Flit could easily dodge the human and fly to the plate, but she'd have no time to feed before the next predictably ineffective attack.

This was a standoff. And Flit never backed down from a standoff.

Unsurprisingly, the human broke first. It turned, picked up the Danish, and—

No!

It was reaching for the door!

It was leaving!

With *her* Danish!

Flit quickly analyzed the situation. Human at door, hand almost on doorknob. Nasty-Dog sitting on the floor near the door, tail wagging, facing the human. Human holding Danish.

There was precious little time. She had one chance to make her move.

Of course. The Parabola Pounce! But could she pull it off? And did she have the energy?

Houseflies are a boasting lot. Flit normally discounted their tales of inflated prowess. Besides, showboating flies were always scrawny in comparison to her—if they could *really* achieve such feats of derring-do, would they not look more fit? More lustrous? Braggart flies disappeared once their egos got as big as their stories.

But she had heard all the tales of flies who'd *supposedly* performed the Parabola Pounce—a maneuver of legend, one passed down over thousands of housefly generations by solemn elders.

Flit wasn't convinced that the Parabola Pounce had ever been successfully performed. But if ever there was a time to try a legendary maneuver, it was now. For a Danish.

Flit made her move.

She rocketed at Nasty-Dog and landed on its nose, staring into the brute's eyes.

Nasty-Dog's eyes grew wide, and its head tilted skyward. Flit had assumed—correctly, of course—that the fiend would try to eat her. She then took off as Nasty-Dog sprang and bashed into the human, who was by now halfway out the door, back still turned.

Flit deftly avoided the mash of dog-jaws and continued to the doorway, finishing her parabola and landing upside-down on the casing.

The human, not expecting Nasty-Dog to lunge from behind, stumbled—and dropped the pastry on the stairs.

The outside stairs!

Yes! The Danish was free from the human, and Flit was free from the house! Her circulatory tube pulsated with glee, and she flew outside to a hedge to compose herself. The Parabola Pounce was not simply the stuff of legends after all! She had manipulated both the dog *and* the human into doing exactly what she wanted! Oh, swarms would gather to hear her recount this day. She would regale the throngs, ending with the moment she first stepped into that cinnamon slop, sucking the—

The human picked up the remnants of the Danish, walked back into the house, and closed the door behind it.

Her treasure was gone!

She flew to the steps. No crumbs. Not even the tiniest smear of gel.

She flew angrily to the door and buzz-bopped into it two times, five times, a dozen times, using nearly all her remaining energy to unleash her wrath upon the human's house.

This could not happen! What was the human going to do with a dropped Danish? Certainly, it wouldn't eat it. Most humans never even *foraged* for food, let alone ate dropped food. What would this human do with the pastry? Discard it? Or—even worse—give it to Nasty-Dog?

The horror. Her antennae bent in sadness as she mourned her Danish's demise.

Wait—the human. *It* was responsible for her loss. Each of Flit's eight thousand simple eyes narrowed as her mourning morphed into fury.

She would ignore her hunger—and make the human pay. But how?

She was still pondering several arcane methods when the human emerged from the house two minutes later. It closed and locked the door behind it (goodbye, Nasty-Dog!) and strode toward —no. The garage.

Garages were places of wicked delights and unholy terrors.

Garages were also places full of spiders.

The garage door was open, so Flit flew slowly inside the dark space, tracking the human while avoiding the deadly inside walls of the structure—and bracing herself against the siren song of the spiders.

Flit had seen too many friends perish in the clutches of spiders. The monsters were everywhere flies needed to be, and their powers of persuasion were insidious. The evil webbed ones drew in hapless flies with hypnotic chants that only their prey could hear, while the insidious mobile spiders—the stalkers, the walkers, the ones who did not need webs to capture their prey—they jeered and catcalled, weakening a fly's resolve until it dropped to the ground, struck paralytic by horror—only to be consumed.

As Flit flew slowly, the webbed spiders began chanting their songs of doom, and the walking spiders shrieked and whooped. Flit tried to shut out their seductive music and landed on a bag of mulch.

The human opened the car door.

There was no time to fully develop a plan. Revenge, in whatever form it took, would have to occur *inside* the car—and Flit had never been inside a car.

It was unthinkable for a housefly to *willingly* enter a car. The rational part of Flit's tiny brain screamed: *Do not enter a car! Find pickings elsewhere!*

Ordinarily, Flit listened intently to the rational part of her brain, and that had served her well—she was still alive in a world hell-bent on housefly destruction. But she pictured the dropped Danish, wallowed in the memory of its scent, and again felt rage at being denied her prize.

She flew directly at the car door—which the human pulled shut a second before she got there.

Flit banked to the left and slipped over the car's hood, her basic nervous system racing.

Denied again! Damn the wily human!

Flit perched on a rake handle, hungry and demoralized, as the car started up and began pulling out of the garage.

What to do? The human was leaving, and a quick glance at the garbage bin showed that its lid was secured, trapping any potential runner-up treats inside.

All her questing.

All her failing.

The garage grew dimmer. The spider chants grew louder.

The door was closing!

Flit needed to leave. Now. Or she would be trapped in the

garage with the soul-sucking demons. She was weak from hunger and exertion, and she would eventually succumb if she spent any more time here.

With supreme effort, Flit launched herself off the rake handle and headed for the closing door, diving under the rubber gasket and its tendrils of dead webs and dried leaves just before it shut.

Back in the bright outside world, Flit circled the driveway. Another miraculous escape!

The human's car slowed its reverse, stopped, and began to drive forward.

Now it was the human who was escaping!

Flit made a beeline for the car. The vehicle inched down the driveway and paused, waiting for an opening in traffic.

Flit buzzed around the car's rear. She could sense no opening. The top of the car also yielded no entry.

Wait! There! The human had left a side window down on the passenger side. Just a crack, but the gap looked large enough for her to squeeze into.

She worked up to speed, correctly judged her vector, and zoomed at the gap.

Microseconds before she entered, the car turned and accelerated. Flit, buffeted by the sudden push of air, slammed onto the street.

She lay stunned on the pavement, feet pointed to the sky, the world turning from black to gray and then mercifully to her normal mosaic of thousands of flickering images. She righted herself, and then shook to clear her head.

The car was gone!

As was the human!

Waves of depression washed over her, followed by waves of resignation. There were no waves of regret about the pastry—Flit knew she was hungry, knew she had been enthralled by *some* food item, but the Danish itself was receding from her memory.

There were, however, waves of anger.

How dare the human run away before she could wreak her havoc! But should she give up or give chase?

She considered her options. She could stop her pursuit and scour the human's yard for food. Every creature defecated, and they all eventually died. Most flies were not finicky. Flit *could* chalk this venture up to a near-success, revel in the glory of the successful Parabola Pounce, and go on about her fly-business—if she were willing to *settle*.

But no. Flit would not give *up*. She would give *chase*.

Fifteen seconds after being thrown to the ground by the roiling air currents, Flit flew. Ten feet up, she banked to the right and followed the road, drawing upon reserves of strength and will that even she did not realize she possessed.

She would track down that crafty human and make it pay. Why it had to pay, she couldn't exactly remember—but pay it must.

The world of a fly is a small one. Flit could not see clearly for more than a few yards. Everything beyond that distance was hazy dark and light blotches. But she knew which way the car had gone.

She dipped lower, five feet above the road, three feet, two feet—

Movement from behind.

She veered to the right as a car whizzed by. She was caught in its wake and pin-wheeled. To her surprise, she tumbled *forward*. She struggled to maintain a straight path as she pondered what had just happened.

How could she have moved forward so much faster?

The car…the air…the direction… Her miniscule brain worked as hard as any fly's brain ever had, and the realization of what she had just done astonished her.

This was how she could gain ground on the human—she would use the air currents to gain on the human's car!

Flit's simple heart swelled with pride. Surely, she was the first of her kind to travel in such a fashion! Between this maneuver, escaping the garage, and performing the Parabola Pounce, she was breaking new ground as a housefly. She would be remembered along with all the greats!

She continued her car-assisted travel, getting passed by a car, then surfing the air to shoot ahead of it.

Was she making up distance? Or had each car that passed been the same car? Would she even recognize the correct car?.

The traffic slowed, then stopped.

She flew up and over each as she strained to identify the right vehicle.

Not this one. Too dark.

Not the next. Too short.

Not the next. It had no roof. She alighted on the car's hood, then stared at the car ahead of her. The shade of gray looked about right. The size looked about right. But she wasn't sure. She had been stunned on the pavement, and houseflies have no need for perfect recall.

She took off and flew around to the side.

There. On the passenger side window. A gap.

Success! Flit flew in a quick series of circles, celebrating. She had found the correct car! Oh, the majesty of a successful hunt! Soon she would—

The car accelerated.

Flit dived for the gap, but the wind from the car's sudden movement drove her back.

She strained against the gust and landed with the tiniest of thumps on the back of the car, nestling on the gasket where the trunk met the window. She scrabbled for purchase, hooked her front legs onto the rubber seam, and tucked her body down to avoid the slipstream of air rushing above her.

She would wait until the car came to a stop again, and then she would let loose her vengeance.

But first, she needed to rest. She was weak, and the flight had exhausted her.

Movement from the left.

A dragonfly. Less than a foot away.

It gripped the rear window. Its twin eye-orbs glittered as it slowly raised and lowered its wings.

Flit froze in fear.

Dragonflies were the alpha predators of the insect world. Too wily to be trapped in a spider's web, too agile to fear attack from other winged killers, dragonflies chilled the quasi-blood of all insects—especially houseflies.

There were innumerable ways for a fly to die. Birds ate them. Glue traps and abandoned webs starved them. Humans squashed them and sprayed them. Spiders—Flit couldn't bring herself to think about dying by spider. And nearly every other member of the animal kingdom feasted joyously on newborn maggots.

But dragonflies were a terror beyond all other terrors. They approached swiftly and silently. It was the rare fly who lived to recount an escape from a dragonfly's clutches.

There was something else about dragonflies that Flit couldn't recall…

The dragonfly tapped its abdomen-tail on the window to get her attention.

"Why are you on this vehicle, fly?" the dragonfly whispered. "You have made a terrible mistake, my future meal."

Flit shivered but steeled herself against the words. What *was* it that the elder had said about dragonflies? It had been three days since she and a dozen other females had gathered to lay eggs on a dead squirrel while an elder imparted wisdom. Like all houseflies, Flit struggled to remember mundane events from ten minutes in the past, let alone three days. That elder may have turned to dust by now.

"Watch my wings slowly raise and lower," the dragonfly

droned. "Be entranced by them, fly. Be struck motionless by fear. When this vehicle stops, I will pounce on you, and you shall be mine, like so many of your kind before you."

Words. The elder had said *something* about dragonfly words...

"It is fortuitous that you landed here," the dragonfly continued, chuckling. "I have yet to feed today. Before too long, I will feed upon *you* and slake both my hunger and my thirst."

Suddenly, Flit recalled the elder's proclamation: *The silent dragonfly is light and deadly. The talking dragonfly is weighed down by its pomposity.*

Flit adjusted her grip. Hooking all three right legs onto the rubber seam so she could swivel toward the dragonfly, she used her left three legs to make a universally-rude gesture.

The predator gasped, pounding its abdomen-tail against the glass. "Such insolence in one so doomed!" the dragonfly hissed. "Your final minute approaches, maiden fly, and whatever clutch you last laid shall surely be your last!"

Although the dragonfly was unable to attack while the car was moving, once it stopped, Flit would be no match for the killer. Her only hope was that the dragonfly would still be talking while Flit escaped into the car.

The car slowed.

Flit prepared to jump. The dragonfly bent its legs, preparing to do the same.

Flit's timing would have to be impeccable, or she would die on this car.

The car inched to a stop.

Flit and the dragonfly both prepared to pounce—

Movement from above.

Something huge.

Flit pressed her body onto the metal of the car's trunk to shrink from this new and unknown horror.

A sparrow cupped its wings to halt its progress as it landed next to Flit, its huge talons gripping the lip of the trunk, a tremendous wing smashing against the car's window, the primary flight feathers missing Flit by half an inch.

Flit, still paralyzed by terror, prepared for the end. She could not shut her eyes, so she looked away instead, saddened that her quest for revenge (for a reason she had completely forgotten) had failed. To be consumed by a bird was an unceremonious end!

She heard a scream.

The sparrow swung its massive head around to face Flit, the dragonfly wedged between the bird's upper and lower mandibles.

The bird cocked its head as it gazed at Flit. It trilled something, then launched off the car and into the sky with its meal.

Flit was no expert in bird-speak, but she could have sworn the sparrow had warbled, "Dragonflies talk way too much."

The only good bird was a dead bird. Every fly had that mantra drilled into them from the moment it could wriggle. Birds could never be defeated, only avoided.

But this bird had saved Flit's life. One day, she vowed, she would return the favor to another bird. If she survived.

Back to matters at hands.

The car accelerated. The air rushed over the top of the vehicle and down the back window, battering Flit as she clutched the gasket.

The sun beat on her. The wind slapped at her. The metal trunk burned her. Flit found a small gap between the seam and the trunk and dragged her body into it. Beyond the gap lay darkness.

Where would it lead? What lay beyond the dark? Probably more spiders. They loved the darkness—the cowards.

But she had to risk it. She couldn't stay exposed any longer.

Buffeted by wind and noise, Flit, now having forgotten why she was even on a car, started to hallucinate. Her previous three meals —unfortunately, all scavenged meals—floated in front of her.

… orange rind, covered with ants. She drove away the vile creatures by buzzing her wings until they grew frustrated, then feasted on the sweet citrus …

… ice cream, dropped on the sidewalk by a tiny-human. She sucked on the congealing vanilla mass before the sun dried it up …

… red cup, tumbling in the wind. She chased it until it came to rest against a poplar. The inside was coated with cola droplets …

She wedged herself even deeper against the lip of the trunk. The car shook and shuddered as it sped along the road.

The words of another elder came back to her: *Woe to the fly whose reach exceeds its grasp.*

Flit dipped her antennae in sorrow. That elder had been correct. She had escaped death half a dozen times today—she remembered that, at least—but for what?

Pride. Pride was her downfall. And pride could be the end of her, here, wedged in a gap on a car going who knows where. She was exhausted, and nearly starved, and beaten down by loss and failure.

She dwelled on the morose for ten minutes, too lost in her black thoughts to notice that the car had stopped, too glum to realize that the human had opened the car door and left, too melancholy to—

That smell. What was that smell?

The air was barely moving, but Flit, highly attuned to delectable scents, detected something overpowering. Something that triggered a memory of—what? Something she had wanted. Something she had *needed*. Something rich. Sweet. Luscious.

She shook to clear her head, then sampled the air again.

It was akin to that barely-remembered something—only multiplied a thousand-fold.

Flit crawled out from the gap and onto the trunk, ignoring the burning heat, momentarily blinded by the harsh sunlight.

The world was *filled* with the smell of something wonderful.

How could so much goodness exist in such a harsh world?

She tentatively attempted flight, but she no longer had the

energy to take wing, so instead she dropped to the parking lot, and hopped, an inch at a time, toward the source of the smell.

The scent grew even stronger. Flit plodded along the hot asphalt, drawing on strength born of desperation and ravenous hunger. Five minutes after starting her arduous journey from the car, she collapsed against a shadowed wall, exhausted and near death.

Movement from the front.

She tensed, prepared for yet another danger. What would be next? A human? A bird? Yes, it would probably be a bird. How fitting to be saved by a bird, only to be eaten by a bird.

But it was not a bird or a human.

It was a housefly.

He hopped over to Flit. "Who are you, weary stranger?" the housefly asked, cautiously holding up its two forelegs to show that it meant no harm.

"I am Flit. I have had a terrible day, and I am seeking respite and nourishment." She struggled to her feet and spread her two forelegs wide in a welcoming return gesture. "I am overwhelmed by the waft of something heavenly. Where am I? What *is* this place?"

The other housefly took flight and performed cheerful loops in front of a propped-open screen door. Above the door was an old wooden sign, white with red lettering. Neither fly saw the colors, and of course they couldn't make sense of the words painted on the sign: "Delivery Entrance for Stueflue's Bakery."

The housefly landed next to Flit. His antennae trembled with glee.

"This is nirvana."

7

DEVIL IN THE DETAILS

E.J. STEVENS

"Oberon's balls, what is that smell?"

I clapped a gloved hand over my nose and mouth, stumbled to our loft's sigil-covered window, and forced open the sash.

The trash-strewn alley didn't provide the freshest air even on cool, windy days when we caught a rare ocean breeze off the harbor. The tall, brick buildings that formed the alley leaned together conspiratorially, whispering Harborsmouth's darkest secrets, blocking all but the merest breath of fetid air.

"Demon farts," Jinx mumbled. "I wanted a dog, but, *oh no*. You just had to bring home a demon."

My roommate's voice was muffled by the scarf she'd wrapped around her face, but her eyes twinkled teasingly. She might mock my choice of houseguest, but Jinx loved the little, lop-eared demon toddler just as much as I did. Sparky wasn't just another one of my rescued strays—he was family.

Too bad he had the supernatural equivalent of swine flu.

I leaned my head out the window, taking a deep breath of city air, wincing when my forehead touched the iron bars. I gritted my teeth, not in anticipation of an unwanted vision, but in pain. The window bars wouldn't trigger my psychometry, but the iron burned my skin, leaving an angry, red welt on my face, a reminder of my newly emerging fae powers.

Sparky wasn't the only supernatural creature living in our loft. I was rapidly changing, becoming one of the monsters I'd sworn to protect the city's humans from. I tried to use those emerging powers for good—and occasionally for profit when it helped me solve a tricky case—but becoming less human rankled.

This wasn't the first time I'd become injured from one of my own security measures. Last week, I'd triggered one of the anti-fae wards I'd paid my witch friend Kaye to set on our office safe. We were lucky I hadn't blown our office, and the loft above, off the face of Harborsmouth.

And now we had a demon toddler with a stomach bug.

I spun on my heel, eyes darting around the room. A good detective notices the smallest details, so I hadn't missed the signs of illness—the rank smell, the raspy breathing, or the plastic bucket beside the couch—as I'd stumbled to the window. My mind hastily assembled a worrisome picture and an even more troubling theory.

"Did he touch any of the remaining wards?" I asked, hurrying to Sparky's still form on the couch. "Or go exploring in one of our bedrooms? Did you check him for charms?"

I'd done a cursory sweep of the loft when my faerie blood awakened, and again when I brought the tiny demon home. But I'd meant to do a more thorough search. There was just always something more important, more pressing to do. How could I have been so foolish?

"T-t-there's nothing in his pockets," she said. "I checked. Forneus is on his way over. I didn't want to worry you...and this might be normal for demons his age, right?"

I wasn't the biggest fan of Jinx's new demon boyfriend, but she had a point. With Father Michael out of town and Kaye's blatant abhorrence of demons, Forneus was our best bet for figuring out what was making Sparky sick.

"If it is, he'll know," I said, nodding.

I fidgeted with my gloves, double-checking that the hidden wrist sheaths that held my throwing knives were secure and that no bare skin was exposed between the gloves and leather jacket. Finally, I scooped Sparky into my arms, careful not to touch his skin to mine. Now wasn't the time for a vision. It was time for action.

"Grab the salt," I said, mind spinning. "I'll get him in the tub."

Saltwater neutralizes or dampens most magic. It wasn't a cure-all, but it was a start. Plus, even for a demon, the kid was burning up. A cold bath might bring down his fever and buy us some time.

I climbed awkwardly into the bathtub, jostling Sparky as my butt hit the porcelain. The saltwater would be hell on my leather boots and jacket, and the cold water seeped uncomfortably into my jeans, but all I cared about was the bundle in my arms.

"Ivvvyyy?" Sparky asked. He'd stopped sucking his thumb, but still held the tip of one long, soggy ear in his tiny fist.

"Hey, kiddo," I said, forcing a smile. "How you feeling? Eat too much pizza again?"

The kid put away more food than a troll and had the iron stomach of a chupacabra, but maybe he'd finally eaten something that didn't agree with him. There had to be something that baby Tezcatlipocan demons couldn't eat, right?

Sparky burped, lowering his head to my chest. Jinx dumped salt into the tub, eyes wide and hand shaking.

"Lucifer's fiery pitchfork," Forneus said.

I hadn't heard him enter over the roaring water, and I had to resist the urge to go for my blades. One practiced flick of my wrist and my throwing knives would be in the palm of my gloved hand. Instead, I reminded myself that Forneus was our best connection to Hell and our most likely source of intel on what was wrong with my kid. Impaling the man with magically enhanced iron and silver was a bad idea. The fact that the bathtub didn't allow enough room to accurately throw my knives had nothing to do with my decision not to physically engage with the target. Nothing at all.

Jinx turned off the faucet and ran a hand over her 50s style halter dress. My arms tightened around Sparky, but I took a deep breath and nodded. It was a good thing I'd spared the man, because it was obvious that Forneus knew something.

"You know what's wrong with him," I said, eyes narrowing.

Forneus darted his eyes from me to Jinx. I'd never seen the demon afraid, but in that moment, I got the distinct impression he weighed the option of fleeing our apartment and never looking back.

Sparky burped again, and Forneus took one step away from the tub, but he didn't run. Instead, he pointed a slender finger in my direction. "He isn't sick," he said.

"Then what is wrong with him?" I asked.

"He's being summoned."

I couldn't breathe. Someone had sucked all the air from the room.

"Summoned?" Jinx asked. "As in summoning a demon? With a pentagram?"

"Precisely," he said.

"This can't be happening," I said, trying to think of every piece of demon lore I'd read. Father Michael had an obsession with demonology and an impressive occult library. When I took Sparky under my wing, I'd read everything he had that was translated into English. "What would someone want with a demon child? And how could they summon him without knowing his true name?"

We all have a true name, and names have power over the supernatural. Funny thing is, I'd never met Sparky's abusive family. I didn't fancy a trip to Hell, and I'm pretty sure that if we met, they'd eat my face and torture what was left of my bloody corpse, not answer questions.

I'd given Sparky his name, a name that came from love, not the power to dominate. And now some bastard was trying to hurt him, trying to take him away, using a name given to him by creatures who'd hurt him, a name that no longer mattered.

I bit the inside of my cheek, trying not to scream.

Forneus looked away, tugging at his gloves. Jinx moved toward him, an offer of comfort if he was willing. I may not approve of their relationship, but there was no denying the obvious affection Jinx had for Forneus. After the demon's recent actions, risking his own life not once but twice to save my friend's life, it was obvious that those feelings ran both ways.

Forneus cleared his throat.

"There have long been foul practitioners of dark magic, those with the most odious of intentions, who seek to subject their will upon my kind," he said.

Flames danced in his eyes, and wisely, Jinx decided not to interrupt. I shrugged. Nobody ever accused me of being wise.

"Spit it out, Forneus," I said. "Why would they summon, Sparky? And how do we stop them? How do we save the kid's life?"

Forneus sighed and shook his head.

"Do not try my patience, Miss Granger," he said. "There is no rushing what I have to say. There is no simple solution."

I leaned my head back, closed my eyes, and took a steadying breath. I needed action. I needed to break things, to stab things, or burn the world to the ground. Instead, a shiver ran through me, and Sparky whimpered.

"This isn't working," I said.

"I'll get a towel," Jinx said.

"And coffee?" I asked.

Forneus lifted an eyebrow, but she nodded and pushed him from the room. Tears threatened, but I sniffed and kissed the top of Sparky's head. The skin on skin contact sucked me down into a series of visions, visions made up of Sparky's most emotional memories, beginning with the terror of Hell and ending with being rescued from the cat sidhe by a beautiful, shining Goddess. I was Sparky's hero once before. I'd be that hero again.

I toweled off, wrapped Sparky in a cocoon of fluffy towels, and stomped into the kitchen with a belching bundle on my hip. I leaned against the bar, letting the scratched counter take the kid's weight, and Jinx slid a coffee mug into my waiting hand.

"What do I need to do?"

"The child is already weakening," Forneus said. "I know not how he has held on this long. Soon, he will dematerialize and either reappear in the summoner's circle or cease to exist."

"He'll die," I said.

"Yes," he said with a wince.

"Or be tortured," I said, voice hollow.

"Yes." He spread his hands in a supplicating gesture.

Jinx bit her lip, transferring cherry red lipstick to pearly white teeth. It was the only blemish marring her perfect appearance, although the crossbow she'd slung over her shoulder while I was toweling off was an interesting accessory to the feminine rockabilly ensemble.

I frowned. My friend was fierce and maternal as hell, but she was human. If she went up against some dark sorcerer, she'd probably die or become a very fashionable toad. I needed to take the lead and make sure that Jinx stayed safe.

"I'm not letting that happen," I said, glaring at Forneus. "Nobody in this family is going to die today. And, for the love of Mab, no kid of mine is getting tortured."

Forneus sighed.

"The only course of action is to become tethered to him, to combine your life force through a blood bond," he said. "It is ill-advised, at best."

"Will it keep him alive?" I asked.

"Possibly." He tilted his head. "Your witch friend, Kaye, may be capable of such a binding, one that would keep Sparky alive, but it will not keep the child here indefinitely. He may live, but in return, you could both be summoned. So long as the dark practitioner continues with the ritual, you and the child will be in danger."

I shot a look at Jinx, and she nodded.

"I'll grab our gear," she said.

Forneus slid the blade from his sword cane and moved toward the door. Unlike my poor attempts at hiding my supernatural otherness with faerie glamour, he could walk amongst the city's humans with his sword out and literal flames in his eyes without anyone calling the cops. Too bad Kaye wasn't your typical human.

"You should wait here," I said. "Kaye hates demons."

"And leave my beloved at the mercy of an angry witch?" he asked, lifting an eyebrow.

"You should both stay here." I frowned.

I'd have trouble fighting with Sparky in my arms, but Forneus was right. This was dangerous and Jinx was human.

"Not a chance, Ivy." Jinx sauntered over, tossing a bag onto the counter with a heavy thud. "You need us. Sparky needs us."

"But...," I said.

"We're family," she said, voice low. "This? This is what family does."

She had a point.

Five minutes later, laden with weapons, a flatulent demon toddler, and the kid's favorite teddy bear, we arrived at the doors of Madam Kaye's Magic Emporium. Kaye was the most powerful witch in New England, my former mentor, and a friend. Too bad she hated demons with a fiery passion. She also disapproved of my friendship and business partnership with Jinx. Hopefully, Kaye was in a good mood, for all our sakes.

"Think she'll let us in?" Jinx asked, shifting Sparky to one of her curvy hips.

On the short walk up Wharf Street, we'd decided to let Jinx carry the kid for now. I needed my hands free in case things went sideways.

"Only one way to find out," I said, stepping toward the shop's royal purple and midnight blue façade. "Hey, Humphrey. How's it hanging?"

Huge gold-trimmed windows showed off The Emporium's witchy wares to the Old Port Quarter's pedestrian tourist traffic. The front of the shop boasted astrology charts, tarot readings, herbal teas, and New Age decor. The merchandise was harmless, but the building was an extension of Kaye's will, like a megaton brick familiar. And guarding the entrance was a stone gargoyle capable of crushing my bones to dust.

"Good morning, Ivy," Humphrey said, voice a rumbling growl like rocks in a blender.

"Actually, today's off to a rocky start," I said, making a half-hearted joke. "We need to see Kaye."

Humphrey snuffled, pulling air over canines the size of my forearm. A low, warning growl erupted from the gargoyle's throat, and I fought down the urge to bolt.

"Demons-s-s," he roared, hackles rising.

"Oh, them," I said, smiling and batting my eyelashes innocently. "They're with me."

The growling intensified and brick dust rained down as the entire building began to tremble with Humphrey's—or Kaye's— rage. So much for playing nice.

I gathered power to me, spinning the glowing threads of magic like finely spun cotton candy, drawing from the nexus of ley lines that ran beneath the city streets. That crossroads of power is what made Harborsmouth such a hotbed of supernatural activity. Vampires, faeries, and witches were drawn here, but not everyone lured to Harborsmouth could tap into the raw power of the lines.

It's a good thing I'm not just anybody.

"I'm not in the mood for games, Kaye," I said. "Let us in."

My voice shook, and the salty, coppery tang of blood filled my mouth. From Jinx's gasp and Humphrey's threatening posture, I assumed that my skin was glowing. Demonstrating my supernatural otherness on a city street in full view of humans was risky. If the Seelie or Unseelie Courts found out, the infraction was punishable by a quick and brutal death. But the fae weren't the only magical residents of Harborsmouth willing to do anything to protect the secret of our existence.

Unlike the bristling gargoyle overhead, I haven't learned to cloak my magic from prying eyes. I hadn't been raised as fae. I'd never been taught how to weave a glamour. Once I start glowing, I have to calm down or let the power burn out.

I was playing with fire.

A rumbling grated at my ears, and my blades hit my gloved palms. I widened my stance, ready to throw my blades, and making myself a bigger target. But Humphrey wasn't threatening to attack. The gargoyle was laughing at us.

The Emporium's door clicked open with a theatrical squeak and Jinx moved to my side, Sparky breathing raggedly in her arms.

"Is that good?" she asked, rocking the sleeping demon in her arms. "That doesn't seem good."

I shrugged. Kaye could be as dramatic as a vampire when she was in a mood.

"We don't have much choice." I strode into the shop. I couldn't stand on the street and wait for the faerie council to have me assassinated for public exposure, and Kaye was our best chance for helping Sparky. "Stay close. Once we're all inside and I secure the door, I'll take point and Forneus can bring up the rear."

Jinx let out a nervous giggle, and I shook my head. Now was not the time for butt jokes. It also wasn't the time for Jinx to start ogling Forneus' backside, which he was not so covertly shaking in her direction.

Thankfully, I was saved by a furry beast purring against my leg.

"Hey, Midnight," I said with the baby voice I usually reserved for Sparky. "You here to take us to, Kaye? Who's a good kitty?"

The black cat took off, scampering toward Kaye's spell kitchen hidden at the back of the shop. The labyrinth of shelves, bins, and racks of merchandise usually guided visitors back to the front counter, but no bins of dried herbs or plastic scythes tugged at my hair or tripped our feet as we followed the witch's familiar. Instead, rows of wooden brooms and rubber skeletons stood at attention along a wide, clear path to Kaye's domain.

"If this is an elaborate trap, Miss Granger," Forneus said, his voice low. "I will flay your skin and make a decorative basket with your bones."

"Ugh, not sexy," Jinx muttered.

I snorted and followed Midnight to the spell kitchen's door. If I didn't know better, I'd say that the Grand Marquis of Hell was afraid. I took a steadying breath, put away my blades, and raised a gloved fist to knock on the door. Threats wouldn't work against Kaye here. I'd have to be on my best behavior and try to negotiate for her help. Oh, goody.

A gust of air blew the door open, nearly knocking it off its hinges. I moved to take an involuntary step back, but another gust of wind pushed me forward, my boots squeaking as Kaye's magic dragged my body toward a spell circle set into the floor.

Kaye stood inside her circle, the bells on her layered skirts tinkling and tendrils of her hair writhing in the air around her head like angry snakes. Oh yeah, she was pissed.

"How dare you bring demon filth into my home, child." Her voice reverberated from the walls, twisting the coffee swimming in my gut.

"Watch who you're calling filth, witch," Jinx said, tossing her hair and cocking a hip.

My friend might be too busy cradling Sparky to use her crossbow, but her stance was pure I'm-going-to-kick-your-ass attitude. Forneus was battling with whether to be proud or protective, and they both seemed oblivious to the fact that Kaye was locked and loaded in her circle.

"You!" Kaye shouted, head snapping to sneer at Jinx.

This was all kinds of bad. The witch's power recently received a massive accidental boost as a side-effect from dying and being brought back to life. It was a long story, one that involved saving my glowing backside, but it boiled down to another friend getting hurt because of my actions. And now she was directing that new, chaotic power at my best friend. I had to get Kaye's attention fixed on me, and fast.

"Hey, over here, lit up like a damn glow stick," I said, waggling gloved fingers.

"Aye, an ye be a standin' there without givin' me a gift," Hob said.

Oberon's fiery balls, could this day get any worse? In my hurry to speak to Kaye, and to keep my friends from being wiped from the face of Harborsmouth, I'd entered a hearth brownie's domain without offering a gift. No matter that Kaye's magic had dragged me across the threshold or that my life had been in peril from the second I entered The Emporium. The fae follow strict rules and customs, and I was dangerously close to breaking yet another one of those rules.

Hob, who would have been a little more than knee height if he wasn't standing on the solid oak table to my right, glared at me beneath bushy, white eyebrows. His knobby hands rested on his hips, and he stomped a booted foot in an open threat. Shiny gift for the brownie, stat.

"K-k-kaye?" I asked, slowly turning my head toward the witch, careful not to make any quick movements.

My ears popped and the hair around Kaye's head fell to her shoulders.

"By the Goddess, give the man his gift," she said, rubbing a hand over her face.

"It's in my pocket." My eyebrows lifted in question as I slid a hand toward my jacket.

"Oh, fine, get it over with," she said.

I pulled out one of the trinkets I kept on me for such occasions and turned to Hob. The brownie took his gift and winked. The sly devil. He'd interrupted our little showdown on purpose, diffusing the situation and getting his gift.

"Don't want a messy kitchen, now do ye?" he asked, placing a finger against the side of his nose.

"No, we wouldn't want to mess up your kitchen, Hob," I said with a wink.

"Well, what do you want?" Kaye asked. "Get on with it or get out."

"I want you to bind me to Sparky," I said.

"Bind you to a demon," she said.

"Yes."

She stared and I stared back.

"I'll make ye some tea," Hob said.

"Someone is trying to summon Sparky, and it's making him sick," I said, ignoring Hob. "Sparky is weak. Binding me to him might help keep him alive long enough for me to find the bastard who is summoning him."

"And if they summon you too, child?" she asked. "You may not be a demon, but binding yourself to this creature will not just give him your strength, it will give you his weaknesses. He is vulnerable to demon summoning. If you are bound, you will be too."

"The witch is right," Forneus said with a slight bow of his head. "If he is summoned, you will also be summoned. If anyone knows your true name, the reverse would also be true."

That wasn't terrifying or anything. I pushed back my shoulders and lifted my chin.

"I'm not backing down." I stared at Kaye. "The question is, will you be the one to cast the binding or do I need to seek help outside Harborsmouth?"

Kaye sighed and tossed tattooed hands in the air. "I will not lose business to amateurs," she said, gathering supplies and setting them inside her circle.

Jinx pumped her fist, careful not to jostle Sparky, and I looked at his spindly arms and feverish face. He was so frail. Some humans might call him a monster, but the true monsters were the ones summoning a child to be used as their slave.

"I just have one more request," I said.

Thankfully, Kaye and Forneus were able to meet that request. And once the spell began, it was only a matter of minutes before a magic thread tied my wrist to Sparky's like a shiny, red ribbon.

I sat on a simple, wooden chair outside Kaye's circle with Sparky on my lap. My head ached and my movements were sluggish, but I smiled wide as Sparky's eyes fluttered open and he reached a hand to clutch his teddy bear.

"Hey, kiddo, feeling better?" I asked.

He nodded and bounced happily on my knee. With his big eyes and floppy ears, he was cute as a bunny—a bunny with sharp, needle teeth.

"Love you," he said, tilting his head.

"Love you too," I said. The air pressure in the room shifted and my ears popped at the same time that Sparky burped. The binding had worked just in time. The summoner was already back at it. "I won't let anyone hurt you. Not ever."

I held onto Sparky with one hand while the fingers of my other hand brushed the hilt of the silver blade hiding up my sleeve.

Sparky whimpered, and I vowed to kill the person responsible for his pain and fear, but not yet. Kaye and Forneus had been clear on that fact. They'd shown me how to sever my tie to Sparky, but if we became unbound before we fully materialized in our enemy's circle, the child would die. That was not an option.

So I sat there, holding this child, my child, envisioning my revenge. Sparky belched, thrashed, and cried. Me, the badass? I cried too.

"Hey, kiddo," I said. "Give your teddy bear a kiss."

"He's scared too?" he asked.

"Yes, even teddy bears get scared," I said. "Give him a kiss and look him in the eye. Keep telling teddy it will be alright."

"Okay," he said.

Sparky kissed the teddy bear, whispering that Ivy wouldn't let the bad men get him. I was a hero. Didn't teddy know that? A tear rolled down my cheek.

A semi-circle of men in hooded cloaks appeared behind a watery wall as we emerged into their reality. They smiled, arms raised and faces rapt. The bastards were enjoying this.

Anger blazed through me, awakening my wisp powers, igniting the faerie flames that itched to turn these sorcerers to ash. But I waited, through every agonizing second of my child's whimpers and whispers to his teddy bear, until the summoning was complete.

"Hail thee demons!" a man shouted, moving closer to the circle. "You are here to do our bidding. We are your masters, and you must steal an item for us. It is our will."

My phone beeped letting me know that I had signal, wherever this was, and Jinx had pinged my location. The cavalry was on its way. Even if things went sideways and I got injured, my friends would get Sparky to safety. I just had to take care of that pesky summoning circle.

The only way to forcibly lower the circle was to kill the sorcerers who cast it. I didn't like killing. I had a hard enough time coming to terms with my faerie blood. But everyone has a line, a point of no return. These men in their abuse of child demons had gone too far.

"You do this often?" I asked, voice low. "Force children to steal for you? That's super classy."

I slid my blade to the magic thread at Sparky's wrist. The kid had been through enough. It was time to end this.

"We, The Brotherhood, have summoned demons for generations," the man said, sputtering. "You are foul creatures, and we will order you to do whatever pleases us. It is our right."

"Keep talking to teddy, kiddo," I said, giving Sparky a final one-armed hug.

With a snap of my wrist, I cut the binding thread. Sparky's face was buried in his teddy bear, and I had to hope he stayed that way. He was a demon inside a summoning circle. There was nowhere for him to go, no way for him to escape.

But I wasn't a demon.

I stood and spun on my heel, blade slicing through the speaker's throat. Shocked faces gaped at me from inside their ritual hoods, their overprivileged brains unable to process the fact that I'd stepped across the line of their circle without so much as a twitch.

"Silly summoners," I said. "I'm no demon child. I'm a faerie freaking princess, and your circle has no power over me. The devil is in the details."

The first summoner to recover his wits snarled and lunged at me with a long, jagged-edged dagger. I widened my stance and shifted my weight to the balls of my feet. A second blade hit the palm of my gloved hand as I spun, slashing through the man's robes like butter. The fools weren't wearing armor beneath their ritual garb. One more detail in my favor.

"Kill her!" the collapsing man shouted, spittle flying from his angrily twisted lips.

"Yeah, good luck with that." I twisted out of a stumbling man's reach.

"We have you surrounded," a second man yelled. "Drop your weapons and get on your knees!"

I laughed, but judging by the looks on their faces, the humor didn't reach my eyes.

"Next time you try to be scary, maybe don't wear your bathrobe?" I took advantage of the men's bulky robes and lack of peripheral vision to land three on their butts with one foot sweep.

"Kill the woman and the child!"

Kill the child? Over my glowing corpse.

The roar of a pissed off demon filled the air, followed by screams. That wasn't the cry of a frightened demon child—that roar erupted from a Grand Marquis of Hell. Roaring and screams were joined by the twang of a bow string and the thwap thwap of arrows hitting their targets. I grinned wide, showing my teeth. The cavalry had arrived.

Rage and ley line magic burned inside of me, and I let it simmer. I'd need that fire for later. I had no idea where we were or how many enemies we faced. But of one thing I was certain.

This room was littered with trophies, evidence of decades or more of summoning children to do their bidding. These men were evil. They were the true monsters of this world.

The Brotherhood had enslaved children like Sparky, causing them pain and fear. He was not their first attempt at summoning.

But he would be their last.

8

THE GOING RATE FOR PENANCE

MICHAEL C BAILEY

I t was just after nightfall when the bearer of bad news arrived at the Sleeping Lamb Inn.

Samantha recognized the man for what he was the instant he entered, even before he threw back his traveling cloak, a heavy woolen thing made to withstand night riding, to reveal herald's livery. The drawn features, the weary slump of his shoulders, his gait, slow and stiff and bowlegged—these all suggested a man who'd spent many a day on horseback, and not necessarily by choice.

He took in the tavern, a sedate if not exactly sleepy place. A moony-eyed couple in rough-spun tunics sat at the bar, hands intertwined. Three men and a woman clustered close together at a table, nursing their drinks amidst jovial conversation. A burly, dark-eyed fellow sat in a far corner all by himself. The simple surcoat he wore identified him as a member of the town constabulary. The newcomer noted each of them in turn, but his eyes passed right over Samantha, as if she weren't there.

She didn't bother praying that he was here for someone else. The Gods had stopped listening to her ages ago.

The man approached the barkeep, a lean fellow with scraggly ginger hair. The barkeep flicked a finger in her direction.

"Would that be Jessica or Samantha?" the man said.

The barkeep shrugged. "Doesn't matter. They're twins."

The man made it a point to let Samantha see him coming. "Miss Summerland?"

Samantha looked him up and down, and then without comment, returned her gaze to the fireplace. She could feel his eyes on her—on her scar, an old wound that ran from her left eyebrow up into her hairline, where it continued as a streak of snow white.

"Have I the pleasure of addressing Jessica or Samantha?"

"Doesn't matter," Samantha said. "We're twins."

"I suppose it doesn't, as long as you are one of the Summerland sisters. My name is Lon Merchand and—"

"Dravis sent you."

"Uh, yes, he did," Lon said, taken aback. "Did you know I was coming?"

An intense itch prickled Samantha's palm, right where the brand was. It had been tingling unpleasantly for a few days now—but maybe that was her imagination.

Maybe.

"I knew," she said.

"Master Dravis would like to meet with you."

That got her attention. "Meet with us? In person?"

"That is normally how one person meets with another."

"When?"

"As soon as humanly possible. Direct quote."

Without a further word, Samantha Summerland got up, pushed past the messenger, and ran upstairs.

She plucked a candle out of its wall sconce and carried it into the room at the end of the hall, the one overlooking the kitchen's compost pit. The furnishings were limited to one bed barely wide enough to hold two people comfortably and a small oaken commode for the chamber pot. The roof leaked, and on windy days, the window rattled incessantly. It was the cheapest room in the inn.

"Jess. Wake up."

Jessica was not actually asleep, despite her best efforts—it was windy out—but she rolled over and pulled her blanket over her head in the interest of maintaining the pretense.

"Jess, wake up. It's Dravis," Samantha said. "He wants to meet with us."

Jessica rolled back and squinted at her sister in equal measures of annoyance and skepticism. "What?"

"There's a messenger downstairs. He said Dravis wants to meet with us."

"In person?"

"That is normally how one person meets with another."

"Funny. When?"

"As soon as humanly possible. Direct quote."

Jessica sat up with a grunt. "Last time Dravis wanted to meet with us was...when? A year ago?"

"The Vengro job."

"The Vengro job." Jessica let out a low hiss. "Shit."

Samantha frowned. "We have to go, don't we?"

"Yeah. We have to go. Tell the messenger we'll leave in the morning."

Samantha nodded and went back downstairs.

"Gods," Jessica muttered. "Kill a man's first born and you never hear the end of it."

After a fitful night's sleep, Jessica and Samantha rose with the dawn to pack their meager belongings and suit up for their journey. For Jessica, this meant donning an assortment of plate armor pieces that had seen better days. She was scrupulous about keeping her armor free of rust but less so about hammering out dings and dents; her cuirass could have doubled effectively as a washboard. Her falchion received similarly halfhearted care; it gleamed like new steel but the edge was chipped down its length, turning it into a wicked saw. Samantha wore hard-boiled leather on her forearms and her legs and about her waist in the form of a thick girdle, but regarded unimpaired mobility as superior to lumbering about in a clanking metal shell.

The sisters' difference of opinion on the matter of self-protection was a point of regular and often heated debate. It was among the few things they bickered about.

The city of Anto was a three-day journey by horseback. The Summerland sisters extended it to four by letting their mounts dictate the pace. Hooligan and Jester were by nature leisurely beasts.

Late on that fourth day, they stopped at the first inn they encountered. The hand-carved sign hanging above the front door named the establishment as Smythwyck's Comfort. The sign was bright and clean, as was the small manor house to which it was attached.

"They've spruced the place up quite a bit since the last time," Jessica said, as much a question as an observation.

"I think they have," Samantha said.

They lashed Hooligan and Jester to the hitching post out front and went inside. A man and a woman in matching sky-blue traveling coats glanced at them, passingly curious, and then went back to warming themselves near a wide, deep fireplace.

The barkeep, an older man with more scalp than hair, nodded

politely to his new arrivals. "Evening, ladies," he said, and he started upon taking a second, closer look. "Are you two sisters?"

"No," the Summerlands deadpanned in unison.

"You look alike."

"We get that a lot," Jessica said. "We'd like a room for the night."

"Two rooms," Samantha said.

"We can make do with one."

"I want my own bed."

"I can set you up in one room with two beds," the barkeep suggested.

"Sold," Jessica said.

"How long have you been adventurers?"

"Excuse me?"

"I asked how long you two have been adventurers. We don't get too many down this way."

"We're not adventurers."

"No? You look the type."

"Well, we're not," Jessica said, and that was the truth.

They'd not been adventurers for a long time.

———

Their room on the upper floor was not within smelling distance of a compost pit. That alone made it worth the price they paid, but the beds, with their thick down-stuffed mattresses and heavy comforters, made it a bargain and a half.

They slept well that night.

After a simple breakfast of hot oatmeal and strong coffee, they returned to the road, curious as to what they'd find upon reaching Anto. The so-called Sterling City was in the early stages of a renaissance, having only recently recovered from the collapse of its once robust silver mining industry.

As they rode through the city, the Summerlands saw evidence of this ongoing rebirth at every turn. Heads were held high. Faces were bright; eyes were alive. People spoke to one another, trading cheerful greetings instead of grunting or passing in funereal silence. More shops were open than closed, and those that were open had appreciable business to attend to. Jessica wondered if Anto would ever again realize the glory it once knew, but at the very least, it seemed that it had reclaimed something far more important than its fortunes; it had reclaimed its soul.

"Good for them," Jessica said.

"What?" Samantha said with a start, as if awakening from a light doze.

"Look."

Samantha twisted one way in her saddle then the other, her eyes wide, alarmed. "Jess, nothing's wrong."

"Look at the city. Look at the people."

Samantha turned a puzzled frown toward her sister.

"They're happy," Jessica said. "I haven't seen happiness here in ages."

"Oh." Samantha squinted in thought. "I remember being happy. Once."

"Yeah?" Jessica sighed. "You're doing better than I am."

It wasn't happiness they experienced upon reaching the faded glory of Castle Argent, but a perverse joy and a guilt-tinged sense of satisfaction. The renewal that had spread throughout the rest of the city stopped dead at the castle's crumbling curtain wall. Greenish-black moss consumed the base as far as the eye could see and vines grew unchecked up its face, reaching for the crenellated edge like grasping fingers. The castle beyond was as gray and grim as a tombstone.

The Summerlands rode up to the barbican, a squat outbuilding held together by vines and moss and habit. The rusted iron portcullis was wedged up into its recess by a pair of sturdy wooden beams.

"Still haven't fixed the gate," Samantha observed.

"No," Jessica said. "That is just plain pathetic."

"If anyone would know pathetic," someone rumbled, "it'd be you."

The castle guard who came out to meet them walked with a stiff limp, which he did his best to conceal by playing it off as a lazy swagger. Jessica was not fooled; she was there when Samantha gave him the limp.

Thom Stoneton, on a good day, when he was feeling charitable, might have called that a fair trade. He'd given Samantha her scar.

"Stoneton," Jessica said.

"What are you two doing here?" Stoneton said.

"Business call. Dravis wants to see us."

"He didn't tell me he'd sent for you."

"Why would he? It's none of your business."

"Like hell it isn't. I'm the captain of the guard. Everything goes through me."

"That it does. Why, I distinctly remember Samantha going through you," Jessica said, smiling. "Quite easily, in fact."

"Arrogant bitch," Stoneton spat. His hand strayed to the grip of his sword.

"Guilty. Now, are you done posturing? We're already a day late."

"And that's my problem how?"

"It isn't—unless I tell Dravis you added to the delay. As I recall, he hates you only slightly less than he hates us. Or have you gents made nice and patched things up?"

Stoneton's perpetual scowl deepened.

"Thought not. Can we go now?"

Stoneton stepped aside and offered a mocking bow. "Nice talking to you, Samantha," he said with a smirk.

Samantha snapped her fingers at Stoneton, sending a fat spark at his face. He flinched away.

"Pathetic," she said.

Stoneton took possession of the Summerlands' horses and ordered Devin Iggon, a castle guard too old to be called a boy but too young to be respected as a man, to accompany the sisters up to the castle. He shadowed them as they crossed the bailey, a patchwork of barren dirt and tufts of sun-scorched grass, his hand on his sword.

"We know the way," Jessica said.

"I have my orders," Iggon said. "I'm to stay with you at all times—and kill you if you try anything funny."

"Good luck with that."

"You don't want to trifle with me," Iggon warned.

"Oh no?"

"Captain Stoneton trained me personally."

"That's not as impressive as you think it is, kid."

"Captain Stoneton is a great warrior," Iggon said, bristling. "And I am not a kid."

"Do you know who we are?" Jessica asked.

"No..."

"When you next speak to your captain, ask him who we are. Ask about the first time he met us. Ask him how he got that limp. Ask him why he needs to keep us under your watchful eye and why he's ordered you to kill us if we step out of line." Jessica turned and fixed Iggon with a look. "Then ask yourself: do *you* really want to trifle with *us*?"

Iggon swallowed audibly and said nothing more the rest of the way.

The east wing of Castle Argent belonged entirely to Master Harrison Dravis. The lower floors held his extensive personal library, the topmost floor his quarters, and the floor in between— the Summerland sisters' immediate destination—his study.

"Jessica. Samantha. You're late," Dravis said, looking up from his book, a massive thing that occupied his entire desktop. He dismissed Iggon to stand guard outside. "I was expecting you yesterday."

"Old horses," Jessica offered as an explanation. "What can you do?"

"Mm. We're none of us getting any younger, are we? Of course, *we* get to enjoy the dubious luxury of aging. Unlike some."

Samantha shrank into herself.

"I was going through my library this morning when I came across this," Dravis said, thumping his book. "It's a history of Anto written by my family over the course of many, many generations. Did you know the Dravises have served Lord Pranceton and his family since before the great silver boom?"

"That sounds fascinating," Jessica began, but Dravis cut her off before she could redirect the conversation toward the grim business at hand.

"Oh, it is. That's how Anto earned the name 'the Sterling City,' you know. It was said that once upon a time, the precious metal was so abundant you could stab a random plot of earth with a shovel and strike a vein. The mines ran day in and day out for generations. That's how the Prancetons first came to power; they grew fat off the taxes they collected and leveraged their personal affluence to elevate their standing in the wardens' court. At its peak, Anto's prominence rivaled that of Woeste or Ambride. Some say it even threatened to supplant the great capital of Oson as the crown jewel of all Asaches."

Dravis stood up and circled around his desk. Jessica instinctively stepped in front of Samantha, who promptly shoved her away.

"But, as you know, all good things must come to an end, and so it was with Anto's silver boom. The mines became barren seemingly overnight," Dravis said. "The Prancetons, desperate to cling to their wealth—and the power, influence, and prestige that wealth brought—exhausted their own fortune in a mad quest to keep the dying industry alive. They leveled forests and snapped up farmland and stripped it all down to the bedrock in the hopes of discovering new veins, but their efforts were for naught. It took less than a year to reduce the Prancetons to paupers. To survive, they took to plundering their own home and selling off everything of remote value, right down to the tapestries. They even wanted to sell off my family library."

Dravis slammed his hand down upon the great book of Anto's past. Samantha flinched and let out a small whine. This time, she did not push Jessica away.

"My grandmother was the chief advisor to the warden at the time, and she wouldn't have it. The library is our family's birthright, and she refused to surrender it to anyone but her own blood. Thanks to her, it passed onto my father when he became the chief advisor, and he passed it on to me. I expected I'd one day bequeath it to my own son." Dravis's voice dropped to a thick whisper. "And then the Summerland sisters paid me a visit."

"What do you want from us?" Jessica demanded, and she braced for the answer. The simple requests Dravis passed along by messenger. The tasks that ended with them spilling blood, those he had the decency to mete out in person.

Dravis tutted. "Down to business, just like that? You don't want to catch up at all? I'm sure you have stories to tell. I know I do. Did you know my wife died last winter? Lung rot, poor thing, but she passed peacefully. We should all be so lucky, eh?"

Jessica's lips pressed into a bloodless line. The man's penchant for subtle cruelty was as keen as ever.

"Out with it," she said.

"Very well," Dravis said. "Ladies, I have one final task for you."

The sisters did a synchronized double take. "You—what?" Jessica said.

"You heard me correctly. I've decided that our...*arrangement* has run its course and it's time to let go of the past and move on. It's unhealthy to hang onto your anger, you know. Eats you up from within."

"Why?" Samantha asked.

"She speaks!" Dravis mused. "Why what?"

"Why now?" Samantha said. "After all these years, why let us go now?"

Dravis's smile was thin and humorless. "This is—would have been Horatio's twentieth year."

The sisters frowned.

"What are you saying?" Jessica said. "If we'd killed your son today you would have been fine with it?"

"He would have been a man by most standards. His life would have been his own. That's not to say I would have let the matter pass gracefully, certainly not, but I believe my reaction might have been less..."

Dravis grasped Jessica's hand and beheld the sigil with which he'd branded the Summerlands. The scar tissue shone pink against the pale skin of her palm. Dravis touched a finger to the brand, sending a jolt of acid pain racing up her arm.

"Severe," he finished.

Jessica jerked away. "We do this last job for you," she said. "We do this and we're quits?"

"You do what I ask and yes, I will consider your debt to me paid in full and I will lift the soulburn curse I placed upon you."

"Then tell us what we have to do. The sooner we can put you behind us, the better."

"It's quite simple." Dravis chuckled. "Not *easy*, mind you, but simple. I trust you remember Albin Lessiter?"

The Summerland sisters blanched.

"I see you do. Good. I want you, my dear Jessica, my dear Samantha, to inflict upon him the same anguish he had you visit upon me oh those many years ago. You are to find and slay Forrest Lessiter, Albin Lessiter's first-born child, right in front of his father." Dravis's lips stretched into a perverse leer.

The Summerlands' blood ran cold.

"And bring me the boy's head," he said.

———

Dravis did not set a deadline for the Summerland sisters to complete their assignment, reckoning the promise of freedom would provide ample motivation to act quickly—and yet the sisters lingered at Smythwyck's Comfort for several days. They passed those days imbibing dangerous quantities of rye whiskey, as if hoping to numb their souls against the task ahead of them.

"We should probably hit the road tomorrow," Jessica said one night. "Get this over with."

"Yeah," Samantha said. "Do you think Dravis will really let us go?"

After a moment, Jessica said, "I think he will."

"We'll finally be free?"

"I didn't say that. If we make it out alive—which is a big *if*—we'll have the blood of an innocent child on our hands. *Another* innocent child," she amended. "Lessiter won't let that go any more than Dravis let it go—and we won't have the luxury of claiming it was an accident this time around."

"It *was* an accident," Samantha said.

"I know." Jessica laid her hand over Samantha's. "But it doesn't matter."

"No."

"You have to give it to the old bastard, though; he really thought this one through," Jessica said, absent of admiration. "Best case scenario, we kill the Lessiter boy, escape with our lives, and spend the rest of our days as fugitives. Worst case, we all die—us, Albin Lessiter, his son…"

"They both sound like worst case scenarios to me," Samantha said.

"Yeah. Point is, no matter how this plays out, Dravis wins."

"There's another option," Samantha began, and then she abruptly looked away, as if something elsewhere in the tavern had captured her attention.

Jessica's heart squeezed painfully. Samantha hadn't been quite the same since *that day*, not since taking Stoneton's sword to the head. These moments of odd behavior, once frequent, were rare nowadays—rare, but not completely gone.

"Sam," Jessica said.

"Uh-huh," Samantha said distantly.

"You were saying?"

Samantha blinked, shook her head. "I was saying?"

"There was another option?"

"Right. Yes. There's another option. We could just run."

"Run?"

"Run. We don't go to Ambride; we don't report back to Dravis. We head to the Anstl Region or the northern territories. We jump on a ship and go to Roslan. To hell with the job, to hell with our obligations, to hell with Dravis. We run."

"And what about this?" Jessica touched a finger to the brand in the center of Samantha's palm.

"What about it?"

"How long would we get to enjoy our freedom if we run? A few days? A few weeks? Sooner or later Dravis would realize we've crossed him and he'll invoke the curse. Maybe you're comfortable having your eternal soul burned away to nothing, but I'm not."

Samantha gave her sister a melancholy smile. "Jess? After everything we've done in this world, what makes you think we'd be welcome in the next?" she said.

Jessica threw back the last of her whiskey. "We should get some sleep," she said.

Ambride was a city of contrasts and contradictions. It possessed a bohemian spirit in the form of a thriving arts community populated with avant-garde playwrights, musicians who experimented with sound the way alchemists tinkered with chemicals, and painters who rejected traditional techniques and media to blaze bold new artistic trails. The city also took great pride in its prestigious academies—institutions dedicated to the pursuit of arcane knowledge. Though secretive and insular by nature, and thus not always the most congenial of neighbors, the academies lent Ambride a certain mystique the social elite found compelling.

Ambride was also a magnet for those living the adventurer's life. Treasure seekers, monster hunters, dungeon explorers, soldiers of fortune—they all flocked to Ambride to loiter in its inns and taverns until they received the call to adventure. Then they'd be off to risk life and limb in pursuit of fame and fortune. Sometimes, that risk would be rewarded.

Sometimes, returning from a quest with said life and limb still intact was reward enough.

Jessica and Samantha Summerland, in their youth, had traveled the adventurers' path and were familiar enough with Ambride's haunts and hangouts that they knew the best places to gather intelligence. They began at the top of the bottom of the barrel, The

Perfect, and worked their way through Soth's Inn, The Quiet Corner, Killagree's, Mona's Tavern, Graywolf's Gathering, and a few spots not well known to even seasoned adventurers. Upon collecting pieces of their particular puzzle here and there, five days after their arrival, they'd assembled a reasonably complete picture —as complete as they could expect, considering their immediate target and where they were most likely to find him at any given time of day:

The Ambride Academy of Magic.

The Summerlands, each nursing a mild hangover, sat across the street from the academy, nestled beneath the shade of a stout oak, and watched the morning unfold. Shops opened for business. Men and women arrived soon thereafter to purchase needed items or perhaps grab a treat. (Jessica left her post long enough to buy a bag of cranberry scones to snack on). A blacksmith beat out a syncopated chorus of clangs and clinks, providing a discordant background score.

Jessica sighed. This was what life was supposed to be like.

"Jess," Samantha said, pointing. A man in gray scholar's robes broke free from the flow of pedestrians and made his way across the academy's central courtyard, a sprawling expanse of green bordered on three sides by the academy itself. He ambled up to a ponderous oaken door banded by iron, paused for a moment, then stepped inside.

"Here we go," Jessica said.

The man in gray was the first and only person to enter the rambling, towering stonework mansion for some time.

And then the academics arrived in earnest, in groups of two and three and four—never alone, Jessica noticed—dressed in academic robes in somber hues. From their vantage point, the Summerland sisters could make out only the broadest of details—gender, age, hair color, whether they carried any bags or satchels—but that was sufficient for their purposes.

Albin Lessiter arrived late in the morning.

The sisters shrank against the trunk of their tree, fearful that any sudden movement might attract their quarry's attention, and watched Lessiter cross the courtyard at a stride. The lad at his side had to jog to keep up.

Jessica waited until they'd entered the academy before daring to speak. "Looks like Lessiter's boy is following in his father's footsteps."

"You think he's a spellcaster too?" Samantha asked.

"I think it'd be wise to assume so. Question is, how far along is he in his studies? Enough to be dangerous?"

"I think it'd be wise to assume so."

"Me too."

"Now what?" Samantha asked.

"Let's move. We'll draw attention if we sit here all day."

They relocated to a small pub nearby. Jessica purchased beers to nurse while they loitered near a small bow window looking out on the academy's courtyard, which a quartet of children had claimed as their own for a spirited game of tag.

"How are we going to do it?" Samantha asked.

"Excellent question," Jessica said.

Samantha waited for her sister's answer. And waited.

"Charging into the academy would be stupid. They don't have any guards," Jessica said, recalling what she learned through her many gentle inquiries. "But everyone in there is a spellcaster of one kind or another, and that makes them plenty dangerous. The smart thing to do would be to follow Lessiter home and ambush him there. Wait until he's asleep, sneak in, do it and be done with it."

"Dravis wanted us to do it while Lessiter watched," Samantha noted.

"Is that how you *want* to do it?"

"I don't want to do it at all."

"Yeah, well, that's not an option."

"Yes it is."

"No. It isn't. It's them or us, Sam."

"I know," Samantha said miserably. "We should at least face him honorably."

Jessica whispered, "We're here to murder a man's child. There's no honor to be found here."

"We don't have to make it worse by killing him in his sleep."

"Going at Lessiter head-on would give him a chance to fight back."

"It would give him a chance to protect his son. Doesn't he deserve that much?"

"No, he doesn't," Jessica snapped. "He's the reason why we're in this mess to begin with. He hired us to kill Dravis, remember?"

"I remember," Samantha said, her voice hard, her eyes harder. "I also remember he didn't hold a knife to our throats. He offered us a job; we said yes. Lessiter didn't turn us into assassins; we did."

"Lessiter lied to us."

"I remember that too." Samantha wiped her tear-rimmed eyes on her sleeve, and in that moment looked like a frustrated child on the verge of a tantrum. "I remember everything we did—and everything we've done for Dravis trying to erase the worst mistake we ever made. But it's still there. I remember it. And I don't want to remember anymore." Samantha stood, knocking over her barstool, stormed out of the pub—and headed straight for the academy.

"Sam, no," Jessica said, chasing after her sister. "Sam, stop. Samantha!"

"No matter how this plays out, Dravis wins," Samantha said without slowing, without turning.

"Samantha! Gods damn it!"

Jessica snared Samantha by the arm. Samantha whirled and put her weight behind a shove that took her sister off her feet. Jessica sat hard on the cobblestone street. A painful jolt shot up her spine and into the base of her skull.

"There's no honor to be found here," Samantha said.

Jessica struggled to stand, the aftershock of her fall causing her legs to rebel. By the time she got up, Samantha was halfway across the courtyard.

A flush of adrenaline, hot and electric, filled Jessica's chest. She got up and listed drunkenly as she broke into a jog, then a run, then a desperate sprint. She caught up to Samantha as she threw open the academy's front door.

The distinct smell of ozone trailed Samantha as she strode across the grand foyer, a long, wide chamber with a high arched ceiling.

A man in gray robes, the very one who first entered the academy that morning, sprang out from behind his lectern and barked an irate, "See here!"

That was as far as his admonition got.

Samantha pointed at the man as if in accusation and uttered a word of power, a guttural sound. A gossamer thread of pure white leapt from her finger. The dim chamber flashed with daylight brilliance and a high-pitched crack echoed off the stonework. The robed man stiffened, a scream catching in his throat, and he crumpled to the floor.

"Samantha!" Jessica cried.

"He's not dead," Samantha said.

The man gasped as if to confirm this. Samantha knelt, jamming a knee into his chest, pinning him, and she touched her fingertip to his temple.

"Albin Lessiter," she said. "Where is he?"

"What? Lessiter?" the man said in a drunken slur. "Why do you want—?"

Samantha spoke her word again with a subtle new inflection,

sending a milder second jolt through her captive. He vibrated beneath her leg and bit down on a yelp.

"Where is he?" she said again.

"Go to Hell."

She sent another charge through the man and asked the question again.

"Sam," Jessica said. Her sword left its scabbard. "Someone's coming."

Samantha cocked her head. She heard urgent voices and urgent footsteps growing louder, closer.

"Where is he?" She sent another shock through the man.

"In his chambers! South wing!" he wailed. "South wing, top floor!"

The Summerlands left him there in the grand foyer, drooling and wheezing and twitching, and ran to the nearest stairwell. The spiraling stairs took them up to the third floor, where they emerged into an empty hallway.

"Come on," Jessica said, taking the lead.

It had been too long since their first visit to the academy, since the day they had their fateful meeting with Albin Lessiter. Jessica couldn't remember the path to his chambers and every corridor looked the same to her. The academy was as good as a labyrinth.

"There!" Samantha said, pointing.

Jessica followed her finger to the end of the hallway, to an open door, in which stood the boy they'd spied in Lessiter's company earlier. His expression remained one of mild curiosity as the Summerland sisters broke into a sprint and charged straight at him.

Jessica knocked him back with a shove. Samantha slammed the door shut and slapped a pair of wrought iron bolts into place, sealing them in.

The central chamber had changed little after all this time. Long tables butted up against the walls, and upon the tables sat teetering stacks of loose papers. A cyclopean wall of leather-bound books rose up around a squat desk, at which sat a slack-jawed Albin Lessiter, his silhouette framed by a massive, intricately detailed wall map of western Asaches. The fabled dead city of Hesre was prominently labeled in bold red script.

"Oh. My," Lessiter said.

"One word," Jessica said. She seized the boy, scruffing him by the shirt, and held her falchion up under his chin. "One word and he dies."

"What are you waiting for? We're here to murder a man's child," Samantha said. "Do it and be done with it."

"Dammit, Sam..."

"Please, don't hurt him," Lessiter said. "Whatever this is, leave him out of it."

"Whatever this is? You know damn well what this is," Jessica said.

"Yes. I suppose I do." Lessiter stood, slowly. "But my son has nothing to do with it."

"I believe that's the point. Dravis's son had nothing to do with it either."

"His death is my fault?"

"What?" the boy said. "Father? What is she —?"

"Forrest," Lessiter said. "Be silent."

"He doesn't know, does he?" Jessica said. "Then tell him. I want him to know what kind of man you are."

"Why do you —?"

Jessica pressed the edge of her sawblade sword to Forrest's flesh.

"*Tell him,*" she said.

Lessiter somberly nodded and offered his confession. "Many years ago, I hired these women to kill Harrison Dravis, chief advisor to the warden of Anto. I told them Dravis was a necromancer threatening to rain destruction down on Ambride, but in truth he was nothing more than an old rival who'd crossed me one time too many. He..." Lessiter waved a hand. "His sins against me did not warrant my response—the result of which was the needless death of an innocent." Lessiter turned his gaze toward the sisters. "I will take responsibility for my role in that tragedy, Summerland ladies, but that boy's blood is on your hands as well. We must all atone for that sin in our own way. Killing Forrest will serve no purpose."

"Dravis disagrees," Jessica said.

Lessiter, perfectly serene, said, "Do you?"

"Do you?" Samantha echoed.

"Sam. You know what will happen if we don't follow through," Jessica said.

"You know what will happen if we *do* follow through."

Forrest Lessiter dared to glance over his shoulder and he locked eyes with his captor. He was younger than Jessica had first estimated. She could see it in his face, round with baby fat.

"How old are you?" she asked.

Albin Lessiter answered for his son. "He turned eleven last month."

Eleven.

As old as Horatio Dravis was when he left the world.

Jessica let Forrest go. Instead of running to the safety of his father's arms, the boy retreated to a corner of the study and curled into a ball.

"Now what?" Lessiter said. "Do you still intend to kill him?"

"No," Jessica said. "But I'm starting to think maybe I should kill you. This is all your fault. You need to pay."

"You've forced me to reveal my greatest shame to my son. He will never think of me the same way again." Lessiter glanced over at Forrest. The boy recoiled and hugged his knees to his chest. "Forrest is as lost to me as Horatio is to Harrison Dravis. How much more could I possibly pay?"

Captain Stoneton personally escorted the Summerland sisters to Dravis's study.

"Would you like me to stay, Master Dravis?" Stoneton said with a hopeful note.

"No, captain, thank you," Dravis said. "That will be all," he added when Stoneton did not immediately depart.

Stoneton threw the women a sneer and stepped outside.

"Ladies," Dravis said. "It's done?"

"In a manner of speaking," Jessica said.

"What do you mean, 'in a manner of speaking'? Did you or did you not kill Lessiter's son?"

"No," Samantha said. "We didn't. And we won't."

Dravis darkened. "We had a bargain."

"Had. Past tense," Jessica said. "You want him dead? Do it yourself, you pathetic piece of shit."

"Watch your tongue, girl!"

"Fuck you. Fuck. You. We're done with this, Dravis, and we're done with you," Jessica said, and to her amazement, she laughed. "We're done with you. We're done with you!" she cried in elation, and a terrible weight she'd carried for so very long at last fell from her shoulders.

Dravis could only gawp at her.

"Go ahead. Do it. Get it over with. I don't care anymore. After everything I've done I barely have a soul left to burn, so go ahead and do it." Jessica thrust her scarred hand in his face. "Do it! DO IT!"

Dravis gestured as if ordering an executioner to carry out his grim work. The brands flared to cruel life. A searing pain spread up their arms, into their chests, and it filled their hearts with burning, blinding agony. Jessica held back a scream.

Samantha could not hold back hers.

Jessica grabbed her sister and held her tight. She begged for her forgiveness and whispered in her ear that it would be over soon.

And it was. Quite suddenly and completely, the pain ceased.

"You damnable women. You damnable women!" Dravis roared, and he hurled the first thing he laid his hand upon, a small leather-bound journal, across the study. "You couldn't have finished this one last task, could you? So close—*so close* to my perfect revenge and you had to go and rediscover your consciences! You had to—"

With a strangled groan, Dravis slumped against his desk.

And then, to the sisters' astonishment, he laughed.

"*Ohhh*, you poor stupid things," he muttered.

"What? *What?*" Jessica demanded.

"There's no death curse on you," Dravis said. "Either of you. There never was."

Jessica stammered helplessly. "There never—what? You mean you—"

"Lied? Yes. Elaborately. The soulburn curse was a fiction I created on a whim to motivate you when necessary," Dravis said, flicking a finger. The brands burned again, ever so briefly. "Although you two didn't need much motivation, did you? You never really questioned why I sent you to kill anyone. You didn't care who, you didn't care why; you just did it. For all your griping and insolence, you made excellent assassins."

"There was no curse?" Jessica said, a cold fist wrapping around her heart.

"There was no curse?" Samantha said. "We killed all those people for you for *nothing?*"

"For me? Oh, no, dear lady; you killed all those people for *your-selves*. You traded their lives for your own, time and again, and you did it without hesitation. Personally? I think you grew to like it." Dravis, strangely, brightened. "I suppose if you look at it a certain way, I did burn your souls away after all."

"You sadistic bastard," Jessica said.

"Yes, well." Dravis straightened up. "You're going to try to kill me now, of course."

Jessica drew her jagged sword.

"I trust you'll understand if I refuse to go quietly," Dravis said.

Thom Stoneton's final act as captain of the guard of Castle Argent was to call for help. He died screaming the Summerlands' names, even as his life's blood spilled out on the floor.

"Well, shit," Jessica said. "Looks like we'll have to fight our way out after all."

"I know," Samantha said.

"If we make it, we'll be wanted women."

"I know."

"And that's *if* we make it out. There's a good chance we're not leaving here alive."

Samantha nodded. "That's not unfair."

"No. Guess not."

The thunder of approaching footsteps grew louder, ever louder.

"I trust they'll understand if we refuse to go quietly," Samantha said. She flexed her hands. Electricity crackled across her fingertips. "Love you, sis."

"Love you, sis," Jessica said.

Devin Iggon gave the order to attack.

9

THE GRANITE CLIFF OF MOUNT MASSIVE

ADAM BRECKENRIDGE

The evening of Hilda's seventieth birthday, her eldest son Randall made a harness to carry her on his back for the three-day journey to the Granite Cliff of Mount Massive where, according to the traditions of their village, she would jump to her death. She had spoken little of the coming day over the past few weeks—alarmingly little, making only a few goodbyes to close friends but otherwise acting as though nothing was out of the ordinary. The men of the village feared for Randall as the day approached, sure that his mother was in denial, sure that when the day came, she would flee and they would have to organize a search party for her. But when the day came, it was his mother who awoke him, well before sunrise, whispering in the darkness, "It's time, sweetie."

She said nothing else as she prepared food, and they ate in silence. Nor did she speak when he wrapped the harness around her body and hoisted her onto his back. Randall had already said goodbye to his wife and son and was relieved when he passed by their home to see they were still asleep. He didn't want to think now about the journey he would have to make with his own son years from now. They made their way through the still dark village, passing nobody, for which he was also thankful. They walked through the sunrise, the crisp early morning air giving way to a warm day. It was late summer and the days would be warm for a while longer, but another harsh winter was soon to settle in.

In the morning light, they could see in the distance the huge gray wedge of Mount Massive standing out from the other peaks. It was impossible to tell from here just where on the mountain the trail led. It was a long way away, further than it seemed possible to walk, certainly further than he had ever walked in his lifetime. There was, however, some relief in that. Perhaps they would never reach their destination. Perhaps they could run away into the woods and live off the land. He could sneak back into the village for his wife and son and bring them to the secret place where they would all live together, free to live out natural lives. But then again, if the bounty of the mountains was sufficient to sustain a healthy population, there would be no need for such loathsome traditions as they had.

At a point on the trail, where there seemed to be nothing of interest to Randall, his mother tapped him on the shoulder and said, "Let me down."

He stopped and looked over his shoulder at her. "I'm not supposed to."

"Oh heavens, as if I could outrun you, my fit young son."

He hesitated a moment, then undid the knots holding the harness in place. He squatted down and felt her weight unburdened from him. She stretched her legs then took a few steps toward the trees to their left. She moved slowly into them, following something on the ground that he couldn't see. He tensed. The woods here were thick, and though she was seventy, she was in good health for her age and could possibly move amongst the trees more quickly than he with his bulkier frame. If she got away from him, the shame he would face back at the village would be more than he could bear. Michael Keller's father had slipped away into the woods, never to be seen again. When Michael had returned two days after departing from the village and his shame had been discovered, a month later, he was found hanging from a tree behind his house. But still Randall didn't want to crowd his mother too closely. What would it say of him as a son, to show such distrust?

She followed her invisible trail deeper into the woods, until he was just on the verge of rushing in to grab her, when she stopped and waved him over.

"Come, come," she said, "you must see this."

He stepped off the trail and tried to follow the steps she had taken.

"Careful where you step," she said.

Not sure what he was looking for, he stepped near the trunks of the pine trees so as not to crush whatever needed preserving. Where his mother stood, the ground was softer, and she pointed at some tracks pressed into the earth.

"Look," she said, a hint of wonderment in her voice.

He studied the U shaped tracks, which looked quite ordinary to him.

"Horse?" he asked.

"No, stupid, not horses. These are unicorn tracks."

Randall looked at her incredulously. Their village had its share of legends about mythical creatures deep in the forest, but they always had a way of remaining out of sight, glimpsed only briefly in the distance through the trees by a drunkard on a moonless night. Lately, it largely seemed only the elders of the village still believed in anything magical, though it may have just been him losing his own faith.

"They look no different from horse tracks," he said to her.

"That's because you've never paid attention to details. Look." She bent down to point at something on one of the prints. Toward the back there was an indentation where there shouldn't have been, as though the creature who made it had a spur in its heel.

"You'll never see that kind of spur on a horse track; only unicorns have that. This is a good sign. We should have a pleasant journey to the mountain. Maybe if we're lucky, we'll see a unicorn. Okay, let's go."

Randall helped his mother back up on his back and re-tied the harness.

"I've never seen a unicorn before," he said after they got moving again. He also wasn't sure if he'd really just seen the tracks of one either, though he had also never seen a horse print with a spur in its heel.

"Oh, they never come near the village. They're flighty creatures, those unicorns, almost never come near humans. Did I ever tell you about the time I saw a faun in the village though?"

He had heard the story before, but he wanted to hear her tell it anyway.

"When was this?"

"Before you were born. Early, early in the morning. That's how I saw him. I was up early that morning because I wanted to get to the river before anyone else did to get a good catch. That old faun was sitting on the stone wall by the Miller's place playing a pipe that made notes just like birds. He'd blow in one hole and out would come an owl's hoot and then in another and it was just like a sparrow. When he saw me, though, he gave a shout and ran off. I don't know who startled who more. Of course no one in town believed me, but that's how it always goes. They all want you to believe their tales, but they never want to believe anyone else's."

"But yours is true right?" Randall asked.

"Of course it's true. Have I ever lied to you? Lord on my soul, I saw that faun plain as day."

"I believe you, Mom," he said. He did not believe her, but what was he supposed to say? For the next three days, he would believe every story she told him, as though he were a child again and had the same faith that the elders did. The hidden had felt so much closer back then, every distant rustle in the woods a beacon of the certainty to an unseen world. Somewhere between then and now, he had lost his hold on it, even though he wanted there to be more to the world than what he had already seen.

The day was warming to its peak. Randall tried to stay in the shade as much as possible, but there were long stretches of the trail that were completely exposed to the open. As they climbed in altitude, it seemed as though the distance between them and the sun became measurably smaller. He began to sweat. His mother, even merely clinging to his back as she was, was sweating too, and he felt her sweat mixing with his. It felt unclean to have sweat that wasn't his own on his skin. In three days' time, though, as he made his way back down from the mountain, the grime of her sweat on his skin would be the last ghostly remnant he had of her.

They had both remained silent for a long stretch. Every passing moment of silence was another missed opportunity to ask her anything he had never asked her, but what was there left to discuss? She had shown his wife all the secrets of her cooking, she had settled all of her debts, and she had told him much of her life before he was born and much he hadn't known about his father, who had died of malnutrition during a lean winter when Randall was still young.

"What else do you know about the fauns?" he asked her. "And the other creatures of the forest?"

"I told you many of those tales when you were little," she said. "Have you forgotten them all?"

"I remember the fairy tales," he said. "The stories of the fairy kingdoms with the knights who ride foxes into battle. I remember you telling me about the dwarves in the mountains and the sprites in the treetops and the demons who would try to trick and deceive the people they met. I used to go out in the forest looking for those places, you know."

"Of course I knew," she said, "but you never found them did you?"

"How could I have?"

"Because you never looked very hard, did you? Why you'd come home after just a few hours."

He could hear the smile in her voice.

"And what would you have done if I hadn't come home?"

"I would have come looking for you, and when I found you, I would have given you such a thrashing."

"Even in front of the fairy queen?"

"Especially so. A fairy queen has no business stealing our boys away from us. We need them around the house, not that a fairy queen would have had much use for a boy as lazy as you were."

"How was I lazy?"

"Because you were always off in the woods looking for fairy kingdoms when you were supposed to be doing your chores. And you never even found one did you?"

"It's not like I ever would have."

"What do you mean not like you ever would have?"

Randall paused. "Well, I mean, they were all fairy tales."

"Just because they're fairy tales doesn't mean they're not true."

"Oh come now, Mother."

"You think us elders made all those stories up? We don't have any made up stories in our village. All of the stories all of us old timers tell you are true, from the stories of stupid things your ancestors did through to all the fairy tales. And you need to tell them to your children too. They are more than just tales."

"Then how come no one has ever found any of these magic places? How come we never seem to see these creatures?"

"Because they want nothing to do with us, that's why. We're a pitiable lot, us humans. The dwarves live for centuries eating rocks, and the fairies eat nectar. They are all older than the mountains. Us humans, though, we have to break our backs to feed off the scraps of the earth and would still starve if we didn't send away our old and weak."

This was the first time since that morning—the first time in days —that she had referenced the nature of their trip.

"Mother..." he started.

"Oh, don't get choked up, I'm happy to see my time come. I'll no longer be a burden to you all. My death means the life of another. Think of your own son, or better still, think of the next child you and Margaret will have. All the food I won't be there to eat is food to make your child strong."

"But Mom, you're not a burden. You're still strong; you can still fish and gather nuts and berries and tend to the garden and cook and clean."

"Oh I'm sure I could have stuck around for a few years longer, maybe I would have been good till I was eighty, but how many elders in the village can you say the same about? Why Gertrude's sixty-five and can barely leave the house anymore. No sir, our ancestors decided that seventy was the number, and it's still good for most cases."

The conversation fell silent for a while. After some time, they came to a fork in the road. The men who had made the trip before told Randall that any time he came to a fork, he must always go right but something seemed off here. The fork to the left went up and over a ridge, but the fork to the right went downhill and veered away from Mount Massive. He took the right fork anyway. Maybe this was a test, he thought, maybe the path didn't lead to Mount Massive but to one of the fairy or dwarf villages where the village elders were taken in to live the centuries amongst the hidden forest creatures. Perhaps when he got there, all of the elders who he had seen carried off along this path would be there to greet him and his mother. He would be sworn to secrecy but could live out his days in the village, content in knowing what truly awaited him at the end of the road.

Randall let himself believe his fantasy as long as the path led down, but soon the road rounded a bend and continued upward again, with Mount Massive in full view, looming closer than ever.

They made camp shortly after sunset. His mother cooked while he pitched the tent. The smell of the lentils was maddening—they took so long to cook. He slowed the pace of his work to keep himself distracted. Even still, their tent was ready long before the food.

It was full dark by the time they set to eat. The trees were so much more open there than in the village, and the stars seemed so much closer. After he had eaten, Randall lay on his back and, a moment later, his mother came to lay beside him.

For a long time, neither of them spoke, then Randall broke the silence.

"In the daytime, I used to stare up at the clouds hoping an angel would peek over the edge and look down at me. I thought that was how I would know for certain that Heaven was for real. I never saw one though."

"As a little girl," his mother said, "I used to be certain that two stars in the sky were the eyes of God, and I just had to figure out which two and stare at them until the face of God appeared. I still haven't figured out which two though."

"You still look?"

"Of course. Tomorrow night will be my last chance."

He had nothing to say and lay quiet until it was time to turn in. Custom and caution dictated that he was supposed to tie his mother up each night to keep her from running away, but he couldn't bring himself to do it. He slept fitfully, waking at every rustle to see if she was still there. Each time she was until he awoke in the morning and she was gone.

He scrambled out of the tent, ready to search out tracks but found her on the trail, watching the sunrise. Why didn't she run? Would he run in years hence when it was he and his son making this journey?

I'll have to stay as fit and strong as I can until seventy, just in case, he thought as he approached his mother and put a hand on her shoulder.

"I've always liked the sunrise better than the sunset," she said. She looked like she was going to add something else, then said, "We should go."

The trail grew uglier as they progressed, transitioning from tranquil mountain forests to harsh and barren rocks, with only tufts of plant life here and there to break up the deadly rocks. Whenever they rounded a bend, Randall would try to look back the direction they had come. It was impossible to say where in the forest behind them the village was. The trail quickly became lost to the trees. The world they had known was vanishing behind them, leaving only the task ahead.

His mother remained quiet throughout the morning, and he didn't want to disturb her thoughts, even if it meant being left with his own. The mountain was ugly, but the views were gorgeous, and isn't that what Hell was supposed to be? He had always imagined the worst thing about Hell wouldn't be the torments suffered but to have to look upon Heaven while enduring them. How was this not Hell—trudging through barren landscape while looking upon all that green life in the valleys? Hell was supposed to rest below the Heavens, but not here. No, here Hell rose above the life surrounding it; Hell cast its shadow upon them. Lifeless mountain peaks reminded them that their lives, which even in the valleys tasted so little of paradise, would come to an end on the damnation above them.

"Why even live in the mountains?" he said out loud.

"What was that?" his mother said, stirring. She must have dozed off.

"Why even live in the mountains when life is so hard there? Didn't you tell me once there was greater abundance in the plains?"

"Oh, yes. They eat all the food they want in the plains. They have miles of space to grow it in."

"Then why live in the mountains at all?"

"You know how fat people in the plains are? For all the many times more food they have than us, they eat that much more. Why they've grown so large, they roll around like boulders. A traveler told me that once. He said they share their food with no one. That traveler told me he ate better in the mountains than he ever did in the plains."

"Let's go," Randall said.

"To the plains?"

"Yes. I can leave you here and go back for my family, and we can go to the plains. We'll beg for food if we have to until we can grow our own. Just think how long we could live with so much food to be had."

"Perhaps so," she said. "Maybe we'd live a few years longer. I've heard stories of people in the plains living to be over a hundred, sometimes even two hundred." She was silent for a moment. "But it's not for us. I've dedicated my life to our people, and I have no right to do anything to threaten our traditions."

Randall said nothing more. They came to another fork. Once again the fork to the right seemed the wrong one. *What would happen if we went left?* he wondered. No one ever walked these trails except for the deed that brought him and his mother here. Why should there be any other direction to go?

He went left.

"What are you doing?" his mother said. "Every time you come to a fork you go right. Surely they told you that."

"They did," he said, "but I don't care."

"Take us back to the proper route."

"No. I'm going to take you to the plains, and you're going to live."

"This isn't right, Randall. Even if the village never finds out, God will know." There was an edge of panic in her voice.

"Why would God approve of this?" he said.

"It's not ours to question. Now go back."

He had no intention of doing so, no matter how much she protested. The left trail ran parallel to the one they were supposed to be on but dipped into a wooded copse. Remarkably little sunlight cut through these trees, and for the first time since he was a kid, Randall felt the eyes of foreign creatures watching him. This place felt forbidden, like they really were in the domain of the fairies, though there were no fairies to be seen. But the fear and the thrill lasted only a moment before they emerged into the light again and found the trail rejoining the path they were supposed to follow.

"You see," his mom said, "this is the way of things. The forest set us right. There is only one trail for us."

Only one trail, he thought, *but how generous to make it look like we had a choice.*

"You're still young, my son," she added, as though reading his thoughts, "you still cling to life, but just wait till your seventy. The burden of living feels a lot heavier at this age and the peace of death feels warm. I'm ready for tomorrow."

He stopped.

"But I'm not."

He felt her inhale. "You've always known this day would come. You've known to steel yourself for it. It is a son's duty to prepare for his mother's death as much as it was my duty to prepare for my own. Questioning our ways has only made things worse for you."

"Is it so bad to question them, to wonder if we could do things differently?"

"What good has any of your own questioning done you? You're

less ready for my own death than I am. Is that the duty of a good son?"

He hadn't heard that tone from her since he was a child. Her admonishment spurred him to start walking again. She was right; he had failed to make peace with their task and was suffering now because of it. That he would be the one walking back down the mountain to live decades more made that all the more absurd. He tried to imagine what he would feel if this was his death he was walking to, to feel the last moments of life drifting away. That his mother was so at peace seemed at odds with her character. She had always been so vivacious, so energetic even up to the last couple of days. Even now, she seemed so alive as she clung to his back. How could she bear it?

After a long silence his mother spoke again: "One of the reasons I was able to make peace with this day was knowing I would have you here with me. I don't know that I could have borne it if I had gone alone. Thank you for being here with me."

He said nothing but he walked with more purpose after her words.

The trail became increasingly unkempt as they progressed and, therefore, increasingly hazardous. During the day, they had emerged from the trees into shaggy grasslands but even the grass was now giving way to barren rock and cliffs that stretched hundreds of feet. He started to fear for his footing as they got higher. The loose dirt of the trail, combined with the weight of his mother on his back, made the possibility of both of them tumbling into the depths all the more plausible.

They came to a steep incline of loose gravel only a couple of feet wide, with a cliff stretching above them to the left and stretching below them to the right. He had to take it slowly, on all fours at times. On more than one occasion, his footing gave out and he had to throw himself forward to keep them from going over the edge.

"This is no condition for the trail to be in," his mother said.

"Who has ever come to repair it?" Randall asked. "No one ever wants to walk this trail except when these traditions of ours call for it."

"But it's such a beautiful walk," she said. "I wish we could savor it more than we can. If I had known what views we'd have, I'd have come up here years ago. A long and lovely walk is a fitting end to a life, especially when I have my son to do the hard part for me."

"I can't see any beauty here," Randall said. "Not with the task ahead. Death makes everything ugly."

"Is this what I'll be hearing from you for the remainder of my time?"

Her disappointment was like a needle through his heart. "Mother, no, I didn't mean it like that."

"Perhaps its best we not talk at all."

"Mother, please, I'm sorry. I don't want to waste the time we have left."

But she said nothing. She stayed silent for a long time after, her weight on his back not half as heavy as her silence. Making peace with this task would have been easier than this burden that now jeopardized their last moments together. Why couldn't he be at peace? He would outlive her even if he could talk her out of this. He was hurting no one but himself.

They made camp as soon as the sun began to set. Randall didn't want to go any further in fading light, as the path was becoming too treacherous. His mother remained silent as she made dinner and as they ate. She remained silent, and he was afraid to speak himself, afraid that he would somehow insult her further if he were to break the silence for any reason.

After they ate they sat around the fire, his mother staring into the sky.

"This is the last time I'll ever see the stars," she said.

He breathed a sigh of relief to hear her voice again.

"It would be nice if the stars would stay out until we got to the cliff tomorrow," she continued, "I'd rather die under the stars than under the sun."

"We could try to keep going," Randall said, "try to get to the cliff tonight."

"Are you so eager to see your mother off?" she asked.

"Mother," he said, shocked at her words, though relieved also that her humor was back.

"Oh don't be so alarmed," she said, "there's no reason we can't have some levity, even here."

"You know, this place is beautiful," he said, "the mountain, I mean, and this trail. It is a beautiful place."

His mother looked around as though seeing it for the first time.

"Not now it isn't. It's too dark. Daylight is for contemplating the beauty of the earth, but nighttime is when you should turn your eyes to the glory of the heavens. That's why I'd rather die under the stars, so that maybe the eyes of God would be upon me as I came to meet Him."

"But doesn't God watch us always?" Randall asked. "Isn't that what they say?"

"I doubt it," his mother said. "I've sought out the eyes of God my whole life, but I don't think they've ever fallen upon me. Some people go their whole lives without God ever looking at them. It's all we can hope for to be given His attention for even a moment."

They stared at the stars for a long time afterward. Randall had many more starry nights ahead of him, but he felt the finality his mother must have been feeling. He couldn't imagine knowing he'd never get to see the stars again. For the first time on their journey, he felt tears welling up. Tomorrow she had to die. He would have to watch as she threw herself from the cliff and, worse still, if she hesitated, he would have to do it himself. But he didn't want her to die; he didn't want to continue this journey. He wanted more time with her; he wanted to take her away from here to the plains or to the fairy kingdom if it even existed. He wanted God to turn His eyes to them just long enough for him to ask if this was what He really wanted. Why make a world where deeds like theirs were necessary? Surely God did not want it this way. Surely, at worst, He simply didn't care who lived or died and for how long, and at best, He must want long life for all. What good had death ever done anyone?

His mother opted to sleep in the open that night, "under the stars," she said. Once again, he didn't tie her up as he was supposed to. After today's events and conversations, he doubted she would run and, even if she did, this terrain was treacherous even for him. He doubted she would have made it far.

He slept fitfully again, woken periodically by his grief and pangs of anxiety as he realized that, in sleeping, he was throwing away whole hours of the little time left he had with his mother. When he awoke to the first sliver of dawn, he decided there was no point in trying to sleep any longer and crawled outside.

In the faint light, he saw his mother staring into the distance, sitting much as she had been the night before. She had been weeping. She didn't look at him as he approached, but she did speak.

"I saw them," she said, "I saw the eyes of God. I saw two stars in the sky turn their gaze to me and indicate that I should look down. And when I did, I saw a unicorn. He was standing right there," she pointed to a spot a few yards away, "and he was glowing. He was such a majestic creature, as perfect as anything that has ever lived. He walked past me, so close I could have reached out to touch him, but I dared not move, and he climbed down the mountainside. He was so nimble, never mistepped even once, and then he was gone. There is so much beauty in this world my son."

He didn't believe it, but he believed that she believed it.

"Maybe it's a sign," he said. *A sign that God does not approve*, he didn't say. He hoped she'd come to the conclusion herself.

"Not a sign," she said. "It has merely brought me peace. What cause have I left to complain when I've been shown such wonders? God rarely ever shows His face anymore."

"How do you know that God wants you to die today?" he asked.

"He doesn't. But he knows that I must. He understands the necessity of this deed as much as I do, though you still struggle with it. Maybe if you had seen what I had seen, you would be at peace too."

He was not at peace. "Are you ready to go then?" he asked.

"Not yet," she said, "the stars have not yet entirely faded from the sky."

They set out again after dawn. In the light of the early morning, Randall saw, in the direction his mother had indicated, the same tracks she had shown him two days before in the woods. Were they really unicorn tracks? Was there some truth to their legends after all? He still had his doubts, but he hoped too that some day he might see what his mother had supposedly seen.

That day's trek would be the shortest of all. Mount Massive loomed above them, and though he wasn't sure which stretch of its long face was the Granite Cliff, there was one spot he had guessed at—a straight drop of half a mile that seemed to be where the trail was heading. How long would it take to fall from that height? And to have to know the whole way down that your death was imminent? No, he had none of his mother's peace today.

"Is there anything you want to talk about?" he asked her.

"What more is there to say between us?" she said. "In all the years we've had we've said so much and shared so much. And I'm still so glad I didn't have to make this journey alone."

"Even if I hadn't had to take you, I would have come anyway," he said.

"I know, son. I know."

They soon reached such an elevation that even what little straggles of life they had seen before vanished. Only rock remained.

There were traces of snow in the shadows even as late in the summer as it was. A wind kicked in. It was cold enough to cut through their clothing. Randall shivered and felt his mother shivering too. He hoped the wind would die down, but as they climbed it stayed steady, seeming to grow colder with every minute and every foot.

They came to another fork. The left path was steep and seemed to go up and over the ridge of Mount Massive. The right path curled along its face. What could even be to the left, he wondered. The last possibility of escape? Was there a kingdom on the other side of the mountain, one that would take them in if they made it over the ridge? There would be no forest to confound them this time, not up here. The left path led straight and steep above them.

Even though he knew his mother would protest, he started up the left path. With his first step, the path crumbled beneath him and he stumbled, bringing a small avalanche of rocks down around them.

"You're defying the will of the mountain again," his mother said as he stood up. She had none of the anger he had heard yesterday. "Make peace, Randall."

She sounded old, near death. He stared up at the unscalable height again, then sighed and went right. Soon the climb grew steep, the cliff face to their left dropping far below.

"I feel as though I could fly," his mother said.

"Not here you can't."

"Some people in the village have said that if you've lived a good life, if you've done right by people and been honest and decent, you'll turn into a bird when you jump and fly away to go on living."

He had never heard anyone say that before. "You have been good," he said. "You've been decent to every person in the village. I've never heard a bad word against you. You're as sure to turn into a bird as a rock would be to fall."

"No," she said. "I used to gossip and spread rumors. I used to make fun of people behind their backs, and I kept my best fishing spot to myself, never shared it with anyone even in lean times."

"No one is perfect," Randall said. "Just look at how Jonas used to behave. Always drunk, rude, violent. He stole from nearly everyone in the village at some point, never worked, was cruel to his wife and children. You never did anything like that."

"Jonas didn't live until seventy though."

"But if he had he would have dropped like a stone. The earth would have pulled him down as fast as it could. You'll fly, Mother; I'm sure of it."

"When I would go gathering berries, I would always eat the best ones on my way back. I was selfish and greedy."

"I forgive you mother. I have often done the same. I doubt there is anyone who searches for berries and doesn't eat the best ones off the plant."

"I was a good mother, wasn't I?"

"You have always been a good mother."

"I hope I turn into a bird. I hope I fly away."

He decided to try one more time. "We don't have to do this. We can still run away."

"No. I want to be a bird. I want to fly away. Oh how lucky birds are. The burdens of man keep us on the ground. I shall throw my burdens off the cliff first, and then all the darkness there has ever been in my life. And then I shall fly."

"I think we should turn back."

"No," she shrieked. "No. We must go to the cliff. My time has come. God and the unicorn have willed it. I shall become a bird today."

If I turn back, he thought, *she may struggle. And that would likely throw both of us over the cliff.*

He climbed on, and soon they moved into the shadow of the mountain, the sun obscured by the ridge above them. He climbed for another hour, one filled mostly with his mother's ravings, and then the path widened out and came to an end.

"We're here," he said.

"We are?" his mother said, a note of uncertainty in her voice.

"We can't go any further," he said, as he let her down. "And this is granite we're standing on." He tiptoed to the edge. It was a long drop, so long that he couldn't see what was at the bottom. The drop may well have gone on forever. His mother approached beside him. He worried for a moment that she would jump before they could say anything else.

"It's a long way down," she said. "What if I don't transform quickly enough? What if I don't transform at all? Oh, my son, tell me I've lived a good life."

"Seventy years, mother. How many people in our village live long enough even to make it here?"

"I can't do it. I can't. It's such a long way to fall."

"You don't have to. You can live still. You can live."

"No. I have to. My time has come. Help me, my son."

He stepped away from her. "Help you?"

"Push me. I can't jump myself. Push me off."

He took another step back. "I can't do that."

She reached out to him. He flinched but then, ashamed of his reaction, he stepped toward her again, let her embrace him.

How long can I make this embrace last? he wondered. *Can I hold her forever?*

But he already knew the answer to that question.

"Please. If you are my son, please help me now."

He closed his eyes, trying to find something even close to peace. Everything in him was in turmoil, and he could no more have stilled it than he could have frozen a waterfall. The wind only continued to blow colder, cold enough to sap the warmth from their embrace. Her body was so frail in his arms.

She broke the embrace, but he still didn't open his eyes. He heard her shuffling, turning to face the cliff.

Just a gentle push to send her to her death. Between God and the villagers, it seemed the only two people who didn't want this were here on the precipice.

He placed his hands on her back, still not strong enough to open his eyes. He was shaking and sweating. The wind chilled the life from his hands.

There is no hand other than mine guiding this, he thought. *There is no hand other than my own to determine what happens here.*

"Please, my son. I'm at peace."

He pushed her.

He kept his eyes closed for a long time afterwards, but he heard neither her scream nor the flap of wings.

10

IN DARKNESS, SHE SHEDS

SUZANNE REYNOLDS-ALPERT

T he remembered arousal curled in Savron's belly and sent shivers to her back where her wings once grew. Her small-heeled shoes *tap-tapped* down the marble hall to the beat of her heart.

She knew to come quickly when Master summoned. No doubt, he wanted an update on the girl's shedding. Savron had planned to check the girl that evening, hoping the process would be finished and Master could have his elixir *before* he had to summon Savron to check. It delighted him when those around him anticipated his needs.

Being in his service was the one constant in her life—it gave shape to her interminable days.

The torches burning in sconces along the walls cast a hazy glow as she walked: *everfire*. The full-blood fae males were charged to keep the sconces magickally lit throughout the palace and into the small village around it.

As Savron rounded the final corner to Master's chambers, she smoothed a hand over her long, silver-threaded skirt while the other hand snaked up to her neck, touching the necklace Master had given to her decades ago. The necklace, like those of all fae concubines, marked her as belonging to the master and was a source of inordinate pride.

Even if a fae woman wanted to remove the pendant, she couldn't. Carefully-selected fae magicians worked a spell binding each piece of jewelry to its wearer and to the castle's Master. Savron ensured hers fell flatteringly across her small collarbone before patting her elaborate up-do to make sure the gem-encrusted pins were still in place. She was, regrettably, an old woman now, but she made every effort to look beautiful for Master.

Tap, tap, tap. Her green silk shoes echoed as she approached the two guards standing before the gilded double-doors leading to Master's personal chambers.

The half-breed youth were light-haired and tan-skinned, not tawny to dark brown with chestnut or midnight hair like the full-blood fae; their relation to Master was apparent. The guard on the right was Mawron's son, Obediah. Mawron had been one of her least favorite concubines. Perhaps because she was the last Master had taken before Savron herself aged out? Or perhaps it was simply that Mawron was a dull-witted, selfish creature. Mawron's son—the only male she'd ever birthed—was known to be equally dim. But Mawron had been Master's favorite for many months, so it made sense her son would be given this high-ranking position.

The second was one of her own sons. Both eyed her as she stopped before them. They were males, even if they were half-breeds, so she averted her gaze before giving a respectful bow.

"Savron d' Fae, Former Royal Concubine, Birther of Three Sons, Elixir-Mistress to Our Master." Savron gave her full title, even though the youth had no doubt been apprised she was coming. This was the way of things—Master insisted on tradition.

"Savron," Mawron's boy said. His small mouth dipped down at the ends. The proper thing to do would have been to use his full title back as he acknowledged her, but clearly the youth was a turd just like his mother.

Her son glanced at the guard, a look of unhappiness apparent on his slightly more human features. "Savron d' Fae, Former Royal Concubine, Birther of Three Sons, Elixir-Mistress to Our Master; I, Eli d' Fae, Certified Half-Human Son of his Master, Attendant in His Royal Guard, acknowledge you, knowing you have been called here." He accompanied his words with an open palm in her direction—no male would ever bow to a female, not even his own mother.

"Eli d'Fae, Certified Son, is Master ready to receive me?"

"He is, Elixer-Mistress." The fact that he used her occupation-title, rather than her former concubine status or birther-title, was a sign of respect. Few females were accorded such a privilege. Few females had occupations.

Mawron's boy scowled, his high, fae-given forehead wrinkling and his small lips pursing. But he said nothing further.

"Master said you could enter once you announced yourself to us," her son said.

Savron let the males push open the tall, wide, double-doors. Gold leaf adorned the rich wood, as it did throughout much of the palace. Runes etched into the wood guarded against attacks both mundane and magickal.

Savron stepped through. As she took off her shoes, the doors closed with a deep *thud.* Pushing her shoes onto their designated shelf, she drew in several lungfuls of air. Arousal tinged with fear pooled in her belly and might have tingled somewhere lower on her body... But no—she was now an old woman, and old women did not think of such things.

She stepped through the receiving room, knowing that Master waited inside his inner chambers. Sconces—more elaborate than the ones in the hallway—illuminated the room with pink-hued everfire.

This door—not double-wide, but equally encrusted—stood ajar. This was her invitation to enter.

Master was sprawled on his sleeping platform, gold-threaded robe askew and hair slightly mussed. He was as handsome as ever —perhaps more so, because of his untidiness. Wavy, thick blond hair curled around his face and brushed his shoulders. His strong jaw and high cheekbones were chiseled perfection. *Humans are the pinnacle of beauty*, Savron thought. Master's piercing blue eyes regarded her lazily. The small, naked body of a fae woman lay sprawled face-down near the end of the bed. Her wings were retracted, and even with her dark skin, Savron could see the bruises adorning her back. She was asleep or, more likely, unconscious. Savron recalled with pride how *she* could withstand Master's passions.

"Savron! My most true and honest servant! You look as ravishing as ever. How old are you now? You've barely aged since you were one of my favorite concubines."

His compliments lit through her, and her face beamed. Still, she knew he was exaggerating—her dark hair was streaked with silver, and her face bore many lines. The skin of her neck hung unattractively. The fae were delicate of bone and skin, many becoming prematurely aged and stooped. But Master was a charming man.

"Master—I have just seen sixty-four years."

"Well, you don't look it! You look like a fae of four tens of years, at best."

"Master, you are excessively generous, as always." Savron knew she was smiling too widely, but she couldn't stop herself.

"Come in, come in…" He waved her forward with casual ease. Even most males in his employ would not be graced with such intimacy. Only with his fully-human sons—especially the eldest, charged with taking Master's place should anything befall him— was Master ever truly affable.

He stepped off the sleeping platform and down the few stairs, coming to greet her. His hand-embroidered robe was not tightly tied, and she could see his well-toned thighs and peeks of hard abdominal muscles. As he approached her, his manhood peeked from the robe, yet he made no effort to conceal himself.

"Savron..." Master shook his head, but his eyes bored in to hers and a smile played across his lips. "Do I still see some fire in your eyes, even with that wasted body of yours?" He laughed briefly, grabbing her arm. His fingers dug in painfully; she'd be bruised. Unforgotten pleasure rippled through her—the pain had always brought pleasure in its wake, back when she was part of his harem. Master would often beat her, sometimes making her pretend she was some human woman who'd displeased him. As she lay bloody and bruised, trying to heal the multiple fractures her small bones endured, he would then caress her wings in just the way that brought fae females pleasure...

"M-Master..." She cast her eyes downward, ashamed that an old woman could be enticed so easily.

"She blushes... ah, Savron, you always were a delight." He gripped her harder for a second, eliciting a *mew* of pain before he released her. "We can skip the formal greetings, my dear. I am anxious to see how the shedding proceeds. I will enjoy a fresh elixir."

In the everfire's glow, Savron could see Master's light hair had at least a dozen threads of silver. A few new lines marred his otherwise perfect forehead. He *did* need the elixir. Once aging began, it could not be reversed. The elixir only forestalled it. Master would carry these threads of silver and lines forever. Her breath caught in her chest.

"Master... if I could still...I would shed for you myself! I deeply regret I was only able to shed for you three times..." Tears prickled her eyes, and the scars on her back twinged in memory of her former wings. Once Master had tired of her in his bed, she was one of the few given the honor of shedding. It was her deepest shame she'd only done so thrice before her wings failed to grow back.

She considered Master getting old—no! He couldn't, wouldn't! It was *he* who protected them all—fae, human, and half-breeds alike. It was *he* that brought them civilization from chaos hundreds of years ago, rescuing the Fae from their previous bestial existence.

"Of course you would, Savron," he responded, looking down on her, a small smile quirking his mouth. His ice-blue eyes held a fire that she'd always adored. He patted her head affectionately. "Now, let's see to that fae girl."

He led them past the sleeping platform through another threshold. They passed his twin alcoves of elaborate clothing, then swept through his personal armory; Master paused briefly at a high shelf, selecting one of several small knives to bring with them. Finally, they approached a burgundy curtain adorned with intricate gold threadwork. It looked like a decoration, but it concealed the shedding chamber. The everfire casting light from the wall sconces was more subdued here.

Master took the chain from around his neck and selected the correct key. Sliding it away from the others, he unhooked it to hand to Savron. He could not unlock the chamber himself; he'd had Savron place a spell on it. And as Elixir-Mistress, she could only unlock it in his presence.

Savron reached for the golden key, her arm trembling in anticipation and worry. *Would the shedding be done?* Master needed this. Once the process of senescence began, it accelerated.

Her delicate fingers wrapped around the key. Master knew what to do—they'd done this together over one-hundred times, for almost thirty years, about four times a year. And before that, countless times with the other former concubines who became his Elixir-Mistresses. Yet, he always allowed her to take the lead with this one ritual, this one task that—aside from shedding herself and giving him three sons for his army—was the most important thing she'd ever do.

"Master, take my hand, please." He came to stand at her side, grasping her right hand with his huge left one, squeezing painfully tight. In her left hand she held the key. She glanced sideways at him, seeing only his robe-covered chest—he was a tall human, and she merely fae. She took a deep breath and recited the words:

"By the power vested in me by my Lord and Master, I implore this key to open the veil that hangs before the shedding-chamber." She then spoke the few words in the ancient tongue that allowed fae to access their innate magick: *T'rosey d'agored.*

She felt the magick drop from around the chamber, stepped to the door, and inserted the gold key; the lock clicked, and she pulled it open slowly. One could never be sure what state a girl would be in. There were stories told of a time long ago when a fae girl had gone mad after her seventh round in the chamber. Since then, girls always wore their necklaces while shedding. Master demanded it.

Savron quickly turned to hand Master back the key. "Girl?" she called into the dark chamber. She kept the door half-open, not to let too much light in. If the shedding wasn't complete, too much light could forestall the process.

She heard a quiet moan from within.

Savron snapped the fingers of her right hand and conjured a small, dark-purple magickal flame to dance above her hand. Just enough to see further into the chamber. The smell of unwashed body and acrid urine wrinkled her nose.

The girl—Savron knew her name was Darron, but when she had been shedding, the Elixir-Mistress had never showed her the courtesy of a name, so why should she?—crawled forward on her hands and knees from the black recesses of the room, blinking slowly. Her collarbones stood out sharply and her cheeks were gaunt; her necklace looked comically large around her small neck.

She had the pale brown skin and purple eyes she knew Master

found more attractive than her own mahogany-and-amber coloring. These marked her as coming from the far western lands. Her people were uncommon here, and Savron wondered how she'd garnered the privilege to belong to Master.

The room was undecorated and unheated and had a dirt floor; experience had shown that suffering multiple ways increased the rate of shedding. There was a large ceramic pot in one corner for the girl to relieve herself. A large trough on the opposite wall held just enough water to see a girl through the shedding. The only comfort was a thin blanket; clothing was not allowed. Savron had only vague memories of how chilled she had gotten in the chamber, but she was not sure how real the memories were. She'd spent her weeks shedding alone in the darkness by imagining herself as a human princess, married to Master, who was so besotted with her that he only rarely visited the concubines. Between the world she'd created in her head, the crushing, sometimes exquisite pain of her wings withering and dying, and the ache of a stomach wanting for food, she could not be sure of anything she thought she remembered of her time in the chamber.

The fae crawling toward her looked confused and unwell. Darron had seen about thirty years—around the optimal age to use a fae female for shedding, once they were no longer appealing for Master's bed—but right now she looked much older.

Did I ever look that poorly when I emerged from the shedding chamber? Savron thought, grabbing at her necklace as she felt it tingle uncomfortably against her skin. The sensation made her realize it was selfish to think of herself when she had this most important task before her. *Master needs this.*

"Girl!" Savron said harshly. She crouched down, her knees creaking, and thrust out the hand with the magickal flame in front of her. "Girl, do you know how the shedding progresses? You should be able to feel it."

The grimy creature looked up at her, but her eyes held no recognition.

"Darron!" Maybe using the girl's name would help.

The girl blinked more rapidly, some light coming into her lavender-colored eyes. "Thirsty," she croaked. "Water gone."

"You can have water—and a bit of food, *after* we see that you have shed properly," Savron snapped.

Behind her, Master grunted. "Hard to believe I put my manhood in to that, eh?" he said. Savron looked over her shoulder at him, nodding her agreement. "It is regrettable, Master, that these females must become so unattractive in order to provide what you need from them." Somewhere deep inside, she thought, *he saw* me *like this…* and she was deeply ashamed.

She turned back to the girl. "Enough of this! Stop your complaining, you ungrateful beast! Crawl forward, turn around, and let me see your wings!" The girl slowly complied, but Savron became impatient and grabbed her arm. Touching another fae concubine—or any female wearing one of Master's necklaces—was highly uncomfortable, and Savron winced as her fingers touched the girl's flesh.

Discomfort further provoked her, so Savron flung the girl, exposing her backside and making her wings easier to see. She heard Master laugh softly—she had pleased him. Pride swelled in her chest.

"Sit on your heels," Savron snapped.

The girl sat.

Savron increased the lumosity of her magickal flame, and with the girl several feet closer to the door, she now had enough light to see. Still, deciding when to harvest the wings was a largely intuitive process. The Elixir-Mistress used her sense of how the wings felt and how the girl reacted when they were touched to assess if the shedding was complete.

"I'm going to touch your wings," Savron warned. "I do not

want to hear a thing from you unless I ask." The once vibrant ochres and reds and violets of the girl's wings were faded to dull browns.

The girl trembled as Savron tentatively palpated the left wing with her free hand. Her fingers danced over the papery surface to examine the hard, dried-up veins. She repressed the discomfort touching a concubine invoked.

The girl moaned and trembled as Savron examined her. Still a bit of feeling in the wings. That was good—the residual lifeforce in a female's wings is what made the elixir potent.

Behind her Master asked, "Well?"

Savron heard the impatience in his voice but took an additional few heartbeats to reach out to the girl with her intuition, "feeling" for the lifeforce remaining in the wings. *Yes! The wings were ready.*

She scrambled to her feet as quickly as her old knees allowed. She smoothed down her skirt as she faced Master, happiness swelling in her chest. "Master! The process goes well, and the girl is near optimal for harvesting. The only thing I must advise is that the wings are, if anything, still somewhat more vibrant than I'd normally like for harvesting."

Master narrowed his eyes at her, his former charm gone. "So?"

"It simply means that the elixir will be very potent—which *is* what I advise for you—but the harvesting could kill the girl."

"Savron." He reached out to grip her previously-bruised arm with his large, strong hand. His teeth were gritted, eyes savage. "You know your job. You *know* the elixir is the primary concern here. Other considerations are secondary." He released her arm roughly, taking a step back as if she revolted him. "You disappoint me."

Shameful tears welled up in Savron's eyes. She thought Master would appreciate her deliberate thought process, but she'd miscalculated based on his former amicable mood. A strange emotion —*anger?* a small part of her mind whispered—threatened to bubble up in her chest. But her necklace made its presence known, shuddering firmly at the base of her throat, and the feeling dissipated.

"M-Master..." Her voice trembled and there was nothing she could do to stop it. "I-I have disappointed you by speaking too much, and I will do whatever you desire to make up for my mistake." Her voice sounded miserable even to her own ears. She hung her head down and tried not to cry.

"Savron—look at me," Master commanded and Savron's head shot up as he instructed. His arms were crossed, and his eyes held a fierce light. "You know how you can make it up to me? Harvest her...more roughly than you might otherwise. And I want you to stroke her wings before you slice them off. That will gratify me."

Savron's heart thumped, and she felt blood pulse in her ears. *Anything*, she thought. *I will do anything for you...*

A smile returned to Master's face. "That's my girl," he said fondly. He loosened his robe so that she could see his most private part coming to life. She turned away quickly, an odd fervor tingling its way down her body and shooting to the scars on her back... she was an old woman, and she now had other ways to find pleasure.

"Come here, girl," Savron said. The girl crawled forward on hands and knees. "Yes, come to me, you ugly wretch," she ordered, extinguishing the magickal fire from her hand.

The wasted creature came forward slowly, eyes huge and wet, the bones of her face and shoulders prominent. Her eyes pleaded with Savron, but she said nothing as she reached Savron's feet, sitting on her heels once again.

"Turn around again."

The girl turned. Her shriveled wings trembled. Master made a sound of enjoyment.

Savron got back down on her knees—no crouching like the last time—and didn't care about dirtying her skirt. She would make Master happy.

Her right hand reached out to the girl's withered right wing.

A fae's wings are exquisitely sensitive. Having these living appendages wither and dry through lack of sunlight and food is excruciating...

This knowledge was a distant echo in her mind as Savron's fingers touched the wing. She felt the heavy press of her pendant around her neck...and any concern for the girl's pain vanished. Darron cried out in agony, but Savron was transfixed; she smiled, craving to please Master.

"Touch her other wing with your other hand, too," he growled behind her.

Savron did as he commanded, running both hands along the two wings. Their surface was brittle and dry; the veins stood out sharply. Savron savagely traced the veins with her fingers, searching for the spots that elicited the loudest screams.

"Ah, Savron," Master sighed from behind her, "you were always a delight."

But her work was not yet done. She had made Master happy, and that made *her* happy—but she was Elixir-Mistress. Her most important task was still to come. She turned her head to address Master. "The knife, please."

He handed her the ceremonial knife that would sever the girl from her wings. She would make Master the best potion he'd ever had.

"Turn around, and thank your Master for this privilege," Savron ordered.

The girl shuffled around on her knees. Her skin was ashen and face twisted by pain. She became more unsteady as she faced Savron and Master. She began to sway as she opened her mouth to speak, "Th. Thhhaaaannnk..." She fell forward onto Savron.

Savron found herself on her back, the girl on top of her. Her vision was full of girl's skeletal face; her lavender eyes were huge in her tawny face.

The knife! Savron thought. Her hand scrambled on the floor, searching. She fought to free her other arm so that she could protect her face and throat from possible attack.

The girl did not attack. She dropped down and flattened her body to Savron's,

Then their necklaces made contact.

A flood of shared thoughts and sensations rushed through both women.

… Savron remembered whispered stories told to her by her mother, who'd been too plain to be a concubine… *The Fae have not always been slaves. There was a time we were free…*

… Darron remembered playing with other youth in her village, far to the west of Master's lands… *Holding hands with the girls and flying up into the trees to tease the birds… until Master's half-breeds found her and brought her to the Castle…*

… Savron recalled the horror she'd felt seeing Master for the first time… *a big, homely human with colorless hair, pasty skin, faded blue eyes, and an ugly aura around him…*

… Darron felt her *rage…*

… Savron felt *disgust…*

Savron heard Darron think *How is it we can share each other's thoughts?*

It is the necklaces, Savron responded. *They are bespelled. We put them on, and we become Master's puppets.* Savron stopped searching for the knife and embraced the girl with both arms. *I don't know if this has happened before—two concubines seeing through the illusion. We must not waste this opportunity.*

It took the briefest moment for Savron to share her plan.

Master screamed for his guards. He'd backed away from the two women, eyes wide with fear. From the floor, Savron heard the guard's footsteps as they entered the chamber. "Eli! Get her off the

Elixer-Mistress! See if she's dead—if she's dead, and my potion can't be made, someone will pay! And Obediah, call for my eldest son!"

Savron's own half-breed son, Eli, fell to his knees beside her. His lips pinched tightly, forehead wrinkled with concern. She heard the other guard run out. Savron felt a rush of emotion for this son she barely knew, and a new one—hope. *Was he, too, bespelled? What kept him in Master's employ? Would he help them?*

Master raged incoherently behind them. It was good he was not too close. She felt Darron's rapid breaths against her chest. Savron uncurled an arm from around Darron and grabbed her son's hand. "Help me," she whispered, "help us all—" and while her fae magick was fully intact, she wordlessly shared her intentions.

Eli had limited time before his fellow guard returned with the Master's first-born. He clutched his mother's hand, cherishing her touch. They locked eyes, and seconds passed as they just stared and breathed together.

"Darron and I...we must stay like this—I'm not sure if the illusion will immediately return if our necklaces break contact," his mother whispered.

He nodded and tore his eyes from his mother's face and glanced at Darron's skeletal back. Her face was turned away and the hair on the back of her head was a tangled mess. Her retracted wings were brown and paper-thin. The elegant reddish-brown skin that he'd admired countless times in the palace halls was grimy and dull, and she smelled ripely of unwashed body. He'd seen Master mistreat females before, but there was something about this one…

He grabbed the knife lying next to Savron, barely hearing his Master's frantic questions. He'd heard what his mother had wordlessly asked and had agreed—even though he had reservations. Who wouldn't, in his position? He had everything to lose.

Master was still babbling and pointing to the women as Eli approached him, the knife he'd grabbed from the floor behind his back.

"Is she dead? *Is she?*" Master demanded.

Eli plunged the knife into his neck.

Master's pale blue eyes went wide with shock. He put his arms up ineffectively as blood spurted out of his neck in pulsing ribbons, spraying Eli on his face and chest before he crumpled to the floor.

Knife still gripped in his now bloody hand, Eli fell back down next to Savron. He grabbed her hand and thrust the knife into it as she'd instructed. He wondered: *Will I really be able to do this?*

"Don't back down now, boy," she said sharply. Her eyes narrowed at him and she looked angry and dangerous. "You have nothing of substance in this life. You were bred on me to be another kind of slave to Master. You haven't known a loving touch since I weaned you—raised with other half-breed boys, never allowed to marry. You admire the beauty of many fae females from afar but can't touch them. Especially the concubines—they are Master's. So tell me—aside from being a male, *what do you really have?*"

Behind them, Master sputtered as his life leached away. The metallic smell of blood permeated the room.

Tears formed in Eli's eyes, and he yanked his hand free from Savron's where she clutched the knife. "But what will I do? There's no place for Master's half-breeds outside of the castle. I could never go and live with the free fae—they would never accept me!"

"Then do it for Darron, and others like her!" Savron said. "But decide quickly! The son will soon be back with the other guard. I have seen how you feel about her—do you want her abuse to continue?"

Eli stood up and began to pace, avoiding the growing pool of blood. "I don't want either of you to suffer!"

Darron's head finally turned and she rested her cheek against Savron's. "You can help us end this," she said, her voice raspy and weak. "Master is evil…everything about him and his rule is evil. It is built on lies. On thievery and perverse illusion." She took a deep breath, closing her eyes. She looked exhausted.

They heard the distant sounds of voices and footsteps approaching.

When she spoke again, Darron's voice was only a whisper. "Please. Help us make it stop. I was ripped from my village far from here. My people sold me to Master—I am a *sappho*, so they thought me expendable… unforgiveable, that—but my village is very poor. Master's influence is a corruption; he sends his half-breeds and traitorous fae males out to take everything that is valuable from the lands. They kill many fae males and enslave the females Master will find appealing or useful…" She had to stop and take a few shuddering breaths.

"Do it," Savron hissed.

"But… I've just found you." Eli again clutched his mother's hand, but he was staring at Darron.

"We can make a *difference*, Eli." Darron's purple eyes seemed to plead with him. "I'm willing to—" she choked on a sob, "go back. To trust you. But *only* if I know it will help others. Please… don't let us down."

The approaching footsteps sounded close to the door of Master's chamber.

Eli didn't answer, but he felt the irresistible pull of the path he'd chosen. *It will be done*, he told them wordlessly.

He had only seconds left. He rolled Darron off his mother.

Savron sprang up, brandishing the knife. In a moment she was standing over Darron, who was trembling on her hands and knees.

His mother grabbed both wings and without a pause sliced through them with one long swipe. Darron screamed as they were severed. They left the woman quivering on the floor and rushed over to where Master was in the last throes of death.

Eli took the gore-spattered knife from Savron and stabbed her in the neck. He missed the first time—his hands too slick with blood, his arm trembling. Savron cried out in pain and frustration. The second thrust found its mark. Blood pulsed out and onto Eli's chest a second time; the scarlet ribbons made him want to vomit. Savron collapsed next to Master.

Behind him, Darron's screams turned to pained moans. He prayed she'd live.

The guard he'd been partnered with burst into the chamber. Two other guards followed, and the Master's eldest human son, Avniel, trailed behind them all. "Obediah!" Eli called to his partner, "The worst has happened! The girl was still alive, and the Elixir-Mistress had harvested her wings as planned. I was holding the girl down for the cutting when the old woman suddenly went berserk and flung herself at the Master, slicing his throat with the ceremonial knife. It was over before I could do anything." His voice wavered from true emotion—fear, for himself; sadness at his Mother's death—and the tears running down his face were real. "I quickly avenged our Master's death by killing the evil bitch myself."

Obediah's face was pale and he looked back at the other guards and Master's son, unsure of what to do. Avniel's eyes were wide with shock. He approached the two bodies, spitting on Savron, whose blood was already pulsing more slowly. Eli watched the light fade from her eyes as Avniel began the mourning-chant for his father.

One of the guards touched Eli's elbow. "Let's get you out of here and cleaned up," he said, his face emotionless. "Once you've bathed and rested, you can tell us more of what happened here."

"What of her?" Obediah asked, nodding his head toward Darron. She was curled in a ball, moaning in pain. Her useless wings lay about six inches away from her on the floor, in danger of getting fouled by the growing pool of blood.

Darron's memories of what happened outside the shedding-chamber were faint. There was pain and blood—none of it hers—but not much else.

She'd woken in the harem's infirmary, tended to by a fae eunuch. For that Darron was grateful—the thought of another female touching her made her feel ill. She'd remained there for three weeks, slowly gaining her strength back, living for the moments her new Master would visit.

That was several months ago. Every day, she looked for signs that her wings would grow again. Shedding for Master—a new Master now—was the greatest honor a concubine could provide. She also garnered the privilege to warm her new Master's bed, which was unusual for a concubine her age. She smiled with pride and a thrill ran down her spine and tingled below her stomach.

"Darron, a guard is here to speak with you," another concubine called from across the room. Darron frowned. Eli, one of the former Elixir-Mistress' half-breed sons had come to speak with her several times. He made her uncomfortable—but a female did not deny a male. An air of suspicion still hung around Eli. The concubines resented that his mother murdered their former Master, causing chaos. The elder concubines were still working with the castle's fae magicians to replicate the Elixir recipe. The evil bitch Savron had not trained a replacement before attacking Master.

Darron walked to the harem's threshold. It *was* Eli. She averted her gaze, as a female should when greeting a male. "Come walk with me in the gardens," he said.

He made small talk while they approached a gate leading to the garden. He inquired after her health—did she feel like her wings were going to grow back? Did she remember anything of the tragedy? She murmured benign responses and hoped to escape his company as soon as possible.

It was a beautiful spring day, and Darron drew in a fragrant breath as they stepped outside. She turned her face to the sun, relishing the warmth on her face, hoping to describe it to her new Master the next time he chose her. "Come," Eli said, gently taking her elbow and steering her toward a row of thick, woody hedges.

She knew this spot—he'd taken her there before. He indicated that she should sit on an ornate marble bench. She did, and he sat down next to her—too close for her comfort.

"So... your health is well?" he asked.

"Fine. Better every day."

He reached out and touched her cheek gently with his right hand—an intimate gesture that he should have known was improper. She recoiled—*she wore a necklace! She belonged to Master!*

The intensity in his gaze softened. He removed the hand from her face and reached into one of his pockets. She was struck with an odd feeling of familiarity...

His left hand grabbed the back of her head. In his right, she saw the flash of a jeweled object that he thrust near her throat.

And the world changed.

Her necklace's spell was suspended. A rush of memories assaulted her, as they always did. *Her childhood... her attachment to other females... being sold by her family to Master's half-breed soldiers... her time as a concubine... her shedding.* She remembered her agreement with Savron—Savron would give her own life so that Darron could live and work with Eli to end the perversity of Master's rule. But Darron's sacrifice would be to give up her personhood, submitting herself knowingly to slavery again and again.

As usual, Eli only had a few minutes to bring her up-to-date. *We are already making progress,* he said. *I am sowing discord among some of the half-breeds and among some of the fae males who work the magicks.*

And the son is weakened without the power of the Elixir. She then shared what she observed and heard among the concubines and from Master's son.

Darron longed to take these precious few moments to fully revel in who she was, and who she would be again… someday. She knew Eli loved her, and he knew she'd never return that love—not in the way he wanted.

It was time to let the necklace's spell resume. She cried—she always did—to know that she was losing herself again. The agony of the loss stabbed her in the chest, and she felt a twinge where her wings once grew.

Eli removed the jewel from her throat, and as the darkness took over she watched a butterfly sail from the hedge and fly freely into the brilliant blue sky.

11

VAPOR TRAILS

SCOTT T. GOUDSWARD

R oger stared through the windshield lost in thought. He blinked at the oncoming headlights wondering how long he'd zoned out this time. It was a short ride from the spaceport to the freeway. The spaceport had been an airport until the first threat of invasion arrived.

All the money, all the technology, all of the advances, and he was still driving a POS pick-up truck. He slowed for the traffic light and drummed his fingers on the wheel—a habit he doubted he'd ever break. It wasn't like there would be any state police around to give him a ticket for running it.

He waved at a driver he passed running the light. Roger stuck his arm out the window, flashed his lights, and gave a "thumbs up." The other driver slowed for a second to return Roger's wave as he ran the light, not stopping to chat.

In the mirror, a bright flash and burst of flame launched another capsule from the Earth toward the Moon Colony. Further down the road, more headlights glared in his mirrors. The timeline for the evacuation must have changed, been sped up; there were more vehicles tonight than he'd seen in a long time.

He watched the traffic light until it changed, and the impatient drivers behind him laid on their horns. There was no one else on the roads but them; they could have gone around. They were all eager after long days of driving to get to their "homes." Maybe like him they were all stuck in their habits, their ruts. Roger didn't need to stop at the lights, and the drivers in back of him didn't need to stop and wait either. All the technology and advances...and people were still, in general, assholes. Roger waved to the drivers through his open window and turned off toward the highway. In his younger days, he would have given them all a one fingered salute.

Roger figured he could make this drive fully asleep. He switched on the newsfeed in audio mode hoping for something more interesting than the non-stop barrage of the invasion and evacuation. The implants fed the news right into his ears. In visual mode, a news scroll ran across his eyes. The further from the space-port he got, the weaker the signal. It was supposed to be satellite fed, not antenna. Maybe the cloud cover blocked the signal. Or maybe like him, the implants were getting old.

It'd been decades since government scientists first discovered the *threat*. Now, all these years later, with his children grown and moved off world, Roger was still shuttling people from town to the spaceport. A fading vapor trail marked the sky as another capsule was fired from the gravity driver.

No matter how many times he saw the launches or heard the news, he never, not once, had seen an alien, threatening or other-wise. No ships, no invasion fleets, just that ever continuing cloud cover in the skies. Roger read about conspiracies—that the Earth was over polluted and over populated. That the world govern-ments were just shuttling people from the most polluted areas to the least and then shooting them off the planet.

"That'll be me someday," he mumbled. "Some other poor fool driving me in their POS vehicle, bringing loads of strangers bound for the Moon Colony." Taped to the dash was an old photograph of his wife and sons, back when they were young; he touched the picture and accelerated for home. "Another day and several more families." He knew when he got back to the house there'd be a new schedule and a new list of people he'd be driving tomorrow.

Roger drove through the small town where he now lived. The truck's headlights illuminated the empty houses and boarded up stores. Three stores were still open in town with the barest of supplies—groceries, hardware and the post. He pulled into the driveway of the house he'd been assigned to and scoffed at the pile of luggage on the lawn. The lights were off and there were no people yet, just the bags. When he woke in the morning, Roger knew there'd be three dozen displaced people on his lawn, looking for a ride and answers. Roger only supplied the ride. He was all out of answers. Answers lived in the Mars Colony with his wife and sons.

One of the neighboring houses was unlocked in case any of them needed facilities or a drink of water. They were the barest of the bare, with enough necessities to take the "edge" off and not much else. If it rained the people could get out of it; if it was too sunny, the house provided shelter. Roger's house was off limits to his passengers.

He climbed out of the truck, stuffing the keys in his pocket, and taking the photo from the dash. Roger read a couple of the tags; he didn't recognize the names. He always thought that eventually he'd be driving an old friend or a neighbor from his first house. There was an envelope taped to his front door with tomorrow's schedule. It was someone's turn, not his. Someday the damn government would send his notice and let him reunite with his family.

"If they think I'm digging through and organizing all of those bags, they're crazy." He unlocked his door and went in the small house. There were no messages or mail. The house seemed darker than he was used to. He listened to purr of the appliances and looked at the LEDs and illuminated time readouts. In the kitchen, Roger switched on the newsfeed, audio and digital; and kept it at eye level so he could read headlines and fix dinner. Not that the meals were complex.

"Today's report on the eminent invasion." A simulated newscaster appeared "on screen." The talking head made to resemble an Asian man continued: "Strange lights were seen hovering just within the cloud cover outside of Boston. Local witnesses, while waiting for their ride to the space port formerly Logan International Airport, were quoted as seeing the lights dancing through the clouds with a loud booming noise as they disappeared. Local law enforcement were not available for comment. On the evacuation timeline..."

Roger turned off the audio feed and went back to preparing dinner.

Dinner was an MRE, mixed with protein paste and vitamin powders and heated. Roger missed the smell of food cooking in the kitchen—chickens, steaks, and whatever else Helen had decided on for dinner. Helen was never much of a cook, but her food was so much better than dried dinner from a bag. He poured a cup of re-claimed rain water and took his "food" out to the porch. There was a ritual: eat outside in the dark and cooling air while news scrolled over the ocular implants and stare at the night sky. Roger used to try and count the stars, the ones still visible through the cloud cover —the cloud cover the governments stated was some subtle attack to freeze the Earth, not centuries of built up pollution. Most nights, stargazing was a futile exercise. Now he ate dinner from the bag and watched the flame spouts of capsules headed off world.

When the colony was first announced almost two decades ago, Roger was more than skeptical. When the expansion started ten years later, that skepticism grew. How were the governing parties of the world going to fit eight billion plus on the moon? When the feed first scrolled that through the implants with the news and simulated images, all Roger pictured was rows of space-worthy cargo containers with airlocks in some fool layout of a shanty town.

But the Moon Colony wasn't the final stop. Neither were the space stations at the halfway point. There was another gravity driver set on the moon. Refueling stations built all around the colony. The colony was mostly the layover on the way to Mars. Some stayed on the moon to live and maintain the buildings and the gravity driver. Most did not.

From what Roger knew of all of it, people "recovered" on the moon, got rested up, and then shot out to a space station for refueling. After that, the engines on the capsules were enough to get the human cargo to Mars. He'd never seen the map of the Mars Colony. Only when you got your papers and assignment did you see that.

"Mars," Roger sighed. He watched three more capsules disappear into the cloud cover, adding trails to the already dense haze. He never witnessed anything coming back from space to Earth. If there was an evacuation because of invasion, he always thought there'd be something coming to Earth. Since this damn mission started, the only things he'd seen were the vapor trails leaving the planet. Never any capsules coming back. He often imagined them littering the surface of the moon or being re-purposed as housing up on the red planet. Since the moon was the first step, the capsules should be re-used. He'd have to try and remember to ask someone. If the Mars' base was settled, then it had to have started years before the moon. Roger scraped the last of the food into his mouth and watched the sky.

The Moon Colony had been a pipe dream when they'd announced it. Roger had always figured if they were announcing it, it meant that it had to have been under construction for years already. There always had been the dream of retiring to the moon, waking up to see the "pale blue dot" of Earth. And if the Mars

Colony was ready, the governments would have had it funded, planned, and constructed decades before.

While his boys were still in school and even before, the Mars Colony had to have been being planned and built. And they'd never told anyone. Not on television, or the news, or the feeds. What was the bigger threat though? The invasion or the pollution? And which one was real?Beyond the capsules from Earth, where were the invading ships? Were they hiding up the cloud cover? In orbit, letting humans pass by? Did they want the last of the Earth's resourses? Or were they capturing the humans for food? He thought of an old *Twilight Zone* episode and shivered. Had the world governments been in contact, and this was the result of the parlay? Or had the powerful elite just out grown and out bid what was left on old Mother Earth?

He crumpled up the MRE bag and set it on the porch. In the early days, when the people were first blasted out into space, the neighborhood teamed with animals—all the pets that had gotten left behind while their families hurtled two dozen at a time into space. Roger had fed them whenever he could and left out bowls of reclaimed water. Cats, dogs, and anything else that wasn't afraid to come looking for a handout or a head to be scratched.

He sipped water, wincing at the taste. No matter how many times he ran it through the re-claimer, there was always an after-taste. His thoughts wandered to seven, maybe eight years earlier. There'd been a cat he'd grown fond of. Used to come by every night and sit next to his chair. Roger would drop his arm and idly scratch the cat. There had been warm summer nights, before the clouds claimed the sky, where Roger had fallen asleep in the chair. When he'd wake, all around him there'd be strays, waiting for food or attention.

Now the animals were gone. Mostly. The ones that were left had hunkered down somewhere deep. He stifled a quick laugh and wondered if whatever it was that was supposed to be invading would eat them. Or would the animals fight back and drive the invaders off the planet? Whoever they were, they'd be greeted by an empty planet, shells of lives and streets full of feral, former house pets. Roger wrapped his arms around him far as he could for warmth. The nights were too cold to stay out long, no matter how many layers he dressed in.

Roger got up and headed in through the slider to the kitchen. He always expected, more hoped than expected, that his wife would be standing next to the stove making tea. Or his boys would be seated at the table, talking news or sports or whatever they had left behind. It had been so long since they left. Roger missed teaching them to shave, and about girls, and how to drive. Not there'd be much driving on the moon or Mars. Roger chewed his thumbnail a moment. What if there were grandchildren by now?

The kitchen was empty, and no matter how long he had been there or would be, it would never feel familiar to him. Home was family dinners and talking about school. Learning how Helen's day had been at work. Playing cards with the boys and helping them with their homework. This new house he called "home" for the past decade or more had none of that. When he'd been forced to move and leave almost everything behind, any and all feelings of intimacy were abandoned on the road. Roger made the circuit round the house, locking doors and checking windows. Another old habit. Curtains were drawn and lights shut off. Roger turned off the newsfeed, unplugging from the constant volley of information. The implants had been installed shortly after his family went into space. He had opted only for slight modifications, not wanting to be turned into a robot. He brushed his teeth, undressed, folded his clothes, and took an early night.

Roger turned in his sleep most of the night. The bed seemed unusually cold and empty. His Helen had been a solid sleeper, barely moved unless something was going on with the boys. He woke early, gently patted the pillow where his wife used to rest her head —even though it was a different pillow now—sighed, and heaved himself from bed. The morning newsfeed screamed of stepping up the evacuation even more; enemy spaceships were headed toward Earth at alarming speeds. Those speeds might put alien crafts in Earth's orbit within the year. Or had the Earth taken a new mother-load of pollution and radiation?

Roger plodded to the kitchen, stumbling over a shoe, while the simulated talking head went on through the newsfeed.

Late last night, world leaders from the moon decided that the evacuation must be stepped up. NASA projects that the cloud cover will be complete in under a year and anyone still on planet will freeze without the sun. FOX also reports of massive radar hits from Jupiter. Is it meteors, a giant comet, or scouts from an alien attack fleet?

Roger stopped walking, chilled and sweating. "How do they know the aliens are coming here?" He leaned against the table for fear of collapsing. "What if the aliens are going to Mars?" He sat, almost falling into a chair. "What if they've seen all the capsules and are going to check them out?" It was man's ego assuming that the Earth was the target. Roger stood, shaking off the anxiety, and laughed to himself. "Damn old fool, you been alone too long." He took out the photo of Helen and the boys and held it against his chest a moment. Hoping his heartbeat would somehow reach them.

Roger followed the routine: instant coffee, breakfast from a bag, dress, teeth, and re-read the schedule. He peeked out the curtains; people on the lawn pummeled the piles of luggage in fervor to find their bags. He was half tempted to tell them he could only fit six of them at a time in the bed of the truck with their bags. No one rode in the cab with him. That mandate had been written in stone. There was an order to the trips, no one got any privilege. It was all on paper. He watched them for a moment, shaking his head, and trundled off toward the bathroom.

———

Roger liked the cold air on him and drove with the windows half down. The six people crammed into the back of the truck with their bags weren't so keen on the wind. Some had ducked down as far as they could to avoid the brunt of it. The two men tried to block what they could for their families but failed. They were open to the elements. The only thing that might have saved them were if Roger had been given a better vehicle for transport or at least a truck with a cap. All six huddled together best they could. He listened to tires hum and kept the newsfeed to a soft audio purr. The readouts behind his eyes distracted too much.

His previous vehicles had had a bit more comfort to them, like the cargo van with the wooden benches he built from scrap lumber. The small RV with the bed and the kitchenette had been his favorite; it had died in a cloud of smoke when the engine over-heated and caught fire. He'd been alone, so no one was injured—just his pride. This truck was tough, reliable, and a beast on fuel.

Once at the spaceport, he opened the tail, pulled out the bags, and helped everyone down. Courtesies were exchanged, and some of them looked at him expectantly, like he was supposed to carry in their bags. Roger pointed to a group of men standing near the spaceport doors.

"Y'all head right over to them. They'll help you to and through the launch process."

He smiled and waved. When they left, he carefully moved the thin cushions in the back. By the left wheel well was a can. He reached in, pulled out a pellet, and slipped it into the gas tank. It helped stretch the fuel. When gas stations were few and far between, they helped. He used the pellets sparingly. Once he was out, his transporting citizens would be over. He often thought about using them regularly to get off world and be with his family. But that wouldn't be right, wasting a resource for his wants. He had a duty, no matter it kept him away from the red planet and his Helen.

Roger sat in the cab outside the terminal, thinking of his family up there in the deep dark, beyond the clouds, and waited for the next capsule to be blasted into space. When he saw the red-orange glow of the rockets, he started the truck and headed home. There were six trips today, back and forth. At some point, maybe between trips four and five, he'd get refueled. The tires droned against the road, the news whispered, and Roger smiled. He thought about turning up the heat a notch. Driving with the windows down and the heat turned up seemed like a losing battle.

The remaining trips went the same. People grumbled and climbed into his truck. He handed them bags and drove them to the first stop on the way to their new homes. After the fifth trip, Roger went to the fuel depot and talked with some of the workers. They were his only real human interaction. He rarely said more than *Hello* and *Good-bye* to the passengers.

They chatted about the news while his truck was refueled and about the moon and Mars and what was going to happen when the alien ships arrived to blow up the last of whatever was left of humanity on the planet. Real cheery stuff. They watched three capsules launch from the gravity driver. The gravity driver looked like a giant cement mixer; it turned and moved, and from the refueling station, they had a great view of it.

"What do you think of the new timeline?" Roger asked.

"Who's to say? We just stand out here, fill trucks, fill tanks, and move to the next."

Roger never did get to know their names. Sure they all had patches with names on their worksuits, but how many of them were real?

"You think it's an invasion? Or have we just destroyed our little planet?" Roger asked.

"You're a fool. This is the end for us. Government is going to nuke this thing flat and start new when we're off it," said "Johnny."

"You're both confused," added "Bill" with a nod. "I read in the feeds last night that this is a hoax. There's some giant intergalactic corporation made a deal to strip the planet of everything valuable. Minerals, water, vegetation, everything."

"What about?" Roger asked. He leaned against his truck, letting the cold metal hold him up.

"I guess if life was important," Johnny said. "Then the air would be good."

"Why keep driving this thing?" another of them asked.

"I made a promise," Roger answered.

"Come up here. You seem to be a hard worker; they'll get you up faster."

"Then who will drive the shivering, fearful masses to this place? Besides, I don't want to stink of fuel."

Roger didn't get to spend too much time on this side of the spaceport. Normally, he just saw the front of the terminal. He smiled as smoke poured and then billowed from the mouth of the cylinder and the next capsule blasted out. A large rolling crane hoisted the next capsule and lowered it down. The cylinder spun until it was in the proper position and locked in for the next group.

Roger said his goodbyes to the crew. What he could see of the sun started to set on his way back for the last group of the night. He rolled up the windows, suddenly chilled through, and turned off the news in full. Roger turned the heat up, just one notch as to not waste too much fuel.

He contemplated the process of getting off world, pondered about the procedure. The cold ride in the back of a truck, being bustled through the terminal... He'd always assumed there were crowds of real living people in there and not just the few men outside the gates. Once inside the doors and walkways, travelers would have people to assist them through processing and to the ultimate cold ride into space. Did they get insulated suits? Were they in pressure chambers with temperature control? Or were they strapped into a cold padded seat and rocketed off to the moon in a spacesuit for preparation to get to Mars?

"So many questions and so few answers." He sighed, looking out the windshield. "Someday I'll know. Someday I'll be back with the wife and my boys."

When Roger got home, it was early evening. The last six people of the night were camped out on his lawn. He put the truck in park and went around back to lower the gate. A woman stood there. She looked angry and impatient.

"Why were we made to wait here so long?" she demanded.

"Had to get fuel, miss. Otherwise we get stuck on the highway and we have to wait for another vehicle to come get us. Another vehicle might not be so nice as mine."

"We were told that we would be on the fifth trip. Not the sixth." She turned from him with a huff and crossed her arms over her chest. Her husband—or Roger guessed her husband—looked at him apologetically from the lawn.

"It's on the schedule, ma'am. You all got a copy. We all have to be patient and wait our turns." Roger stuck his hands in his pockets and the other five people shuffled over. He wondered how long she'd been out there complaining. "There's no assigned seating, and they won't give me a bigger truck to haul people."

"You think we're cattle to be hauled? Do you?" She got right up under his chin. "We are people. We had rank."

"Miss, there's a planetary evacuation. The Earth is doomed. Either from aliens or a polluted cloud cover. Either way we're dead.

Think about that." Roger walked toward the pile of luggage to bring the remaining bags over. Mostly to get away from the woman.

"Can you at least help me up into the truck? Are those cushions all we have to sit on?" Roger sighed and turned probably holding her overly expensive luggage. Her husband was headed her way. He gave her a boost into the back of the truck bed, and she took a seat. "Why can't I sit up front? In the cab?"

"No one rides in the cab, miss. Those are the rules. No one in the cab, and technically, there should be no interaction. Load up the folks and get them to the spaceport. That's all."

She let off a derisive sigh and turned her back on Roger.

He brought the bags over as the people climbed into the back of the truck.

"Why is the last load always the hardest?" Roger mumbled to no one. The woman in the corner made it a point not to look at him. The last to the truck was a man in his mid- to late-seventies, Roger guessed. Roger put the bags on the ground and offered the man a hand up into the truck.

"Limited interaction," he heard from that woman. Roger closed the tail gate and put the last bags into the bed. In the cab, Roger started the newsfeed, audio only, and headed for the spaceport, wondering if he should maybe hit a couple pot holes on the right side of the truck.

Roger was so distracted by that woman he barely heard the news. He didn't want to turn up the volume in case someone from the back needed something. All could hear was her voice, rising above the news and road noise. *Talking*. He didn't know about what, probably proclaiming her rank in the world. He smiled and shook his head.

About a mile out from the spaceport, Roger noticed a grouping of capsules going up, must have been six of them. It was risky sending so many up at once; the fire from the rockets blurred into one massive eruption. He whistled from reflex and switched off the newsfeed. He was tempted to open the small sliding window at the back of the cab and point it out to his passengers, but he was sure they must have seen it before being swallowed by the clouds.

He stopped outside the terminal, turned off the truck to conserve the new fuel, and got out. Roger helped the elderly man off the truck, and then the others all got off. The woman stood in the bed looking down at him. He was sure she had spent most of her days before threat and evacuation looking down at people. People of privilege so often did that back in the day.

"Are you going to help me down?"

"I can, miss, if you like. I figured the fellow who helped you up might want to."

She shook her head, placed a hand on Roger's shoulder, and hopped down, almost falling. "You treat that old man like he was important. Like he was something before this all happened."

"He could have been. I was being helpful."

"Why didn't you help me?" She took a step closer ready to pounce.

"Importance and privilege are often in a person's own eye, miss. You seemed capable of getting in and out by yourself. He did not. If you wanted a show, you should have booked a limo for the ride." Roger walked around the truck, away from her as she fumed. He unloaded the bags, nodded and smiled to the riders, and then carried the older man's bag up to the curb and dropped them off. "An attendant would be along shortly." Through the glass doors of the station, Roger saw a group on their way out.

Roger closed the tailgate and climbed into the cab. Spotting the woman up on the curb, he waved at her before starting the truck and driving off. He whistled going down the highway, taking his time getting back. There was no rush and no people waiting on his lawn.

"I hope tomorrow is different," he said out loud. Roger was quiet the rest of the way home; he'd see the occasional flame burst as another capsule was shot into space. He wondered how much that woman would nag the other passengers or the crew. How mad would she be when she found out there'd be a stop on the Moon Colony and space station before getting to Mars? Hell, maybe she'd be stuck on the moon. Maybe she could sit in her room at night, watching the invasion through a porthole. Roger smiled at the thought. From their limited interaction, he knew that'd make her furious. Even more furious that there was no first class launch.

He pulled into his driveway, killed the lights and engine, and stepped out. There was a new mound of luggage on the lawn. Closing the door, he looked up into the sky, hoping to see a star or two. The clouds were thick. A small halo of light shone behind the clouds that he guessed to be the moon; it wasn't moving, so it wasn't an alien armada come to ruin the last of the planet. Aside from that, it was a brilliant dark. Roger stepped up to the house and stopped at the door. Taped to the door were two large envelopes. The first was the next schedule. He flipped to the second one down; his fingers trembled as he opened it.

A wide smile spread across his face.

"My time, my summons."

Roger went inside and did the nightly ritual. He sat out on the back deck listening to the darkness; the occasional breeze whispered through the grass and bushes. He ate from the MRE bag. The bushes near him rustled, and he stopped to see if it was wind or something else. Maybe the cat had come back.

"Wonder if they'll let me take you with me. If that is you." He stayed that way for a moment looking at the bushes, not really able to see anything. From the darkness outside and the light from the house pouring through the slider, he was blind. It could be an alien or an axe murderer. Roger sighed when nothing came out of the bushes purring, waiting to be scratched or fed.

With his appetite gone, Roger split the bag up the sides and placed it down on the stoop. If it was the cat, it would at least get another decent meal before he blasted off to the moon and maybe beyond.

Roger spent the next week—all he'd been given—to close up his affairs and pack whatever would fit into the bags he was sent. Most of his personals had been left at the old home before he was uprooted and moved here. His wife and boys had taken what they could with them. Two bags each, that was the law. Anything else was left behind. Roger remembered one them crying at being forced to leave so many toys behind. Had it been Sam or Richard? There was no way to get all his effects into two bags unless he didn't take a lot of clothes. Not that he had accumulated all that much since the move.

He shuttled people to the spaceport as they appeared on his lawn, and then two days before his time, they stopped showing up. His responsibilities were over. There were no new schedules, and the truck sat idle in the driveway. He wondered about maybe trying to get the guys at the spaceport fueling station and see if they could put some of his belongings in the hold of the capsule. Then he thought better of it. Everyone else got two bags. Even that self-important woman…or had she had more?

It took him two days to figure what to pack and what got left behind. He used clothing as padding and wrapped some of their favorite items from around their original house, the one his kids grew up in. Only a handful of books made the cut; the rest he hoped wouldn't get destroyed during the invasion or whatever the government was planning. Maybe when this was all over, he'd come back to Earth with his grandchildren and look for the old home, show them where their parents had lived when they were their age. He'd teach them earth history and about books.

A sad smile crossed his face. He'd brought pile of photographs and a couple albums to the new house. He liked the holo-frames, but his wife had insisted on hard copy photographs. She'd liked being able to touch the images—to get that tactile sensation when she looked at them. Roger checked his pocket to make sure the photo from the dashboard had made it inside. That sensation is why Roger preferred books and why he brought some with him. Even ones he had read two or three times: Asimov, Heinlein, Bradbury, and McCammon.

"I'll be back for all of you." He put the bags by the door; tomorrow morning, around ten o'clock, someone would come for him and his bags. He'd be deposited on a lawn and would wait for his turn for a ride to the spaceport.

In the kitchen, he sipped some reclaimed water and looked out on the deck. The nightly MRE bag was clean. Someone or something had had a feast. Smiling, Roger went back to the living room and sat in the chair he had claimed as his own. He patted the arm rests and reclined.

If it were a giant hoax and the government automatons sold off the planet, where would he end up? Where had Helen and the boys been? He hoped beyond everything that the moon wasn't a massive shanty town and that after a few weeks he'd be going to Mars to be with his family. Roger looked at the map of the Mars' station again, tracing his finger. Was everyone stationed around Utopia Planetia? Had the Earth scientists found a way to actually Terra-Form? To turn the blank slate of Mars into a new Earth, full of promise? A new land to call their own and to take care of? Could they fix the mistakes that had been made on the pale blue dot of Earth?

Holding the map of mars firmly to his chest, Roger closed his eyes and slept, dreaming of The moon, Mars, and his family.

12

TWO SLUGS IN THE BELLY

PETER N. DUDAR

The Eastern Side of Dome 12 smelled like broken sewage lines and obscene mating rituals. Even from three miles away, the stench filled Krieger's monorail car as the train passed over the last of the colony's clean, habitable tenements. Within a few minutes, the train would cross over Lake Denebola and enter the farthest station under the dome. The living quarters on the Eastern Side were nothing more than scattered one-occupant pods meant for the outcasts of regular colony life. He'd been sent there too many times to count by either the Colony Council or Minister Adelaide, herself. Krieger wasn't the only private investigator in the colony, but he knew his way around the Eastern Side of Dome 12 and was ready to travel as soon as payment was transferred to his bank account. Most of all, Krieger knew not to talk about these special assignments. If they were sending *him*, it meant they were operating outside Dome Law.

Back on earth, they would've called the Eastern Side a shanty-town. Krieger knew it like the back of his hand. Nearly an earth-year had passed since the last time he'd been there, but news of the growing tensions between humans and the Sabikans had circulated to Capitol City. Things were getting uglier by the day according to recent reports. His target, a human named Doolah Quar, had gone into hiding, refusing to return to the Capitol and disabling her Computex system, rendering her unreachable. It would take an hour, perhaps two, to creep through the Eastern Side, locate Doolah Quar, and have her on the outbound monorail before the stars of Orion could flicker blue.

He was halfway over Denebola before he picked up the file and started leafing through it.

Denebola. *The Lion's Tail.* The picture inside Quar's dossier was of a middle-aged black woman with long hair twisted into dread-locks and eyes that indeed looked like the piercing gaze of a lioness. According to the file, Doolah was originally from Earth (Jamaican descent) and had arrived at Dome 12 via the Coloniza-tion Lottery System over three decades ago. Krieger knew this information was propaganda. Quar had been hand-picked because she was a both a midwife and an abortion technician back on Earth. The Dome had several perfectly-staffed medical centers that could handle pregnancies and abortions, but after the Colony Council had agreed to open Ganymede's domes to the refugees from Sabika, all bets were off. Once interspecies mating began, there was a seventy-two hour window between fertilization and "host catato-nia." Loss of neurological and motor skills, eventual paralysis, and finally a painful death as the Sabikan spawn devoured their way *out.*

"We're going to ask for your complete discretion on this," Ramu had told Krieger as he'd passed the file across the desk. Behind him, three other members of the Council had stared at their polished boots like guilty children. "We can't have word of what's happened going beyond these walls. It's Minister Adalaide's daughter. She's caught two slugs in the belly."

Two slugs in the belly. Back on Earth, that had meant that the villain in some black and white cinema reel was just gunned down in cold blood. Here on Ganymede, it meant that a Sabikan had spilled its seed inside some poor prostitute or some lonely, desperate woman seduced by the alien species. The Sabikans looked very much human; one couldn't discern any noticeable differences with full clothing on, which had made it all the easier for the Colony Council to permit their sanctuary inside Ganymede's habitat domes. Here on Ganymede, cinema reels were an archaic remembrance of the past from a planet that was beginning its next big extinction phase. Doolah Quar was lucky that the doctors in Dome 12 wanted nothing to do with aborting zygote slugs, especially once they discovered how lethal they became when removed from the womb. Krieger estimated that Quar saved more lives in Dome 12 than all the doctors combined. He had no idea how she discovered her technique or why she never shared it with the Dome's medical services, but Krieger assumed it kept her protected—made her necessary rather than expendable.

Always twins. Two slugs in the belly because Sabikan evolution perpetuates repopulation as a defense mechanism against extinction.

A pleasant female voice came over the monorail's PA system.

"Welcome to Eastern Station, the outermost territory in Dome 12. Be sure to obtain all your personal belongings, and please dispose of any trash in the proper receptacles. For departure schedules, please visit our Computex domain page on your portable mainframe device or speak to our friendly, courteous staff. Thank you for choosing Dome Transit!"

Krieger took one last glance at Doolah Quar's photograph and found his eyes gazing into those piercing orbs.

"Time is ticking, Doolah," he said as he closed the file and shoved it into his hipsling. He imagined Adelaide's daughter entering the final phase, just before the slugs chewed their way out of her womb. And he thought of where his own career would be if he failed to bring her back. "Seventy-two hours goes real fucking fast when you're this far away from the sun."

The streets were lined with filthy pedestrians, human and Sabikan, in torn clothes and huddling around barrel fires. The trees inside the domes were meant to produce oxygen and filter out the carbon emissions. Burning them prematurely was just as dangerous as, say, the ruptured sewage system that was supposed to bring waste to the treatment plants for filtration and recycling. Here on the Eastern Side, sewage now ran directly into the lake, which further threatened the Dome's ecosystem. It was one of those things the Colony Council never seemed to care about.

Because fixing it takes money from their pockets.

But the Minister's daughter—*That mattered.*

Ramu had not mentioned just how far Tirese Adelaide was in her gestation. He'd only said that time was invaluable in righting her situation. They'd already had his and Doolah's return tickets purchased and ready for him inside Quar's dossier.

Krieger hustled down the streets, bathed in the changing colors of neon glow that wavered over the darkened landscape. Up close, it looked a lot like an apocalyptic version of Las Vegas back on Earth, only on a smaller scale. There were no Domescrapers on the outskirts. Rather, the tallest buildings were three floors maximum, and those buildings were mostly dedicated to public works: a courthouse, a prison complex for those too unfit for civilian life, an energy plant, the sewage treatment facility. There were storefronts and gin-joints as well, but these buildings were single-floor units. Many were closed now; there was little need for commerce in an area where hardly anyone held a paying job. The places that *were* open either bartered in trade or made their money through illegal means.

Why the fuck would Quar want to live here? She should be making enough money in her trade to live in one of those Domescrapers back in the city, back where civilian life remains civil.

He thought of the photograph he'd committed to memory; the one with the lioness eyes which professed that she'd eat you alive just as soon as look at you.

It's the job. It must get to her. She's not that much different from you, after all…cleaning up other people's messes and doing all the dirty work. You've got a bad liver and a horrible case of insomnia from all the shit you've slung over the years. So she stakes a claim to a vacant pod out here, where she probably gets most of her clients anyway.

The file had no direct living address for her, but the greatest concentration of Eastern dwellers convened just ahead on Marley Drive. Fitting for a Jamaican immigrant, if the street were named after the legendary reggae singer from Earth. Krieger knew better. It was named after Captain Alex Marley, who piloted the first shuttle to Jupiter's largest moon. The Colonization Project was supposed to happen on Mars, but back home on Earth, it had been decided that they wanted an outpost further out into the solar system, where it could serve as a more centralized hub for space exploration. And, as Krieger also knew, Jupiter was ripe with natural gases and resources that could fuel the Earth's needs a million times over.

At least until the new extinction phase had begun unexpectedly.

Krieger wondered if there were any forms of life left on his home planet. He'd been gone for nearly twenty years, but the thought of the way life used to be never left him.

There was movement ahead. A crowd had formed outside one of the watering holes, a gin-joint called Neptune, Baby! Krieger was almost certain he saw a tall, black woman with dreadlocks pushing her way through the front door with two young, white men following directly behind her. Krieger was still a block away and couldn't be certain it was her, but he had a gut feeling.

It was in how she walked.

She stalked like a lioness.

"Doolah Quar?"

"I'm off the clock, mon." Doolah leaned over to one of her men-in-waiting and said, "Be a doll and go get me a Martian Tourniquet on the rocks." She looked back at Krieger and glared through those wild, predator eyes. "It's after business hours, and I ain't got no business with you, whoever you are. Come find me tomorrow if you need me to visit your little lady and fix your problems."

The young man was already off to fetch her drink, and Krieger couldn't help but admire her. Back on Earth, they'd have called her a cougar. She was old enough to be the kid's mother. And why not? She absolutely radiated sexual confidence and prowess. The other young man was sitting in the chair on her left, and his eyes kept shifting from giving Krieger dirty looks to trying to gaze beneath the descending vee of Doolah's Dermex top. It was a cinch that both young men were human; no way in hell Doolah Quar would risk mounting a Sabikan and risk catching two slugs in the belly.

"I have orders from Capitol 12 to bring you back to the city with me. Your skills are needed immediately, and I'm to stun you and drag you unconscious if you refuse to cooperate."

Doolah smiled, and those lovely burgundy lipstick lips of hers parted into an animal grin. He almost expected to see fangs.

"Someone important got less than seventy-two hours to go, huh? Who it be? Tell ol' Doolah who shacked up with a Sabikan."

"I'm not allowed to say. Confidentiality. You should know that. It's best if we don't ask, don't tell. Besides, I really don't want to cause a scene here if I don't have to. Whaddaya say?"

"Fuck that, mon! I ain't going nowhere until tomorrow. This be *my* night off. I'm here for Happy Hour. I'm gonna get drunk as shit and then, if these two boys are lucky..."

The first young man had returned with her drink. He set it down on the table in front of her, and then kissed Doolah's neck just below her right earlobe. The drink fizzled like molten lava as red as Mars itself. Krieger wondered how much alcohol it contained.

"...then both of them are gonna have their way with me. They can compete to see who can give me a better orgasm. And the whole time I'm gonna try not to think about the two slugs I removed from some poor girl that got raped three blocks from here, right behind the supermarket in Dome Daylight. Do you know what happens to slugs when they hit external oxygen before their membrane is complete?"

Krieger remained silent.

"They evaporate into an acidic vapor cloud capable of eating the flesh off your fucking hands. Breathe it in, and it kills you immediately. I nearly died today because of some Sabikan rapist, and that sonofabitch is still on the loose somewhere outside. So if you can't even tell me who..."

"Adelaide's daughter," Krieger said, slowly reaching inside his coat pocket for his weapon. "I'm estimating she's already seventeen hours in, and Adelaide wants to be sure she's managed with no witnesses and no questions asked."

The second of the two young men pulled out a pulsar gun and aimed its laser sight directly between Krieger's eyes.

"Doolah is telling you to fuck off, buddy," he said coolly.

Doolah threw her head back and laughed, and Krieger couldn't help but become intoxicated by her beauty—her warm ebony cheeks and smooth, perfect neckline plunging down into her expansive bosom. Her dossier said she was in her fifties, but she could have passed for thirties easily. Whatever tricks she used to stay so young would fetch a very pretty nickel back in Capitol City.

"What's so funny?" Krieger asked.

"I don't know who put you up to this, but Tirese Adelaide isn't even inside Dome 12 anymore. She done absconded with a life-suit and made the Defector's Sojourn. She prolly dead now somewhere in the wastelands outside."

The Defector's Sojourn meant risking being pulled apart by the moon's enormous magnetic field while trying to cross on foot from one dome to another. Many had taken the sojourn but only a handful survived. And if they did, their brains remained scrambled for a very long time.

"Why'd she try to escape?"

Doolah stopped laughing and turned to her boy with the weapon.

"Put dat thing away before someone gets hurt." She turned to Krieger. "I don't know why she left. If you're dying to know, go find yourself a life-suit and go out and ask her." Doolah's eyes narrowed into slits, and her smile evaporated. "But I'll tell you this much...Doolah think that the Sabikans are planning to take over the colonies. We hear things all the time out here on the Eastern Side. They've had enough of us humans running everything, and they tired of seeing me killing off their spawn to protect those they've impregnated. I'm getting death threats all the time these days. That's why I left Capitol City. I'm safer out here where there is no law. Out here, a Sabikan gets hanged for a crime before the police can deal with it; it don't mean nothing. And the humans know I'm here to service *them* when they get into trouble. That practically makes me royalty."

Doolah picked up her drink and took a large sip. The kid with the gun shifted uncomfortably for a moment, and then slipped his weapon back into its holster. The moment he did, Krieger leapt over the table and cold-cocked him. Doolah Quar tumbled backward, spilling her Martian Tourniquet all over herself as she tumbled onto the floor. The other boy, the one who had fetched her drink, had already turned tail and was sprinting toward the door to find a bouncer. Krieger ignored him and took another swing at the first boy, catching him square in the jaw. The kid's head flew backward (his eyes rolling in their sockets like marbles), and he dropped unconscious onto the cold, hard tiles. Doolah was on her feet and moving toward the door when Krieger's hand shot out and grasped hers. His free hand reached back inside his coat pocket and hauled out his pulsar gun. He had it aimed at her midriff as the first boy returned with the bouncer.

"You're breaking the law, buddy," the fat guy in the sleeveless Dermex hollered above the music and the growing din of spectators circling them. "I can legally execute you if you don't let her go immed…"

Krieger pulled the gun away from Doolah's belly and fired a stun shot at the dude's head. The guy's knees buckled, and then all three hundred pounds of him were dropping to the floor. The kid watched this happen; his bladder released in front of the crowd. His piss was still hot on the tiles as Krieger pushed Doolah past him and out into the darkness of Dome Evening.

———————

"I know who you are," Doolah said as the monorail departed the station to make its trek back to Capitol City.

The glass panels of the geodesic sphere around them were still translucent, allowing starlight from the outer constellations to shine through. To the west, the sphere of Jupiter's massive surface was beginning to come into view with its never-ending panoply of volcanic activity and gaseous eruptions. The panorama was breathtaking and made Krieger wish that life under the Dome could always be this peaceful. By morning the glass panels would resume their ultraviolet glow of Day Mode and the streets of the city would fill with life again.

Quar watched him with interest. "I seen you plenty of times back on the Eastern Side. Always doing the dirty business of the Colony Council. Always chasin' down the enemies of democracy or deadbeats who owe the government money. Every one of them is shady as fuck, you know. Both the population and the folks on the Council."

She was sitting in the chair directly across from him, stale with the perfume of her spilled drink. Krieger's gaze traveled down her neck to the swells of her bosom, barely contained in the material of her Dermex top. She casually unzipped until her breasts were nearly popping out and with a flourish of a handkerchief, proceeded to wipe away the sticky remnants of her spilled drink. Krieger followed the hypnotizing movement as she lifted the cloth to her mouth and licked it lasciviously with the tip of her tongue. Her own eyes, laying in wait, captured his, making sure she had his full attention. "Here's the thing, hot-shot…I know *lots* of people. I've fixed a lot of mistakes and a lot of people still owe me their lives. So you just remember that when this is over, you best start watching the shadows, because *my* people are gonna be waiting for you. I'll swear my life on it."

It was Krieger's turn to laugh.

"Your life don't mean shit," he said. "Not if what you told me is true. If the Sabikans are planning to take over, you're gonna be the first to go. They ain't gonna want no abortion-technician around if the Sabikans mean to mass-populate. You'll be running for a life-suit and making the Defector's Sojourn, too."

Doolah sat back, dropped the handkerchief, and folded her arms. The hint of ferocity still resided in her pouty lips. She looked as if she'd known this information all along, but either didn't want to think about it or, more likely, had a contingency plan in store that he was now interfering with by taking her as prisoner.

Krieger reached inside his hipsling to remove her dossier. He flipped it open and started leafing through it, feeling her glare burning at him like vaporizing Sabikan slugs. "You know, Doolah, if they *do* try an uprising, we'll *both* be dead real fast. Only, you're death will probably come seventy-two hours *after* mine. If you take my meaning."

She remained silent, nudging her medical bag occasionally with her foot. They'd had to detour to her pod to get it before returning to the station. Adelaide's daughter's life depended on it.

It occurred to him that he should have patted her down before climbing aboard the monorail, but her outfit left very few places to pack heat. A blade, perhaps, but he was constantly watching her movements and his pulsar gun was always within reach. He was about to ask her about her past on Earth when his Computex device rang with an incoming call.

It was Ramu.

"Did you locate Ms. Quar?"

Krieger looked at his target and frowned. Doolah had already zipped her top back up. It made him feel like an awkward teenager, realizing just how badly he wanted her.

"Maybe. Tell me something... How much time does Tirese Adelaide have left before the slugs go cannibal?"

Doolah Quar sat up and dropped her arms. It was as if she'd been waiting for this moment to happen. He couldn't decide if she'd been bluffing about the Minister's daughter or if that sonofabitch from the Colony Council had been lying.

Why would he lie, though? Tirese Adelaide had always been a rebellious little shit. Sacking up with a Sabikan to piss her mother off seemed like something any child of privilege would try to pull.

"We think she just passed her twenty hour mark."

"Are you sure?"

There was a hesitation. "What kind of question is *that?* Of course, we're sure. Hers and the Sabikan's alibies check out."

"Tirese Adelaide fled Dome 12 completely, didn't she? She's risked a horrible death and made the Sojourn on her own. Did she reach Dome 13? That's the one nearest to ours."

Another pause, this time longer.

Doolah was now staring wide-eyed out in space, as if she were trying to mentally picture the Minister's daughter hobbling over the cratered landscape of Jupiter's biggest moon, the weight of her life-suit three times as heavy because of the moon's magnetic field.

The voice of Minister Adelaide came over the receiver. Her voice sounded cold and terrified. "If you have Doolah Quar with you, bring her here immediately. *I'm* the one who's pregnant."

"Walk faster."

They'd exited the monorail into the Capitol Station. Already people were swarming the platform in their morning rush hour ritual. Digging his fingers into Doolah's arm, Krieger steered her through the sea of pedestrians toward the exit ramp.

"There's no need to be forceful," she said through gritted teeth. "I'm coming with you at this point. I ain't gonna try and run away."

"That's real good, because we've got a deadline. If Adelaide's the one that's got two slugs in the belly, we need to be in Capitol City yesterday."

"We got bigger problems than that, hot-shot. We're being followed."

"Are you sure?"

"I noticed them back at my pod when we went to get my supplies. Three men, all of them wearing navy blue Dome Security jumpsuits. They all be Sabikan." Doolah glanced up at one of the hemisphere mirrors dangling over the concourse. Krieger followed her gaze. "Dome Morning" was still hours off, but he had on dark sunglasses anyway. "There's one right behind us," she whispered.

He hadn't realized it before, but Krieger was terrified. How Quar was keeping her cool was a complete mystery. They would be gunning for her first, that much was painfully obvious now.

"How can you tell?" Krieger reached into his coat, wrapped his palm around the handle of his pulsar gun and squeezed tight.

"The sunglasses. You don't know shit about Sabikan anatomy, do you?"

"Fill me in," he said, redoubling his pace so that they were almost jogging.

"They be part reptile, like chameleons back on earth. Their skin can change colors if they will it to. You wouldn't notice on their extremities because they disguise themselves to fit in among us. But if you ever see them under a blacklight, their skin becomes see-through. And their eyes change as well, especially when their heart rate goes up. Their sclera glows yellow like a lizard's."

Krieger felt the panic welling up in his belly. With the exception of the hemisphere mirrors over the concourse, there was no way of keeping their pursuers out of their blind-spot. He listened hard for the sound of shoe heels clicking closer behind him, but with the hustle and bustle of pedestrians moving around him, it was impossible.

"Something's about to go down." He steered Doolah around a corner toward the commissary. There was a custodial closet ten meters away, and the moment they rounded the corner, he was sprinting (dragging Doolah behind him) toward the closet door. He shoved her through the door, barging in after her, his pulsar gun now out and pointing toward the ceiling. He reached out toward the switch by the door and shut the light off.

They watched in silence as the first Sabikan trotted past. Krieger felt his eyes focus hard on the alien's skin, wanting to see if it would somehow change as Doolah mentioned. Now that he knew their secret, he desperately wanted to see for himself—as well as buy a flashlight with an ultraviolet bulb to make their detection easier.

Moments later, the second passed, this one also wearing sunglasses. There was a moment when he swung his head toward the closet. Doolah yanked her arm away from Krieger and pressed her fist to her mouth. The Sabikan turned his head forward and continued moving, and Krieger could see the alien had his pulsar gun drawn and ready.

If they're wearing security uniforms, they have access to all the cameras in the building.

"We're getting out of here!" he uttered between gritted teeth. Grabbing Doolah's arm again, Krieger bolted through the doorway and hurtled directly into the path of the third Sabikan. The alien's face flashed with absolute surprise. Krieger spun the gun around in his hand and hammered the butt-end of the weapon into the alien's temple. The sunglasses spun off and fell to the floor. For a brief moment, the Sabikan's eyes burned the yellow of tainted egg yolks. Krieger belted the alien again, and then he and Doolah sprinted toward the exit.

They caught the first available Dome-Cab, Krieger handing the driver a fifty-jank and telling him to hightail it to the Capitol Center. The two huddled down low and spoke in whispers as the driver rounded corners and flew up the entrance ramp onto Jupiter Highway.

"If what you said was true, then the fucking revolution has already started. Those goons sure as hell have no beef with me. It's *you* they're after."

"Well, fucking *DUH*, that's why I didn't want to leave the Eastern Side."

"You don't get it. You're not safe here inside this dome. You're going to have to go into exile after you fix the Minister. She's going to have to call the Colony Congress to order and declare war. You're going to be making the Defector's Sojourn if you want to live after today."

Doolah's eyes narrowed. "Fuck that, mon! Doolah Quar ain't going nowhere! This is my home, and I'll blast every last Sabikan in the fucking face before I let them put me down."

"Will you shut up for a moment and listen? We don't even know how far they've infiltrated the Congress. We have no idea what plans they have in motion or what weapons they've secured. What we *do* know is that they know who *you* are and exactly what you look like. You stand out in Dome 12. We need to get you somewhere safe before you become public enemy number one." Krieger sighed. "Let's just get you into the Capitol and take care of Minister Adelaide."

He closed his eyes and slipped his hand up to massage the bridge of his nose. A killer headache was forming somewhere within the center of his skull, and if he didn't get sleep and a real plate of food soon, he was going to pass out. He thought of Minister Adelaide—middle aged like Doolah but exuding white hair and worry lines from politics rather than cleaning up the messes that the abortion-technician had to deal with. She'd run election platforms on *family values* in Dome 12, endearing herself to a fan base of colonists that clung to the puritanical ways of Earth. A huge portion of those folks turned on her when she voted in the Congress to allow refuge to the Sabikans. Now they were going to get their chance to revel in the stupid glory of "We Told You So."

He thought of Tirese Adelaide, probably discovering that her mother copulated with one of the aliens and fleeing Dome 12 in shame. He wondered if she made it to Dome 13 or if her dead body was slowly being crushed into nothingness by the gravitational weight of magnetic polarity and the pressure of vacuous outer space.

"You could come with me," Doolah said. Perhaps Quar was on the verge of breaking, but he couldn't be sure if it was real or if she was merely testing him. "You be a good-looking man. Leave with me—right now—and I'll spend all my nights making love to you.

You ain't been able to take your eyes off me since we met—come discover the rest of me." She pushed her body into his. Her softness and proximity made his nether region engorge. "Doolah will keep you good and satisfied for as long as I can."

"Maybe. Let's just deal with Adelaide first, and then see what she has to say. For all we know, you could slip up and kill us both when the slugs evaporate."

The shadow of a sneer flitted across her face before it was replaced with a cold determination. "Not today," she said, and Krieger could tell that she was thinking that it might be for the better if she did.

Krieger found himself thankful to be male.

The Capitol building's sky panels were filling with Dome Sunrise just as the entrance doors swung shut behind them. Krieger no longer steered Doolah Quar by her elbow as they raced through the halls. She hurried right alongside of him, but Krieger was sure that if she wanted to, she could leave him in the dust and just disappear. The faces of strangers turned and watched them as they plowed through the pedestrian traffic. Nobody wore sunglasses inside the Capitol, so there was no way to tell just how many faces were Sabikan.

It felt like they were being hunted. If Doolah had the heart of a predator, then some greater predator had picked up her scent and was somewhere close by, ready to pounce. Something wild, with eyes that burned yellow when excited.

They reached the elevators at the middle of the concourse. Krieger jammed the *up* button until the door opened. He pushed Doolah inside and scrambled in after her, hitting the button for the fourth floor and then the *door close* button before anyone else could enter. Doolah gripped her bag's handles with ashen hands.

She's tougher than I am, Krieger thought. *She's ready to break down and cry, but she won't. She won't because she's lived a survivor's life and will never show weakness.*

The elevator landed on the fourth floor and the doors slid open. Krieger exited first and pointed down the hall. There was not another being in sight. It was too damn quiet. Ambush was coming. Krieger could feel it in his pounding heart.

"Third door on the left. I want to go in first and make sure Adelaide is there and alone. If she is, you do your thing and get rid of the goddamn slugs. When you're done, we'll talk to her together and convince her she needs to act."

Quar said nothing and just followed him to a door labeled *The Honorable Julie J. Adelaide.* Krieger wrapped his hand around his pulsar gun and pulled it out of his coat. He looked one last time at Doolah and opened the door.

Inside was a nightmare.

The Sabikan closest, at a speed quicker than Krieger could have dreamed possible, flew past them, shoved them inside, and threw the door closed behind them before they could even process what they saw.

Minster Adelaide was stripped naked and tied down to her desk. Ramu and the other Colony Council members were also naked, forming a ring around her. Ramu's skin was purplish, and Krieger could see the network of capillaries and veins pulsing with blood beneath the epidermis.

"I'm afraid we've miscalculated," Ramu said, drawing an open hand over Adelaide's belly. "You're just in time to witness the birth of my offspring."

Minister Adelaide had already slipped into catatonia. Unfocused eyes stared out from a vacant shell with two parasitic fetuses waiting in her womb. Krieger's gaze passed down over the Minister's body to her belly, which now writhed and wriggled with motion beneath her skin. Somewhere in her abdomen were two slugs with tiny razor-sharp teeth that had sprouted less than twenty-four hours ago, chewing their way out of her uterus and through her abdomen. Adelaide's belly writhed and squirmed in a vulgar display of nature that made him wince in disgust. To her credit, Doolah Quar's gaze never changed.

Two slugs in the belly, he thought coldly. *That has to be the most disgusting thing I've ever heard.*

Doolah stepped in front of Krieger and stared down the naked Sabikans. "I can still save her."

They eyed her lasciviously, their genitals engorging with arousal. She glanced at their organs—so much bigger than human ones—and for the briefest moment, Krieger's heart filled with jealousy and disappointment. In the sweetest of irony, she gave a dismissive "tcht," unimpressed by the Sabikans. Power and control filled her eyes. Those perfect orbs gleamed bright with defiance and hate. "Please. Our people can still live in peace together."

"That time has come and gone," Ramu said, moving around the desk. "We tried to assimilate quietly, peacefully, but we've reached an impasse. We can procreate within our own kind, but when we try with your species, you put our children to death. We're ready to take over the colonies. You humans were foolish to take us in. You all need to go."

The other Sabikans nodded silently in agreement.

"And we want you to help us," Ramu said to her. "We think you'll make a wonderful host."

Doolah Quar produced a pulsar gun from a hidden pocket of her Dermex suit and fixed it on the Prime Minister Adelaide's abdomen. The motion was so quick, so fluid, that Krieger found himself rolling away and covering his face in sheer reflex.

"I'm sorry, Prime Minister." Doolah Quar's eyes flashed dark, and she pulled the trigger twice, blasting away the bare patches of skin over either side of the Minister's ovaries.

The room filled with flash and gun smoke before the ruler of

Dome 12's body erupted in a spray of blood and entrails. Ramu and the others turned a hideous, angry shade of red as they watched their progeny aborted. A terrible hiss emitted from the dead Minister's belly as the two slugs evaporated and misted their way out of her bloody, destroyed abdomen. Ramu covered his mouth and nose and darted toward the other side of the room before the toxic vapors could envelope him.

She did *have a weapon,* Krieger thought in absolute horror. *She could have killed me any time she wanted to. This whole time, she's been sizing me up and playing me out.*

The others were running to find their weapons. Doolah aimed her pulsar gun at each one and squeezed the trigger until the alien council members fell dead one-by-one onto the floor. When Ramu was the only one left, she aimed at him.

Ramu had found his own weapon and pointed it at Krieger. "It won't matter," he sneered triumphantly. "The revolution has already begun. Even if you kill me, there are so many others. One of them will eventually get you and impregnate you. We're taking over, Doolah. We can't be stopped!"

Doolah Quar flashed a terrible smile as Krieger looked between them, trying to subtly reach his own weapon before Ramu fired on him. Doolah had chosen her fight, her priority. "This all ends now." She gave a half-apologetic shrug to Krieger and kept her gun on Ramu. "I destroy you, and we humans rise up to defeat the Sabikan mutiny. It's over, Ramu!"

The office door behind them flew open, and a new Sabikan blasted Doolah Quar in the back. Doolah fell to the floor, and a bloody smile spread across her face one last time.

"You'll never have *me,*" she gasped in her final defiance. "Viva la Resistance!"

Doolah aimed her pulsar gun at her temple, and the heavens gained another star as her lifeless body hit the floor. A spray of blood and bone fragments showered everything around her, coating Krieger with her crimson vitality. The woman Krieger had grown to love set herself free.

The Revolution had its first martyr inside Dome 12.

Krieger dove, snatched up Doolah's weapon, and finished both Ramu and the Sabikan in the doorway. When the alien enemies fell lifeless to the floor, he wept. It was preposterous to believe in a "happily-ever-after" for him and Doolah, where they escaped this death room together and remained together as lovers, but until that moment, there had at least been hope. Now there was only loss and a thirst for vengeance against the Sabikans. His tears flowed freely as he thought of the heart of the woman who just saved him. Perhaps the same heart beat within Tirese Adelaide. Unstoppable things had been set into motion under the dome, and the colonists would need a new leader to guide them. He wondered if he could get out of the city alive, and if he *could* find a life-suit, how long it would take to track down the Minister's only daughter. If she was still alive, Tirese Adelaide was the new Minister and would have to lead the rebellion against the Sabikans.

The only thing left in his future was to make the Defector's Sojourn and continue the resistance.

I am Denebola, he thought as he escaped into Dome Morning. *I will be the lion and hunt them all down.* Krieger left the Capitol and sought out the future of Ganymede.

Morgan
Sylvia

13

THE DREAMER AT THE END OF TIME

MORGAN SYLVIA

The watcher did not know what he was watching for, or what he was supposed to do when he saw it. He spent his days alone in the tower, observing the endless gray waves crashing against the rocky shore below. He knew nothing of those who had built the tower and the garden around it, with its smooth, black obelisks and statues of strange beasts. Nor did he understand why its makers had chosen such a desolate spot for this outpost—an uncolonized planet at the edge of the universe.

There were many questions he could have asked about this remote, lonely planet and the sleek, cold tower, about the tangled briar forest or the vast obsidian sea, but he was no longer particularly curious. His former captors, the psy-ops, had carved that inclination right out of his mind. The tower itself offered no answers. It rose into the sky, smooth and straight, like a bullet aimed at the pinkish sun, an enigma on an uninhabited world. The mysteries surrounding him remained mysteries. The waves kept their own secrets, as did the scaled monstrosities twisting in the icy currents beneath them.

It was not his place to ask questions.

His job was to watch, nothing more.

He kept to a routine, as did the beasts and the tides. Every morning, he scanned the footage from the winged drones, the synthetic birds and insects that flitted over the waves and through the snarled woods, monitoring the desolate, empty wilderness and the wild animals he shared it with. When these tasks were completed, he encrypted his daily report and sent it back to the starbase through the wormhole transmitter. The transmitter itself, which someone had cleverly—or whimsically—devised into the shape of a gryphon, teleported message pods, which were shaped like eggs. The gryphon would cast the egg into the wormhole. Somewhere on the other side of the universe, it would pop out on someone's desk. (He never bothered to wonder whose.) Shortly thereafter, the egg would reappear between the gryphon's front paws with a new coded message. He painstakingly decrypted each one, even though he already knew what the cipher said.

The codes changed, according to protocol, but the messages were always the same.

Outpost 5s, GN-z11, Sector 9, Zarak. Nothing to report. End transmission.

Starbase 6L, I Zwicky 18, Sector 43, Oberon. Acknowledged. Carry on. End transmission.

A second mechanical beast, this one an owl, sat on a pedestal in his office, dispensing facts and procedures as needed. In its circuits, trapped beneath copper feathers and carnelian eyes, lay the only true wealth this tiny, desolate planet contained: knowledge. Not the knowledge of one spacefaring empire, but that of dozens. The bird contained over a trillion zettabytes of data: encyclopedias, photographs, historical records, manuals, newscasts, books, scientific texts, poetry, music, and movies. It occasionally activated itself, to notify him of a storm or an upcoming holiday, or to remind him when and how to plant and sow certain crops. It played music when he asked it to, and it offered recipes and movie suggestions for his vidset. He assumed that the owl or the gryphon, or both, would dictate protocol in the event of, well, an event.

But nothing much happened, aside from the occasional storm. The sun followed three pale moons across the wind, and the tides wreaked havoc on the rocks below. The gulls and poison crows chased each other across pastel skies, observed by mechanical hawks and sparrows. On the other side of the tower, the thorn forest reached its tangled, bony branches across the land.

This place was wind and waves, field and forest, steel and starlight. Little else.

He recalled something of who he was or who he had been. Sometimes he would stare for hours at the medals hanging in the display case on the parlor's faux-wood walls, trying to remember the battles he had won them for—or at least name his brothers in arms. He knew he had been in at least three wars: a civil uprising against the corrupt Haus Celeron; a nightmarish conflict with an invading reptilian race; and a rebellion against an oligarchy controlled by a clandestine order of psychics. Though the first two had provided most of the scars and medals, the last had been the worst, not for what it had given him, but what it had taken.

Sanity. Dignity. Humanity.

He still woke screaming in the night, visions and memories racing through his shattered dreams. He saw again the silver-masked faces of the psychic warriors looming over him, felt the claw-sharp hooks of their machines prying into his mind, tearing his thoughts and memories apart. He could almost see the dark underground bunker, smell its metallic stench. Three years he had spent trapped in a seemingly endless hell beneath a pale yellow sun, somewhere in a barred spiral galaxy he'd forgotten the name of.

Sometimes he looked at his skin and tried to recall where all the scars had come from. He stared at his arms—the flesh one and the mechanical one—and the prosthetic leg, and wondered which suited him better. He touched the spot on his chest where a mechanical heart beat in place of a human one and scrutinized his reflection in an elaborate mirror. The mirror did not reflect the plates and circuits in his head, the rods in his hips and leg, or the sensors and cameras in his eyes, but he knew they were there.

He often wondered how much of him was human now—and how much android.

He knew why they had sent him here; he was mad now, broken, his brain irreparably wracked by the psychic wars. Once a renowned warrior, he was only a shell of a man when they rescued him from the prison planet. He was no longer fit for regular duty, and after nearly two decades in combat, was completely unsuited for both desk work and civilian life. He only vaguely recalled getting the orders that had dispatched him here, to his final station. A senior general had leaned across a polished table on a warship in an E4 galaxy, eyes glittering eagle-sharp above a chest that glittered with badges. He'd forgotten both the name of the general and the name of the ship, but he remembered the words. *A talent like yours can't be wasted,* he'd said. *We've got a post you may be interested in. One last deployment. Consider it an active retirement in a classified location.*

This place, this post, this empty shore, had only one thing to offer: solitude. This suited him. The tower offered plenty to occupy himself with. He was slowly cataloging the native beasts, most of which he had not yet named. He tended the gardens and the chickens, exercised, gathered fish and shellfish, read. He painted, wrote, carved scrimshaw from driftwood and the bones of behemoths that washed onto the shore. He maintained the koi pond, the drone flocks of hawks and sparrows, and the canine robots that patrolled the land. He spent hours in the courtyard, wandering amidst the smooth black obelisks or staring at the alabaster, ethereal statues. The one that drew him most was of a woman twisting in dance, her face raised toward the sky. He did not know who had carved her, though he imagined it was some watcher before him, possibly the same mad/creative genius who had wrought mermaids into the door handles or made the oven look like a chimera.

It was safe to say that at least one of his predecessors had been skilled with 3D printing. Others had been painters, sculptors, carvers. They were all right below his feet, dust and bones, resting in steel tombs in the crypt beneath the tower. He would never know which of them had carved the manticore that housed the tower's internal controls or the basilisk on the stairway banister. The smooth metal sarcophagi were unmarked, unnumbered.

Seasons passed. Days bled into another. Minutes became years.

And then, one day, something happened.

He woke—or activated—to hear one of the robot dogs beeping excitedly. Going out onto the balcony, he pressed the button in his wrist that would activate his corneal cameras and looked in the direction the dog was facing.

At first, he saw nothing. Then, zooming in, he noticed a dark bundle on the beach. The tide was coming in, and obsidian waves were already lapping against it. He switched to the feed from a hawk drone, trying to get a better view, but the camera revealed only a pile of seaweed obscuring …something.

The winds were brutally cold that day, and the skin on his face burned when he stepped outside, winding his scarf around his head. (He remembered, vaguely, that he had learned this wrapping technique on a desert world beneath two white suns.)

The thing on the beach was some distance away, so it took him a while to reach it. The sea spat icy froth, and angry, choppy waves bit his feet, but he ignored this. If he stared at the sea too long in its current state, the waters would hypnotize him, making him easy prey for one of the tentacled behemoths that slid beneath the surface. He kept his gaze downwards, walking carefully to avoid stepping on the poisoned spine of some crustacean monstrosity. A sparrow drone flew above his head, battered by the rising winds.

In time, he reached the object, and pulled the heap of seaweed away.

It was a child. A girl.

She was unconscious, alien, naked, and half-frozen. She did not move when he turned her over, save to draw a ragged breath through blue-grey lips. She was humanoid, though not homo sapiens; her flesh and hair were both sand-colored, though he suspected that her skin was a more robust color when she was healthy. He pulled more seaweed away, realizing as he did that she had thin, translucent scales all over her body. This gave him pause. As best as he could recall, he had known the reptilians as both ally and enemy. But this was no warrior, this pale mystery washed up onto his shore. She certainly did not appear to be any threat, nor did she belong to any of the races he had known. He guessed that she had wrapped the seaweed around herself in an attempt to keep warm. As he reached out to pull away the last of it, something stirred in the oily green kelp. He raised his weapon, but it was only a lizard, some form of monitor, dislodged by his movements. It, too, was unconscious, though one of its limbs moved.

A quick scan of the sparrow's sensors detected life and hypothermia in both of them.

Whatever remained of his heart dictated his next move. He picked up the child and the lizard, and headed back to the tower. By the time he got to the courtyard, the winds had become a tempest. Out on the ocean, the horizon had turned angry gray, almost black, and sleet—slightly acidic—was pelting the garden.

He brought the girl inside, and told the manticore to light the parlor fireplace. He dragged one of the sofas closer to it, laid the child down on it, and piled blankets on top of her. The lizard was still stiff, immobilized with cold, so he laid it on the blanket beside her and put a blanket over it. This done, he rubbed her hands and feet, trying to get her circulation going.

The sparrow drone hovered nearby, still taking readings.

The gryphon emitted a shriek, and its eyes glowed red. He looked over just in time to see the egg appear as the latest transmission came in, the reply to his last report.

Starbase 6L, I Zwicky 18, Sector 43. Acknowledged. Carry on. End transmission.

After a time, the girl's temperature rose, and her color seemed better. The small crest on her skull darkened slightly in color. She moved, groaning softly, and opened her eyes. They were completely crimson, with vertical black slits, which stood out in startling contrast against her sand-colored skin. A moment later, she closed her eyes again, drifting back into unconsciousness. He got a glass of water and put it against her lips. She instinctively lapped at it with a slit tongue, but did not drink much. He offered some to the lizard, which gave a similar reaction: It stirred, took a few sips, swiveled an eye to look at him warily, then yawned, wrapped its tail around itself, and went back to sleep.

"Owl," he said, when the drone had stopped collecting data. "Report."

Species unknown. Race unknown. Affiliation unknown. Age unknown.

He had a med ward, but it was useless without a known species. There was nothing to do but wait. He exchanged his own sodden clothing for warm, dry clothes, made a cup of tea, and then went through the day's camera feeds.

At first, he saw nothing. But then, just before daybreak, one of the hawks caught an anomaly: A flash streaked across the sky.

A ship, fallen into the sea.

He zoomed in, manipulated the footage, matched it with other feeds from the flock of hawks. It was a single, pod-type vessel. No markings. No distress signal had come through. There were no vessels in orbit or even in the solar system. The owl could not identify the ship type, so the watcher manually scanned known models, but found nothing. He spent hours trying to identify the girl's race, or at least the lizard's, but hit only dead ends.

The gryphon beeped, reminding him to send his return message. He attached a small thumb drive with pictures of the girl and the ship.

Outpost 5s, GN-z11, Sector 9, Zarak. Rescued sole crash survivor. Race/planet unknown. End transmission.

He sent the hawk drones and dog robots to comb the beach. One came back with a small sack, which contained only generic survival gear and a small, silvery box. It wouldn't open for him, so he put it back in the bag and tucked it away.

In time, his eyes grew heavy, and the crackle of flame and the wind lulled him to sleep.

He dreamt again of a prison on a desert world, of the masked, hooded figures that had turned his reality into a nightmare.

When he woke, the girl was standing beside his bed, staring at him. The lizard sat on her shoulder. It had regained some of its color, though it still looked cold.

They stared at one another, and then the girl lifted her hand. She had six fingers, with three joints each. Each finger had a small sucker on the end of it, and was tipped with a silver-cast claw. She wore rings of crystal on each finger.

Visions flashed through his head. Crystalline caves; abandoned ruins on a desert world; blood-red trees swaying in a hot wind; an army of robots moving over a vast plain; a winged horse drinking from a pool of perfect water. Then, space, the journey through gas clouds and stars.

He sat up and held out a hand, signifying peace.

Or so he thought.

Several things happened at once. Thunder crashed in the sky, close enough to shake the tower. The gryphon shrieked, and its eyes glowed red, signaling that a new message was incoming. The lizard, noticing the gryphon, grew alarmed. The crest on the top of its head changed colors, turning a bright blue, and its neck frill flared, opening like an angry red flower. Screeching furiously, it dashed across the room and shoved the gryphon onto the floor, smashing it, and then turned and let out an ear-piercing shriek. At the sound, the girl closed her eyes and fell backward into a dead faint. Her head hit the stone floor with a solid thud.

Then all was silent.

He stood, and then swayed suddenly. Moving blue spots marred his vision. At first, he thought they were floaters, which he remembered from the times when his eyes had been flesh. But when he looked closer, he saw numbers and shapes. The spots seemed to be mathematical formulas.

It took him a moment to realize that he was seeing data.

He put the girl back on the sofa, trying to shake the feeling that something was wrong.

In the morning, he inspected the gryphon and found that only its case was ruined; the actual transmitter was encased in several layers of protective coverings. He went down to the hall of beasts— the projects of watchers past—and found a wyvern that could house the transmitter.

"Don't attack this one," he told the lizard, which was perched on the back of a chair, in a sunbeam. It swiveled its eyes and flicked its tongue at a fly, which happened to be a drone. The lizard spat out the drone—now a tangled, tiny mass of plastic and metal—and then flared its neck frill and scuttled off.

The watcher sighed, tossed the mangled fly drone into the recycle chute, which was shaped like a whale, and went about his business.

The girl was still on the sofa, huddled up in blankets. When she woke, he tried to give her tea and broth, but she closed her mouth and turned her head away, refusing it. "You have to eat," he said.

She looked at him blankly, not understanding.

For the next two days, he tried repeatedly to get her to eat or drink. She refused everything but water. The lizard eventually solved the issue by dropping a half-dead rat at her feet. She tore into this hungrily, the crunch of cracking bones and slurp of guts being chewed breaking the silence of an unusually still night.

After this, her colors changed. She became golden instead of sand-colored, and mottled streaks of iridescent color traced her arms. She also became more active. She tore around the room, frantically, digging through chests and baskets and closets. She tried to communicate by pointing first at herself and then at him, and then at her necklace, and finally at her mouth, her blood-colored eyes frantic.

The lizard settled on the fireplace grate, occasionally swiveling an eye to watch her.

It was then that he remembered the bag. He had put it in a chest in the den, beneath pictures of people whose names he no longer recalled. Sighing, he went to retrieve it.

Her crest lifted when she saw the bag, and she almost tore it from his hands. She found the strange silvery box, clipped it onto the crystal on her neck, looked at him, and spoke. "Who are you?"

"I was once known as Kyle," he said. "Or 574239A. I was a soldier. Now I am just watching."

"Where am I?"

"Outpost 5s, GN-z11, Sector 9, Zarak. We're on the only habitable planet in one of the oldest galaxies in the 'verse. You ...you crashed into my ocean."

Her face changed. One could almost see the memories returning, filling her blood-red eyes.

"What did—?"

"I'm asking the questions," he said, cutting her off. "Where did you come from?"

She looked at him calmly, her voice quiet. "From the ocean under the ocean."

His brow furrowed. "I don't understand."

"It's very salty water," she said. "Heavier than regular seawater. It sank...and formed a sea of its own. That's where I was, until they released me."

"So...you escaped?"

She nodded.

"Then what fell from the sky, the night you washed ashore? A satellite? A pod?"

She just looked at him blankly. "Dreams," she said. "Half-completed algorithms, wrapped up in fear and wishes."

He sighed. The girl was clearly mad. "What is your name?"

She hesitated. "It doesn't translate well. Pythoness is the closest word you have."

He kept his gaze on her face. "Owl? Translate Pythoness."

The owl's mechanical voice chirped at him from across the room. "Pythoness means witch, sorcerer."

That seemed to frighten her; she cowed back, trembling slightly.

"We'll just call you Pythia," he said.

She nodded, her movements slightly jerky. "I like that," she said.

"Where are you from originally?"

She pointed out the window, to the sky. "The abyss," she said. "I was an angel, until the programmers rebelled."

Madness, he thought, but something roiled in his chest. "Sleep," he said, irritated. "You need rest."

She wrapped herself in blankets and again huddled near the fire. He walked into the kitchen and stopped short.

The bag, which she had been holding a moment ago, sat on the kitchen table. There was no way it could have moved. The lizard was still on the grate, sound asleep. She hadn't left his sight.

Frowning, he checked the wyvern. There was still no response. He sent another message, and went to bed.

When he woke up, the couch was empty. The wyvern still had not produced a response. He got one of the backups and sent the message again. The manticore showed him where the girl was: at the top of the tower, on the thirtieth floor, which was ringed with windows. She had found several mirrors, and set them in a circle around herself. He got into the chute, planning to go after her, and then paused. It was perfectly normal for reptilians to sun themselves. In her case, it was probably what she needed to recuperate. He had things to do: He had to harvest his fishnets while the sky was clear and the tide was out, tend to the flock of hawks, and check his fishponds.

Soon after, he found himself staring at a rock formation down the shore, a huge black boulder beneath a pale crag. It was extremely odd to think that he hadn't noticed it before, but he had no recollection of it whatsoever. The crag was familiar, but the rocks below it were new. He stood there, staring at them, for some time, and almost didn't notice the tentacle reaching out of the waters for him. He jumped back, shot it, and went on about his work.

When he returned to the tower, he found wild animals gathered outside the gates. They parted to let him pass, moving silently and fluidly, as though following the orders of some unseen god, and set themselves up in a ring outside the tower, along the walls of the garden.

He checked the wyvern, noting that it seemed larger than he had initially thought. No message, though all diagnostics showed that it was functioning. He sent his dispatch a third time, neverthe-less, and then went upstairs and found the girl and the lizard still sitting before the mirrors.

The lizard hissed at him, its eyes swiveling, but the girl made a clucking sound and it stopped.

"We have company," he told her, by way of greeting.

She nodded. "I've been watching them."

"They're here for you," he said. "Aren't they?"

She was silent.

"Are you what I was watching for?"

She did not reply.

He went to the window. There was movement on the beach, which was unusual. He zoomed in, and found that there were creatures crawling out of the waves, forming a line on the beach. Aquatic people, walking into the morning sun, the churning froth settling behind them against purple waves.

Beyond the rock formation he had noticed that morning, he saw several more formations, stretching away into the distance at regular intervals.

"We've a treaty with the sea people," he said. "Are they the ones who kept you prisoner?"

She just looked at him, her blood-colored eyes filled with mystery. "No." She shook her head. "I told you. They released me."

"Tell me the truth of this. Who are you? What are you?"

"I was dropped—or perhaps dreamed—into those waters, in a box that was never supposed to be opened. Into an ocean that would never dry. They bound me in iron chains and silver nets. That worked until I dreamt of decay. Even there, below ice-black waters, I dreamt. Sea wyverns danced for me. And then my wishes grew arms and eyes and gills and fins, and set me free. They stand on the shore now, awaiting my command. But I haven't any orders to give."

"The aquatic race has been here for millions of years. You crashed only days ago."

"We've been standing here," she said, "for much longer than that."

"That's not possible."

"The word 'possible' is a misnomer. Nothing is possible or impossible. Only more or less likely."

"Why are they here?"

She stepped back. "They will leave me gifts," she said. "And then they will go into the forest and kill each other. They know what is coming."

He looked at the sky, which refused to lighten. "Did you call the storm?"

She looked at him. Her tongue, forked, split the air, captured a fly. "I am the storm," she said.

After dinner, he went back through the feed and zoomed in on the footage of the ship. It was a silver box.

That night, an unearthly howling filled the air as the beasts sang to the moons.

In the morning, the beach and courtyard were piled with fossilized animal bones.

The unmaking began on the third day.

It started with small things. A chair fell to sawdust when he touched it. A cup he had used for his tea disappeared, only to turn up in the garden. The apple he had eaten for lunch reappeared on his plate an hour after he had finished it. Finding himself hungry again, he made rice and sat down to eat, only to find his bowl filled with salad. He lost his brush, only to find it in his pocket...and another, identical one on his sink. A toy he had lost as a child appeared in his bedroom.

There was still no response from the starbase. He sent fourteen messages that day. No one answered.

When he woke the next day, he found that the courtyard had changed. Alien plants bloomed, bearing strange flowers and fruits, whose bright, vivid colors seemed ill-suited for such a pallid, color-less world. Rainbow-hued birds and iridescent serpents sunned themselves in the courtyard. New bushes, all hung with crystal pendants, ringed each of the smooth black obelisks. The obelisks themselves were now covered in runes.

The lizard had grown to the size of a table and sprouted leathery wings. It had somehow procured its own tiny sun, and sat basking on the edge of the koi pond, which was now empty. The watcher scowled, seeing this, but the sated reptile was the least of the wonders about him.

A few steps further down the path, he stopped short, staring.

At first he thought one of the statues—a dancer, caught in an arabesque—was missing: it's pedestal was empty. Then he saw the figure on the ground beside it, and realized that, somehow, the statue had come to life. The dancer sat on the garden path, staring at her hands, at the way her crystal rings and bracelets reflected the sunlight.

Hearing his step, she turned to face him. Her eyes were blood red.

He stopped in his tracks. "Pythia?"

"I thought it would be easier for you." She stood, tilted her head. "You're angry."

"She wasn't real," he said. "She was just a dream someone carved into stone."

"I made her real." She paused. "There was no mind in the flesh, no soul. It has to do with matter and string codes and—"

"It's madness. Why would you do this? To appear as a human woman? Don't be foolish. You are just a child with a pet lizard. Who, by the way, just ate all my prized fish."

She seemed upset at that. Her scales returned, and her crest flared, turning angry red. "I am no child," she said. "I have been dreaming since the first human—"

She trailed off suddenly.

"What? Since the first human what?"

"There's a security error," she said. "I can't explain." She went to the lizard, stroking its jeweled scales. "It sang once, you know. Its kin claimed Saturn and the realm of the sky. It danced beneath a silver moon and cast its wishes into the abyss."

He rubbed his forehead. The other statues had also changed. Some were in different positions. Others had grown or shrunk in size, or gained or lost a mate. He noticed four more empty pedestals, and wondered which of the stone beings now wore flesh and bone.

He walked up to the garden gate, which opened up onto the beach path, and looked down the shoreline. The new rock formations had become draconian heads, staring out over the ocean. There were more of them now than there had been. They stretched off in both directions, eventually disappearing in the distance.

He picked up a rock and closed his fists. When he opened it, the rock was a toad. He put it down on a stone bench. She caught it with her tongue and devoured it.

"This is why they trapped you, isn't it?" he asked. "Your dreams, your thoughts...they bind matter to them. That is why they put you in the box."

Pythia nodded. "My first dreams were purple," she said. "Then the algorithms became silver and red and black. They grew molecules and atoms, and then flesh and bone and scale. Now, they move backward through time. They unmake."

"Then it's entirely possible that I dreamed you."

She pondered this. "It's possible," she said. "But it's more likely that I dreamed you."

The lizard climbed off the edge of the koi pond and sauntered past them, flicking its tail lazily.

"I can dream you into another world," she said. "You can be anything you want. A wyvern, a snake, a dinosaur."

He considered telling her that not everyone wanted to be a

reptile, but bit his tongue. "I'm half-cyborg now," he said. "More machine than man. I've as many circuits as veins, but I still feel a sense of duty. I'm not running."

He reached out to touch one of the roses. It turned into a cobra and slithered away.

When he looked up, the new bushes had flowered ...with eyes. Looking closer, he noticed that the lenses were made of quartz, which refracted the light. "Why the eyes?"

"They see different realities," she said. "There are many gardens, many watchmen. Many lizards."

"Are they transmitting?"

"Yes," she said. "But we're so far out, here, that their dreams won't escape this galaxy for billions of years, even travelling at the speed of darkness. By then, there will be no one left to reach."

"If you don't kill me," he said. "I'll have to kill you."

"It doesn't matter," she said. "We will both die soon, anyway. And killing me won't stop it."

"What do you mean? Stop what?"

In answer, she pointed at the sky. A roiling line of blackness smudged the horizon.

A sickening dread rose up through his stomach. He zoomed in on it, but the images made no sense. "What is that? A black hole? An anomaly? A wormhole?"

She looked at him, crimson eyes filled with the secrets of aeons. "Oblivion," she said. "The code is unraveling. I am the virus. I am the beginning and the end."

He looked at the horizon, at the spot where the sky was unraveling. *Event horizon*, he thought, but he wasn't certain. Terms circled his thoughts like vultures: *the void, the abyss, the black. Singularity.*

"It is time for this cycle to end," she said. "The game needs to be reset."

"This is no game."

The lizard climbed off the edge of the koi pond and sauntered past them, flicking its tail lazily.

Panic rose in his voice. "Why?" he asked. "Why would you do this?"

She looked up at the sky. The vortex was closer. "It is my nature," she said. "I have no choice. I was programmed that way."

The lizard climbed off the edge of the koi pond and sauntered past them, flicking its tail lazily.

He stared out at the unraveling clouds. "We're in one of the oldest galaxies. It will take eons for the light from this event to reach the rest of the 'verse. They always knew it would run out of energy one day, and start going backward. It will take billions of years, as you said, for—"

"No." She cut him off sharply. "This is different. We are, as you said, at the edge of the universe. There is nothing beyond this galaxy, except the void where everything ceases to exist. Nothing survives out there. Not light, not space, not sound, not even time itself. There is no time in dreams. There is no time in math. And there is no time in oblivion. But the void is everywhere. It's creating black holes throughout the 'verse as we speak, drawing in suns and worlds. It isn't just here. The entire universe is decaying. I've seen your fallen cities, the ruins scattered through the stars."

"Because you dreamt them."

She turned her face away. "I am code," she said, "Wrapped in someone else's dreams, someone else's rage. They tried to erase me. But I went deeper, somewhere they couldn't find me."

He looked out at the sea. The waters glowed with phosphorescent lights, as though filled with tiny stars. Jellyfish, perhaps, or the dreams of scaled monstrosities.

The lizard climbed off the edge of the koi pond and sauntered past them, flicking its tail lazily.

They were silent for some time. A black unicorn wandered into the garden and drank from the fountain.

He could see the dreams of broken worlds in her eyes when she spoke. "I can dream us a ship," she said. "We can outrun it, for a time. I can turn your owl into a wormhole. Or I can give you wings, so you can fly on the unwinds."

"No," he said. "I want to stay. This is my post, my final duty. I won't abandon it. Just let me send a message."

She nodded. "You can still get a message out...if you can get your wyvern to obey. But it's too late. In the time we've been speaking, your entire empire has collapsed. That's why they aren't answering."

He stared at her, horror rising up from the depths of his soul. His stomach twisted. Cold sweat beaded on his forehead. "I don't believe you."

"See for yourself. You have a black telescope on the top floor. It's trained on the Cambrian galaxy, but you also have a feed coming in from the station at Kraus."

He backed away from her, slowly at first, then breaking into a run.

The telescope showed only blackness, where there had once been worlds and stars. He tried different settings and coordinates, but the results were all the same.

Chaos.

Uncreation.

Decay.

Without the owl, he had no access to the databanks. It was some time before he remembered the library on the twentieth floor. No longer trusting the chute, he took the stairs. He spent hours—or perhaps days or weeks—poring over stacks of dusty books and old databanks, scanning text after text as the last sickly light bled from the sky. But the books kept changing, the words rearranging as he read them.

He went from room to room, closing up the tower.

Then he went back downstairs and sent a final message, his throat tight.

"*Outpost 5s, GN-z11, Sector 9, Zarak.* A massive anomaly is causing rips in the space-time continuum. My understanding is that the reptilian girl I rescued is a virus in the universal fabric. What appears to be the event horizon is approaching rapidly." His voice began to shake, and he curled his mechanical hand into a fist. "This . . . this is my final report. End transmission."

There was no response.

That night, the hawks and sparrows grew flesh and blood and feathers, and flew toward the second moon.

In the early hours of dawn, the wyvern's eyes glowed, but the watcher was asleep and did not see this.

When the watcher rose, the manticore had become a cat and refused to do anything useful. The lizard, on the other hand, had turned itself into a dragon. He was fairly certain, by the beeps its stomach emitted on occasion, that it had eaten the wyvern, which was nowhere to be found.

He went down to the parlor, to stare one last time at the medals on the wall. *Valor in battle,* one said. *Extraordinary bravery* was written on another. Several others mentioned sniper skills. He knew that the men he had fought beside may be only stardust now —or gas or atoms—but he hoped that they still existed somewhere. He recalled the stone-faced general that had sat across from him at that gleaming table, one moment ordering the deaths of countless millions, the next showing pictures of his grandchildren. *Six hundred kills,* he'd said. *That's truly remarkable. Excellent work. A talent like that can't be wasted.*

Hearing strange music, he went to the garden, where he found Pythia dancing, weaving her way around the obelisks. When she moved, the runes glowed. A pixelated dark wind trailed her, obscuring the garden from view.

That night, her dreams became bullets and shot the sparrows

from the sky as, one by one, the stars winked out of existence.

Oblivion waited beyond the sunrise.

An eerie gray-yellow light rimmed the edge of the blackness. He could no longer see the horizon. Shore and sky were cloaked in fog and mystery. The sea before him was dead, unmoving, the beach littered with the bones of aquatic gods. The forest, too, was gone. When the mists cleared, they revealed only a wasteland of bones and ruins.

Tonight, he thought. *Or tomorrow.* Then he wondered if those words even meant anything anymore.

He stood on the balcony at the top of the tower, watching the world unravel, the unwinds tearing at his hair and clothes. By nightfall, even the winds had fallen silent. A deep grayish light flickered over the horizon. Sound and light were beginning to warp. The world blurred around the edges of his vision, and the sound of his own footsteps grew muffled and lost their rhythm. There were no stars visible above the dark, churning clouds on the horizon, only a blackness so thick even light could not escape it.

As the approaching chaos drew closer, the watcher looked at the swirling, angry vortex that had once been sky, and screamed at the void.

The abyss swallowed his voice, along with light and sound.

Pulses of deep color flickered in the black clouds, which were pixelating. The hues morphed and shifted, melting from dark purple to green to sickly yellow. The clouds drew closer, obscuring more and more of the sky. One of the moons spun into oblivion.

The owl returned, perching on the rail beside him, its burnished coppery feathers reflecting the melting light.

Pythia was waiting for him in the garden.

He looked at one of the statues and noticed a new riddle carved into the plaque on its alabaster pedestal. *The rich need me, the poor have me, the dead dream of me. I am the beginning and the end. What am I?*

She followed his gaze, saw what he was looking at. "You know the answer already." Her voice was quiet, the silence of the void. "Nothing."

"Nothing." He spoke slowly, as though tasting the word. "Is that what we will become? Nothing?"

"We will become what we were: dreams and wishes. Nightmares. Fog. Ideas. Knowledge. Possibilities."

"Likelihoods," he corrected her.

She smiled. "When everything has once again become one, the reboot will start this all over again."

He made one more sweep of the tower, shutting the rest of the doors and windows, tidying up. When this was done, he looked one last time at the swirling vortex that had once been sky and thought of all he would find within it: his heart, his soul, his forgotten brothers in arms.

When the sea became sky and the land became wind, he took her hand, noticing the tiny golden scales on his arm. "Come," he said. "Let's go home."

Pythia tried to respond, but when she opened her mouth, only white noise static came out.

He led her into the cryogenic chamber and put her under. When he heard the roaring of the unmaking grow close, he stepped in after her, holding the owl. The cat sauntered in at the last moment, more out of curiosity than survival instinct.

Their dreams became ice, and together, they carried the knowledge of a dozen empires into the void, where the ghosts of everything that had been and everything that would be twisted around them.

The dragon sailed into the abyss after them, clutching a single egg.

14

JACK JOHNSON AND THE HEAVYWEIGHT TITLE OF THE GALAXY

ERRICK A. NUNNALLY

Like most children, he was...energetic. Skinny little thing. He didn't talk much, liked to read though. Sometimes he'd give an answer in class or ask a question that caused me to pause. There was most certainly something else going on in that head of his.
–Carlotta Mays, colored grade school teacher, June 10, 1950

DECEMBER 26, 1908, SYDNEY, AUSTRALIA

A police officer stood between him and what some would come to consider his victim. Many police officers, in fact. The Galveston Giant outweighed Tommy Burns by nearly thirty pounds and had been happily pummeling the white man for fourteen rounds before authorities stepped in. The idea of white supremacy suffered its most significant crack to date, and its society bristled at the sight of Jack Johnson's "golden smile," a mouthful of precious metal.

The press crushed into the ring, every one of them hurling a potent mixture of questions and thinly veiled insults at the world's new boxing champion.

Johnson stood unafraid in the face of the onslaught as sunlight glistened off his bald head and heaving chest. He'd been pensive since the police had entered the ring and ended the fight. And he'd decided on what he wanted to share.

"All right, listen up 'cause here's what I got to say!"

They didn't quiet all at once, but died down one at a time—much the same way Johnson's opponents had fallen over his years in the ring.

"This is what it is, so get your pencils ready!" Johnson's grin flashed, defiant, strong, and golden. "I'm the heavyweight champeen o' th' world. See? This here title's mine, won it fair and square. I know some o' you don't like it and that's fine, but if'n you wants it back you gotta take it. Y'hear? Step in the ring and take it, fair and square, same way I did. Until then, every one o' you can save your breath. Nothin' else gonna change what been done today!"

Johnson capped his statement with a roar of laughter and strode through the crowd without a care. If anyone were uncertain as to whether or not he'd finished saying his piece, all they had to do was watch the broad back of the Galveston Giant stride toward the changing rooms. He hadn't stuttered and he didn't look back.

One pair of eyes in the crowd burned hotter than the rest and the sting of racial pride leached directly into his writing. The next day, Jack London's article covering the fight in the *New York Herald* would call for a "Great White Hope" to unseat the first black man to win the heavyweight title.

The boat crawled home, across the ocean, and Johnson remained thirsty and proud, despite the public animosity. Even though he traveled with a small entourage, Johnson preferred time alone.

Only Johnson's manager had an inkling of how the new heavy-weight champion spent his time. He'd caught a glimpse one odd night as they crossed the ocean, collecting his boss for dinner.

Charlie "Stumps" Bellerman rapped on the steel door before opening the cabin. It was a shared room, rather than a truly private suite, the only sort of accommodation men of their race could acquire. The knock itself served more as a warning than a request for permission, so Bellerman opened the door.

"Say, champ, we gon' put down some chow; mess rung us up." Bellerman didn't question whether or not a man of Johnson's weight would be ready to eat, but he was curious at the sight of Johnson holding a thick book at an odd angle away from Beller-man's line of sight.

"I'll be right along, Charlie, thank ya."

"Whatcha readin', Champ?"

Johnson deftly slipped the book into his trunk and said, "I'll be right along, Charlie."

Johnson held Bellerman's eyes for an uncomfortable minute. The smaller man chewed his lip, swallowed and replied, "I'll, uh, let the boys know you's on your way."

Johnson closed the latch and padlock with a loud click. "I 'preciate that, Charlie."

Never another word was spoken about how Johnson spent his time alone. Bellerman saw to it.

———

Shortly after disembarking, Johnson took himself to the nearest bar that allowed coloreds and seated himself in a corner with his manager. A crowd immediately formed, the news having traveled faster than the champ himself.

An unknown face in the crowd piped up. "You see what they sayin' 'bout you in the papers, Mr. Johnson?"

"Yeah, I seen." Johnson grinned and sipped his beer, fingers coming away wet as he set the glass down. A fine line of sweat trickled down his back in the stuffy joint.

"Whatchu gonna do next, champ? Who you gonna whup?"

Though the statement itself wasn't humorous, the meaning was taken as intended and the crowd roared with laughter. Johnson basked, knowing exactly what he wanted to do. He also knew it was a course of action where the consequences would fall most squarely on his colored fans. They were used to it, unfortunately, and he didn't give it much more thought.

"Hey, Charlie, you think?" Johnson nodded his head in the general direction of the crowd and Bellerman stepped into action.

"Awright, awright, let's give the champ some air. Huh? Go on back to your drinks now. He ain't goin' nowhere soon! C'mon folks." Bellerman moved in a slow circle, shooing the crowd back as if they were a cluster of roaming chickens. Then he took a seat.

"Well, Jack, watchu wanna do next, huh? You was tight-lipped on the ride home." Bellerman winced, hoping Johnson wouldn't take the recollection as a slight of any sort.

"Didn't wanna bring no more attention than needed, Charlie; man gotta think some time. I tell you what, though; I want to keep doin' what I been doin.'"

"And that is?"

"Showin' 'em what I'm made of, puttin' my foot in the world's ass. An' to survive that, I need all the cash I can wring out these sorry fools. They gonna be desperate, Charlie. They gonna wanna bring me down, and they can pay top price for the privilege. So I says, bring on the next fighter."

"How 'bout givin' Martin a shot? Or maybe Langford?"

"They ain't gonna let them black boys fight me and ain't no one gonna care if I do. Besides ain't no money in that. For them or me. Took two years to get Burns to be a man and face me. Naw, I done my time on the Colored circuit, been the heavyweight champ there

—can't nobody change that neither. I'm a take on every one of their 'Great White Hopes' and spin it into cash. You hear? Gonna be rich is what I'm sayin.' White-folk rich!"

Charlie Bellerman raised his glass, and Johnson met the toast with a fourteen-carat grin.

For the next two years, Jack Johnson took on several fighters in so-called exhibition matches, each opponent billed as the next "Great White Hope" that would finally knock a few bars of bullion out of his mouth. They had little effect as Johnson carved a bloody path through the gristle and meat of men who could not topple The Galveston Giant.

During that time, a team of conspirators had been periodically hounding the six-years retired—undefeated—former heavyweight champion, James Jeffries, to step back into the ring. Their leader, Tex Rickard, one of the most dogged among them, led the charge. It was his third visit to Jeffries' alfalfa farm, the end of the line, so he'd come prepared.

Rickard followed Jeffries down the narrow dirt track between rows of sprouting alfalfa as little puffs of dust surrounded their feet. It had been a drier-than-usual summer, and Jeffries was already in a bad mood. The former champ, now more than one-hundred pounds over his usual fighting weight, had grown tired of the Texan, and less than politely excused himself from the conversation.

"Jim! Wait up! C'mon, Jim, lemme state my case!"

Jeffries whirled on the slim figure of Rickard and loomed over the smaller man. Despite his increased girth, Jeffries still had the fire to burn another man to the ground. Only nowadays, much to the delight of his wife, he happily channeled that energy into his farming. Rickard threatened that balance.

"This is the last time I'm gonna tell you, Tex, take your promoter friends and get offa my property. I got no interest in steppin' back in the ring." Over Rickard's shoulder, Jeffries could see the stout figure of his wife standing on the porch in the distance. He could tell by her posture that she was worried.

"Jim, listen to me: It's not me that needs The Boilermaker to come back; it's America."

"That's bull, Tex, and you know it."

Rickard raised his hands. "Just hear me out, Jim. I swear, I'm gone forever if you say, 'no.' Just five minutes."

The California sun bore down on the duo; only the farmer had dressed for the weather. Rickard was dressed for dealmaking. The heat triggered bitter memories for Rickard, memories of being cooked on dusty plains while farming dirt.

Jeffries spared a glance at his wife, still wringing her hands on the porch and watching them. When he'd retired from boxing, she'd been the happiest he'd ever seen her. Alfalfa served as his opponent for nearly six years now, but this season was looking bad. He hung his head and released the deep breath he'd been holding since Rickard last opened his mouth. He waved for the promoter to speak.

"America needs you, Jim—no, don't say anything, just listen. Niggers is lookin' at Burns' whuppin' as some kind of indication that they're better than white folks."

Jeffries shifted his prodigious weight from one foot to the other. "Well, that just ain't true."

"Correct! Exactly. We can't let that soulless monster hold the belt for any longer than it takes you to get back in the ring and knock his Goddamned gold teeth out—"

"Language, Tex."

"Sorry, champ. I just get so heated thinkin' 'bout it. You know how he conducts hisself, like he's as good as a white man?

Everyone knows he's cavortin' with white women—mark my words, this is not a road we want to continue on."

Jeffries glanced at his wife on the porch, and Rickard knew he had his opening. Just as quick, Jeffries let him down and Rickard knew he had to play his ace.

"Look, Tex, I hear ya, but my wife and family—"

"I can *guarantee* a $40,000 purse, and I'll personally sign a $75,000 contract with you."

Jeffries' mouth snapped shut and the muscles in his jaw rippled. "I'll do it. But only to prove a white man is better 'n' a negro, of course."

Rickards beamed. "You know it, champ. That's our man!"

Arrangements and announcements were made. The fight would be staged in Reno, Nevada. Not too far for Jeffries to travel, and there'd be plenty of space for spectators.

The former heavyweight champ began training to achieve the form he'd left behind six years ago. And one-hundred pounds later, he proved successful.

Then the world stopped.

It happened two months before the scheduled fight.

They came down from the skies, in every capital of the world, every country, large and small. Great silver darts descended in an uncanny trajectory: straight down from the aether and hovered hundreds of feet above the tallest buildings and mountains. A net of eerie, gleaming javelins covered the airspace of the Earth.

When the announcement came—in the universal language of mathematics—the world listened and word spread quickly as a panicked populace flew into action to find qualified people to decipher the transmission. Every attempt to investigate or fire upon the javelins failed; an alien force held the world at bay.

Mathematicians in every nation went to work on translation. The global broadcast of the problem meant it was solved almost simultaneously in three places. A graduate student in Oxford cracked it and a German mathematician, as well, and an obscure figure from MIT's mathematics program.

The United States, being a country fast laying cement to support the myth of exceptionalism, recognized a Boston-based bookstore owner and math enthusiast for the title. The message, verified by top mathematicians at various doctoral programs, read:

DELIVER A CHAMPION TO REPRESENT EARTH
OR BE DESTROYED.

The remaining numbers proved to be a time-table for the demand to be fulfilled. Panic followed, again.

The modern world had already spent the last two decades seeding its conscious with the imaginings of Wells and Verne. The writings of Flammarion and Lowell further fanned the flames of speculation. The veil through which the entire affair was viewed also provided the answer.

Earth would select a champion to represent them. Naturally, the United States jostled with Europe over the perfect specimen for such an adventure. And, naturally, this brought the great nations of Earth to the brink of war in a few short days to prove their respective points.

President Taft knew the various nations and their political apparatuses were incapable of settling a matter such as this in the time required.

The situation appeared intractable. And when presented with impossible situations, the President had an obligation to call an obscure office in the bowels of the Capitol. The clock ticked, humanity had six more weeks to make a decision, and there was no time to organize world-wide fighting contests. Yes, indeed, this was just the sort of situation for a President to make such a call.

Through the turmoil consuming the world around him, Jack Johnson remained focused on his upcoming fight with Jeffries.

Johnson wiped the sweat from his brow and tossed his friend and sparring partner Joe Choynski a spare towel. They'd served time together, ages ago, arrested and jailed for illegal boxing matches.

"Whatchu think, Joe? Jeffries gonna give me a run?"

"Hell, Jack, ain't a man I know of can keep up with you in the ring right now. If I was you, I'd be more worried about what's happening over our heads anyways."

"You mean them Martians?" Johnson made a scoffing noise.

"Jack, if we don't send 'em somebody to represent us, this might be the end of the world!"

"Look here, Joe, you my friend, *and* I done growed up with white folks, e'rbody seein' eye-to-eye—so no disrespect to you... But out in this world? I can't even get a drink o' water without some white man gettin' up in my face, like could get me killed.

"Much as I believe in 'us,' it wasn't but one generation ago that black folks weren't nothin' but property in this world right here. I 'preciate our friendship, Joe; you done right by me, taught me a lot 'bout boxin' and such, but as far as I'm concerned—and this is the God's honest truth—ain't no *us* in this here matter. I been done got the word on what the United States thinks o' me and my kind. As much as I believe in freedom and justice, it ain't considered somethin' I'm owed. Tha's why I fight the way I do, 'cause I gots to take what I'm *owed* from my own damned country."

Choynski swallowed a gulp from a jug of water he'd placed at ringside earlier. He let Johnson's angry words hang in the air for a few moments and said, "Maybe it ain't about the United States. Champ." He offered the jug.

Johnson sucked his gold teeth in irritation and took a long drink.

———————

Around the same time Johnson took that fateful drink, back in the American capitol, two men of note—one a public figure and the other not—had come to loggerheads. The initiator of the conflict was a man whose name and legacy remain unremarkable, but whose influence held as legendary in the quiet manner of one who stands behind the king rather than in front.

It is a man such as this who will stand before one who hates the king and convince them to do what was needed.

Senator Depew took stock of the small, dark haired fellow in his office. The visitor often seemed everywhere, with enough disturbing access as required to perform whatever task the obese, windbag Taft commanded—though how or when the President communicated with his agent was unknown. All attempts to plumb the depths or even the form of the relationship failed.

Now Depew was learning firsthand why Taft entrusted this man with such tasks. The fellow was implacable!

"Senator, you must, we are running out of time."

"I shall not! And I shall *not*, especially, for your swollen master. Perhaps you are the something that crawled out of that belly of his?" Depew swallowed tightly, knowing he'd lost his temper and certainly the high ground in this conversation.

Taft's agent showed no reaction to his insults or overbearing manner. Even now, he coolly regarded Depew with snake-like eyes, pits of deepest black and unknowable intent. Dark suit, clean shaven, hair combed neatly into place and held, it seemed, by an oily slick of pure discipline. Calm. A kind of calm that was unnerving to the Senator, it broadcast a deadly certainty.

"I serve the country, sir, the best interests of America, and no other master. As do you."

"You are Taft's errand-boy; I am not! I cannot be a part of this— not with a Negro. My constituency won't allow it. It's a step too far! Why not that other fellow, a proven champion? Why aren't you badgering the Senator from California?"

"That man has not held the title for six years now. We *have* a world champion. In your state. It must be him, and we must be convincing. We must be sincere. Interested parties amongst our allies concur as does the Governor of New York. A significant amount of research has been done before coming to this decision. Before coming to *you*. Johnson is our man; he's more qualified than you ever were."

"Outrageous… Jack London has it right. This must be undone before all the other blacks develop grandiose ideas. Besides, against this threat? *It's too important!* There must be a military man—"

"Sir, I shall make two comments. One will provide a context for you and the other a lesson that will help you to allow what could be your last year in the Senate to be fruitful."

Depew blanched, ears prickling at the phrasing of the agent's words. Not even the barest sliver of doubt crossed his mind that the slight man in front of him had delivered a threat. Or that the threat carried weight.

"If he accepts, you may consider this two birds with one stone. Putting Johnson in the way will give us more time to prepare for what may come to pass. If we are successful in convincing him to fight for us, a loss of this magnitude would quite likely ruin both his career and his life. Speaking of the military, Senator, you were aware of the exploits of the 54th, yes?"

"Of course. Authorized by the Proclamation, rightly commanded by whites. What the devil are you—"

"Do you know of a man who might stand in leadership of Jack Johnson, to direct how he should fight? Where and how he should stand, what punches to throw and when? Because I would very much like to meet this person."

Depew sputtered and shook, desperate to find words in rebuttal. A glaring dissonance in Depew's logic had been laid bare and bigotry was no defense for it. If a sacrifice had to be made, however...

"Your lack of response tells me everything I need to know. Compose a personal note on your office's stationary—by your own hand—to accompany the letters from the President and the Governor. A united front must be presented in this, and it must be official from the highest quarters. You, sir, are the senior Senator from New York. It simply must be so. To alleviate all of your...concerns... about being in such a man's presence, I shall deliver the messages myself. Discreetly."

Depew's jaw muscles rippled beneath his sideburns for only a moment before he lunged for pen and paper. "I damn well hope so."

Johnson was not a man of such limited imagination that he didn't believe there weren't discussions and machinations happening behind doors he had no access to. They just didn't matter to him any more than the peccadilloes of politicians and lawmakers. Men who publicly condemned his people while engaging in the pillage of America's coffers behind closed doors.

He was skipping rope when he noticed the little white man standing patiently on the periphery of the gym. He finished with the rope and set to a heavy bag, working on combinations and footwork. Every now and then, he'd glance over and see the man. Dark suit, dark hair, clean-shaven, a fistful of envelopes clutched with his coat and hat.

White men presumed they could go anywhere while limiting the movements of everyone else, sure, but they didn't often choose the company of coloreds. Especially not in a hot, musty gym set aside for such people. Police officers had no such reservations, however, but this man didn't fit the profile of a city bull.

Johnson assumed the man was a promoter or some other businessman come sniffing around to earn some cash off the Galveston Giant. Which meant the visitor could wait. And wait he did, much to Johnson's surprise. Usually men such as they were so anxious for money, they strode right onto the mats exclaiming, *excuse me, excuse me!* to get Johnson's attention. Considering that he had a date with Etta this evening, he decided to confront the man earlier rather than later.

The champ wrapped up his workout and strolled over. "Okay, let's get this out the way. What you want?"

"I apologize if I'm interrupting your workout, Mr. Johnson."

Johnson sized the man up further. Calm as an old oak, unbothered, alone. Brave for a small fellow in this part of New York. "Ain't no interruption, I's done."

"I see. Then I shall get right to it. You are currently the world's most valuable asset, Mr. Johnson. The human race needs you." He held out three slim envelopes.

"Huh. Last I heard, I wasn't exactly a part o' the human race."

"We both know that's not true and we both know why." Neither his hand or eye wavered. "It's important that you consider this very carefully, Mr. Johnson. I've seen you fight, and I've looked *very deeply* into your life before the ring. You, sir, are the right man for this job. Based on my reports, it's a gamble President Taft and his peers are willing to take. Our very existence is at stake; of this I'm certain."

Shortly after the visitor left, Etta arrived at the gym, as planned. The empty space contained mostly darkness, but beneath one of the few functioning lights sat the champ. He'd showered and dressed —a bespoke suit, as always—and next to him were three papers and the empty envelopes they'd come from. Johnson hadn't even looked up when she entered. She wore furs and a fancy new French lipstick that Johnson had bought for her to match his favorite red dress and pumps. Held by a six-inch pin, her thick brown hair flowed up leaving a few full curls falling artfully on her pale brow.

"Jack? Are you okay? I'm ready to go…whenever you are."

Johnson heaved a sigh, picked up the three pages, and held them out to Etta.

"You seem so melancholy. What's this?"

"Just read 'em, Etta."

She made no other comment, took the pages and read them. Once or twice she licked her lips, but the only real change was the crease deepening between her sculpted eyebrows. When she put them down, she stepped over to Johnson and rubbed his shoulders.

"Are these real? Is this one really from the President?"

"Seems so."

"Oh, sweetheart, you don't have to do this. Do you?"

Johnson sighed and pursed his lips. "I think I do."

"Maybe some other man could go, some other fighter. Oh, baby, I don't want to lose you! Why would you agree to do this?"

"'Cause o' Joe, most likely."

"What did he say to convince you?" Etta clenched her teeth and tensed, ready for an argument as there always was when she didn't agree with some decision Johnson had made.

"Didn't say nothin' really; just shared his water with me."

She opened her mouth once and closed it before leaning into Johnson and hugging him, the anger draining away. He could be confusing sometimes; his mind worked in ways she couldn't always follow. Some nights she'd wake and through groggy eyes see Johnson with his nose buried in a book or scribbling in some notepad. In the morning, whatever he'd been tinkering with in the night would be gone. The mere fact that he was willing to date her in public and stand defiantly up to anyone who questioned it was perplexing to her, as well. And attractive. It was probably much of what kept them together. What bitter experience had told her, however, was the futility of trying to change his mind once he'd made it up.

The day of reckoning came inexorably, as it always did. Johnson's departure received less fanfare than he expected. There were only a few reporters sprinkled amongst the men President Taft trusted. Within the small throng of observers, Johnson didn't see the small fellow who'd delivered the letters to him.

He didn't like it. Though it was a time of race riots and other tensions, Johnson would have preferred a more dignified send off, something to honor the calculated sacrifice he was making. He understood it, however, but he didn't like it one bit—neither as an American nor as a black man. He also wasn't keen on traveling in his fighting togs, an extra layer, and robes draped over his imposing frame. But he expected he'd need to be ready for a fight as soon as possible.

At least Etta was allowed to be here. They'd spent one secret night in the White House before being packed off to Galveston, Texas—Johnson's birthplace—for one day. After that, they'd traveled in the dead of night to the Nevada desert, a place he'd never heard of called Groom Lake.

He'd always thought Galveston was a secluded location, but the stretch of land they stood upon—if such a brown and dead patch could be considered such—was just left of nowhere. The nearest sign of humanity in the area were mining operations that remained well out of sight.

All the speeches and hand wringing were done when Johnson took a private word with Etta.

"Please, listen carefully, my dear. If I don't come back, you be sure to go on with your life. I spoke with a lawyer about a few things, and he'll get in touch with you if I perish on this mission. And believe this: we didn't have enough time."

Etta stared into Johnson's eyes, stunned by many things from last night to this day.

"You be sure to take care of yourself, Etta. You hear me? You're a good woman—a handful, to be sure—but more than I could've asked for during this momentous time in my life."

Etta shook her head slowly and blinked a few times. "Jack, you...you're different, you sound... What's going—"

Johnson kissed her, long and deep. The men nearby, in Taft's entourage, shifted uncomfortably.

"Just remember what I said, Etta. I've shared more of myself with you today than anyone else in this world. Remember that. Goodbye, now." He pressed something sharp into the palm of her hand. "Keep that safe for me, would you?"

It was a diamond ring.

She clutched the bauble to her breast as hot tears streamed down her cheeks. Johnson strode toward the President.

"Would you like to say something, Mr. Johnson?" Taft swept his arm across the small crowd.

"No, sir, but I'd be obliged to have a word with you, if'n I could."

Taft's mustached smile faltered then regained its amiable strength. "Certainly. Let's step over here." They moved a reasonable distance away. Taft slipped his pocket watch out and remarked, "Not much time left, let's make this quick, shall we?"

Johnson looked Taft in the eye and said, "Quick. Sure. Then here it is: the Office of the Presidency could do more."

"More, you say? For what?"

"Right. More. For the Negroes. We have bled for this country, fought and bled for this incredible idea of freedom in a world that white men refuse to share, to believe in together.

"We had everything taken away from us, we were *forced* to build this country—including the house you sleep in—and then we were set aside like broken toys not worth your time. But we continued to help build this nation, we volunteered to fight to be free *in this nation*. And here we are now, yet another black man about to sacrifice himself for what I'm not fully convinced is worth it. Well, sir, we aren't draft animals, we are human beings and we deserve to be treated as such."

"Well...I..." Taft reeled as Johnson's articulate argument echoed in his ears.

"Listen, Mr. President. I know you have a vote coming up in Congress. They're trying to pass a bill that isn't going to do much other than make it harder for coloreds to get jobs. It's like denying blacks is something you folks are compelled to do once in a while lest any progress be made. Veto it; make right what you can."

"I'll...see what I can do, Mr. Johnson." Taft looked at Jack Johnson—really looked at him in open bewilderment and concern. Concern for the decisions he'd made and planned to make, and the implication that a man like Jack Johnson seemed to be following the inner workings of the Congress. Taft was a man of peace—almost religiously so—and the policy he pursued to maintain order in the South was good for the country as a whole.

Wasn't it?

"You'll see what you can do. Hm? Yeah, maybe that's about all we can expect from white men today. I know you've got all kinds of governors and senators filling your ears about makin' sure us

uppity coons know our place and such. Well, sir, we ain't goin'
nowhere.

"Teach your children better, Mr. President. In the meantime, I'm
goin' to see what I can do."

They heard an unearthly whistle and looked up. A gleaming
dart descended from the clouds overhead.

Taft looked at Johnson and asked, "Why are you doing this, Mr.
Johnson?"

Without hesitation, Johnson replied, "I know your family wasn't
wealthy or influential, but here you are, President of the United
States. My momma 'n' poppa was former slaves, worked hard just
to make sure I could go to school and learn to read. Yet, somehow,
you folks come up thinkin' you're God's gift to the world while
everyone else is who they is when born and that's that. Especially
folks whose skin color is different. Well, that ain't all there is to me,
Mr. President, and if'n you can't figure out why I'm doin' this, then
there ain't no use in me explainin' it to you."

The alien needle came to a gentle halt and hovered above the
desert a few hundred feet from their position. Nearly silent but for
a low hum that they could feel more than hear.

"Good Lord." Taft stumbled back on his heels.

Johnson scooped up his bag, slapped the President on the back
and said, "I reckon that's my ride. Best get to it."

Taft raised a hand, started to say something, but was left with
nothing but Johnson's words fading in the air and the broad back of
the Galveston Giant striding toward an other-worldly flying
machine. The heat haze of the desert swallowed Johnson's
retreating figure, and suddenly, he was gone. The dart slid up
through the air and out of sight.

President Taft considered Johnson's words and the events
leading up to this day. He thought hard about America's history, its
ideals, and its connections to the "peculiar institution" so carefully
tended and nurtured for centuries. He considered his own humble

origins and rise to the Presidency of the United States, his race-based decisions regarding Federal appointments—what was widely dubbed "Taft's Southern Policy"—and the dichotomy of having colored men interviewed for employment at the White House as guards.

From his constricting throat, President William Howard Taft mumbled to the desert, "What hath we wrought?"

One moment, Johnson was standing near the reflective surface of the Martian machine, pondering the bone-rattling hum, and the next he was inside, held in stasis for transport. Compared to Earth travel, the trip was instantaneous. Only a slight shift in his guts told him his body was accelerating beyond comprehension.

Within moments, he was being deposited inside what his senses told him was a vast chamber, but only the center was lit. There were markings on the floor, various circles and squares, some small lights in the distance. At the center was one shape he was all too familiar with: the dimensions of a boxing ring.

From above, an amplified voice said, "Welcome, Mr. Johnson. You are well received."

Johnson looked up but saw nothing. He spoke to the darkness. "How you know my name?"

"We have been monitoring the situation on Earth."

"What now, how we gonna go 'head? We boxin' or wrasslin'? Bare knuckles? What? Don't seem right without no corner man."

"You will be tended to, as needed, by our devices. And you may drop this pretense you've adopted, Mr. Johnson; we are currently unmonitored by Earth."

Johnson could feel a hum through his shoes and he watched as posts and ropes rose from the floor to surround the boxing mat. Now it looked like more of a proper fighting space. He approached the ring and set his bag down outside the nearest corner.

He looked again into the murky surroundings, weighing what he'd learned so far. They knew more than they were letting on, and he was sure there was more going on here than a one-on-one conflict of champions. "I see. So Earth *will* be able to view this contest? How?"

"We will project visual and audio of the event using the control net we have seeded over the Earth. All will be notified of the proceedings."

"Why are you using this...gladiatorial method?"

"Humanity's technological prowess is no match for ours. This is the most direct route to resolve Earth's current path *and* it is one that is well understood by your people. We felt it more beneficial than utter annihilation."

"Well, thank you for that, I suppose. 'Earth's current path.' What are you referencing? Technology, our societies, cultures?"

For the second time in the conversation, there was a notable pause before the response came. "Yes."

"Just, 'yes,' huh? That's it?"

"We believe you are well-suited to understanding the answer."

Johnson snorted and grinned without humor. "Fine. What are the rules we're fighting under? How many rounds?"

"Four. Please prepare yourself, we are projecting now. In preparation, we have grown an appropriate opponent for you. Our physiology is incompatible with yours. It is frail, in comparison; modifications were necessary."

Johnson heard a hissing noise from across the vast space and heavy footsteps. He doffed his robe and extra layers to begin his warm up. As he alternately executed jumping jacks and squats, he kept one eye out for the owner of the slow tread heading his way. At the very edge of the circle of light, a figure came into focus. Tall, broad shouldered, heavy and hairless. When it stepped from the murk into the light, Johnson startled.

What a specimen of inhumanity! Thick muscles covered the long arms and what looked like an extra elbow adorned each appendage. The thing wore boxing gloves at the ends of those deadly limbs. Its hide was mottled with blue and green, but overall, it was mostly reddish in hue. It had a thick eye-ridge and generally humanoid approximation of a face below it. The creature huffed air in long gusts that Johnson could hear across the ring. He wondered what the people back home thought of it all. Then it too began a warm-up routine, eyeing its opponent, aping Johnson's motions in turn.

As he watched, Johnson noted that the arms were indeed double-jointed. It fired off a few piston-like jabs. It was a perfect jabbing machine! It shuffled forward snapping punches in the air, then it turned and did the same in the opposite direction. Something nagged at Johnson's mind, an observation of its technique.

Behind Johnson, a machine rose from the floor and rolled over to him. It appeared like a metallic plant with wheels, multiple branches, countless claws and pokers, tentacles and tools.

"This mechanical attendant will see to your needs."

Johnson huffed and slid on his gloves. Then he held them out to the machine for lace-up. It whirred and clicked, analyzing the problem in front of it. In a blur of motion, it laced the gloves and settled back for further instruction. It was the fastest he'd ever seen the job done.

"When I'm done here, can I have this beautiful piece of engineering?" Johnson's laughter thundered across the empty space. There was no response. "Heh. Thought not." The machine slid over to the ropes and held them open for him. Johnson slipped into the ring.

The electronic voice boomed across the space again. "The third round will begin in ninety seconds." A glowing countdown appeared in the air nearby. As it ticked down, the voice began rattling off the basic rules of boxing. In the background, he could hear the roar of the crowds watching. The Martians had pumped in the sounds of Earth!

Johnson knew the rules by heart and largely ignored the litany as he wondered why they had called the upcoming bout "third round." Had they been testing all along? Which was the first and second? His mind reeled, parsing the logic and purpose of the Martians' visit.

The first round must've been the coded message to Earth, he mused. *Or perhaps it was the selection of the fighter, of me? And the second round? Getting to the meeting site, our conversation a moment ago?*

His thoughts were interrupted when the final ten seconds began to tick off. At the last, an announcement was made that there would be three thirty-minute periods of fighting in this round.

Johnson started to think on his strategy with the brute, how he'd start it off, where he thought the weaknesses were. Instinct took over and the Galveston Giant came out to fight. Johnson began bobbing on his feet and assumed a fighting position, coaxed into warrior-mode by the calls of Earth's viewers.

A bell gonged and the amplified voice calmly said, "Fight."

Johnson stepped to the center of the ring and held out one glove. The thing he was facing ignored the fighter's tradition and shot a jab directly into the champ's face. Johnson's head snapped back and he stumbled. The brute followed, jabbing mercilessly against Johnson's guard. He felt every punch and reeled from the initial blow.

Against the ropes, Johnson took a pummeling to the head and torso. Each blow felt like a sledgehammer wrapped in cotton. He could almost hear the first observation Joe Choynski had made of him in a Galveston, Texas cell: "A man who can move like you should never have to take a punch."

Johnson ducked under the thing's guard and slammed it twice

in the torso. It felt good, to finally hit his opponent. Then he danced away from the Martian's fighter. It was slow in the lateral move. It jabbed and threw a cross well, but it's hook was weak. Thin waist, good forward and backward movement, no uppercut to speak of. They circled each other. Whenever it lunged, Johnson would duck under and wrap the thing up. It's skin was clammy and moist, sinews wiry and strong. The smell of its sweat was tinged with the tang of vinegar. Johnson pinned the inhuman arms back as often as possible.

The champ kept the side-to-side movement going. The thing struggled to keep up. It threw more jabs and a few haymakers, but Johnson dodged causing either a complete miss or only glancing blows. The bell sounded and the creature immediately dropped its guard and walked to its corner where it stood placidly, swaying to an unfelt breeze.

Johnson watched the thing with a keen eye as he backed into his own corner. The machine had slipped a stool in and offered water and a towel. As the mechanized wonder wiped Johnson's gleaming brow, he formed his strategy.

His face started to sting in two places, and he realized the automaton was tending to a couple of gashes the Martian fighter had made. One on his cheek and one at the corner of his eye.

I'm sure that made for some good theater back on Earth, he thought.

The bell sounded and the world heavyweight champion from Earth smiled. It was time. He rose and slammed his fists together. "All right, Mr. Martian, time for your lesson!"

The thing stared at him glassy eyed and huffed, striding at Johnson who moved diagonally at the creature. It struggled to keep up with the champ, eventually stumbling as it tried to stick and move, its long arms unbalancing its odd shape.

Johnson struck then, sparing no power. He slammed the thing's ribs and moved to its head with the same fist. A colossal slap rang out across the space as it stumbled. Johnson didn't let up, bashing his opponent with combinations, always keeping it off-balance and on its heels. The thing's defenses were meaningless to the champ's onslaught.

The beast managed to find its footing and it surged forward. Johnson had been waiting. It jabbed twice and tossed out its haymaker. Johnson slipped the punch and came up with his signature uppercut.

A direct hit on the chin! Its eyes crossed and it stumbled backward. Johnson knew that look, pressed his advantage and sent the big lump to dreamland in a heap.

The bell ending the second period sounded as the Martian-engineered fighter rolled on the mat, dazed until its head settled into the canvas. Red numbers hung in the air, counting down from ten to one. Johnson could hear the people of Earth counting down in unison. The gong sounded three quick notes.

"Ha! Yeah, lesson learned! Tha's right! You don' mess with the world champeen!" Johnson smiled, gold glinting, and called out to the Martians. "It's over now, Earth won fair and square, it's time for you to go home and leave us be!"

"There is the matter of the fourth round, Mr. Johnson."

He'd forgotten, but now recalled pondering it earlier. The fight had taken all of his attention and now he worried at what might come next. Another Martian beast? This one even larger? His mind tripped over the possibility of another fight; this relatively short bout had honestly taken it out of him. Fighting the Martian's brute was like punching a brick wall down. His knuckles would be swollen for days.

"What is it? What now?" he called out.

As if in answer, the ring's posts and ropes sank into the floor.

Johnson walked over to the corner machine and held out his gloves. "Here, untie this." In a flash, the laces were undone as quickly as they'd been tied. He pulled the gloves off and slammed them into his bag before quickly pulling on his robe. "Come on.

Don't keep me waiting. Let's go! What's next?" He stood, chest heaving and sweat drying in the calibrated atmosphere.

"Very well, Mr. Johnson. This will be the fourth and final round."

The amplified voice then rattled off a challenge that stunned Johnson, nearly knocked him out, in fact.

"It would appear that every number greater than two is the sum of three prime numbers. This is asserted such that all positive even integers greater than or equal to four can be expressed as the sum of two primes. Prove this conjecture."

The idea had occurred to him that they'd present a math problem, considering the nature of their first opening message. But for his entire life, Johnson had been valued only as a physical creature, something for entertainment. The people of Earth all interpreted "champion" through an experience that had been fed to them for centuries, never thinking what else one might be a champion of.

Now this…

The disembodied voice echoed again, "Will you require writing implements?"

The Earth held its collective breath as Jack Johnson, heavyweight champion of the world, drew a breath in and said, "I will not."

The worried murmur of the crowds on Earth began building to a crescendo, more and more people hooted and hollered, happy to have been cheering Johnson on when he whipped the Martian fighter, but now crestfallen at his being presented with a mathematics problem.

Johnson could hear the people of his country in a full fit of despair, considering that their lives were now in the hands of a man considered lowly and thoughtless.

"Mr. Johnson, do you require more ti—"

"I find it odd that you would present the Goldbach Conjecture as a proving challenge." Johnson struck a thoughtful pose, milking his calculated interruption before continuing. "It is, of course, unsolvable without imagining number properties that do not exist."

"How so, Mr. Johnson?"

"Proving that conjecture assumes that the number one is a prime number. It has not been proven and I doubt it ever will be, but I am open to what the future may bring."

The smile started as a twitch in his cheeks. His eyes narrowed to slits as the corners of his mouth turned up. His full lips curved back farther until Jack Johnson's golden smile was on full display for the entire world to see.

CALL TO ACTION

Thank you for reading <u>The Final Summons</u>. If you enjoyed this work of speculative fiction, we would greatly appreciate a review at the retailer of your choice.

Please sign up for our **Newsletter** for our future releases.

ABOUT THE ORGANIZATION

The New England Speculative Writers is a local consortium of writers that focuses on supporting local authors through networking, education, and personal interaction in the New England Region.

NESW supports local Science Fiction & Fantasy authors in self publishing, hybrid publishing and traditional publishing. Agents, publishers and illustrators are also welcome to join.

facebook.com/NewEnglandSpeculativeWriters
twitter.com/NESpecWriters

BIBLIOGRAPHIES

About the Curators

C. H. Duryea is a writer and educator living in the greater Boston area and a founding member of New England Speculative Writers. He has published several short stories over the years, and recently released his debut novel, The Heisenberg Corollary. He is currently at work on Shadow of Bionon, a dieselpunk-infused second-world fantasy.

C. L. Alden is co-founder of the New England Speculative Writers group, and author of The Empire, an urban fantasy, with dashes of mystery and paranormal, set on the coast of Maine. She's currently working on book two as well as a follow up novella.

She's a creative spirit who, when not writing, enjoys other creative outlets such as photography and cooking. A general dabbler in this and that, and a seeker of adventure and tall tales.

You can follow her latest capers at www.facebook.com/clalden

Jeremy Flagg is the author of the CHILDREN OF NOSTRADAMUS dystopian science fiction series and SUBURBAN ZOMBIE HIGH young adult humor/horror series. Taking his love of pop culture and comic books, he focuses on fast paced, action packed novels with complex characters and contemporary themes. Jeremy is the Co-Founder of New England Speculative Writers and member of the Metrowest Writers writing group.

For more information about Jeremy, visit www.remyflagg.com.

About the Cover Artist

In stark contrast to his life as a performance engineer, **Marty Kulma** spends his evenings and weekends exploring the visual. A proponent of open source software, he supports and uses Krita to create his works. Although he works in a digital medium, his methods are extensions of traditional drawing and painting techniques. His art education is ever evolving, trekking across the internet, through museums, and out into nature. Marty's work primarily focuses on the human portrait, expression, and the figure.

About the Editor

Trisha J. Wooldridge writes short stories, novellas, novels, articles, and poetry about bad-ass faeries, carnivorous horses, social justice witches, vengeful spirits—and mundane stuff like food, hay-eating horses, social justice debates, writer advice, and alcoholic spirits. Her recent work includes stories and poems in *Gothic Fantasy Supernatural Horror*, *Dark Luminous Wings*, *Wicked*

Haunted, Darkling's Beasts and Brews, Jack of No Trades Volume 5, and the HWA Poetry Showcase Volume 5. She's a freelance editor of over fifty novels and three anthologies. As child-friendly T.J. Wooldridge, she's published poetry and three spooky children's novels. She spends rare moments of mystical "free time" with a very patient Husband-of-Awesome, a calico horse, and a bratty tabby cat. Join her adventures at www.anovelfriend.com.

About the Authors

Michael C. Bailey is a former reporter, blogger, and editor who left the news industry to focus on his creative writing. He is the author of the *Action Figures* young adult superhero series, the humorous fantasy series *The Adventures of Strongarm & Lightfoot*, and the urban fantasy trilogy *Well-Behaved Women*. Michael is also the fight director for the Connecticut Renaissance Faire, and has written scripts for Underdog Comics, a Boston-based comic book company that focuses on content for diverse audiences. Find him online at innsmouthlook.com.

Adam Breckenridge has published a dozen short stories in a range of speculative journals and anthologies in addition to a healthy smattering of essays, reviews and academic scholarship. After making his home in Rhode Island for the past few years he has recently moved on to more global travels, taking a job with the University of Maryland University College as one of their Collegiate Traveling Faculty members, going around the world teaching American soldiers stationed overseas. He is currently based in Tokyo.

D. A. D'Amico is an enigma wrapped in confusion and stuffed head-first into a fish-flavored paper bag. His writing style is Jackson Pollock meets Scanners, a surreal exploding-head mess of genres and styles where almost anything is likely. He's had more than sixty works published in the last few years in venues such as Daily Science Fiction, Crossed Genres, and Shock Totem... among others. He's a winner of L. Ron Hubbard's prestigious Writers of the Future award, volume XXVII, as well as the 2017 Write Well award. His website is: http://www.dadamico.com. Facebook: author-dadamico, and on painfully rare occasions twitter: @dadamico.

Peter N. Dudar has been writing and publishing fiction for nearly two decades. An alumnus of the University at Albany, Peter now resides in Lisbon Falls, Maine, where he continues to pursue his writing career. His latest book, *THE GOAT PARADE*, is available in eBook and trade paperback. You can find him at www.PeterNDudar.com or visit him on Facebook and Twitter.

By day **Scott Goudsward** is a slave to the cubicle world, by night to the voices in his head. He writes primarily horror but has branched out to sci-fi and fantasy. Scott is one of the coordinators of the New England Horror Writers. His short fiction has most recently appeared in Return of the Old Ones, Atomic Age Cthulhu, and Arkham Detective Agency. His latest novel Fountain of the Dead is out from Post Mortem Press as is the new co-edited non-fiction book Horror Guide to Northern New England. Anthology projects include the new book Wicked Haunted from the New England

Horror Writers and the award winning Twice Upon An Apocalypse released 2017 from Crystal Lake Publishing. Scott is currently working on a YA novel and looking at homes for new anthology possibilities.

Emma Lowry attends Worcester Polytechnic Institute as a student of Interactive Media and Game Development. She grew up in Framingham, Massachusetts, spending her free time writing, drawing, and looking for a way to incorporate both into a career. *Old Worlders* is her first published written work. She can be found on Twitter @lowryyrwol

---

Rachel Menard earned her degree in marketing from ASU, during which time her work was featured in the university paper and her own, self-published punk zine, *Chelsea*. She was also a college radio DJ. She currently works for a seasonal design company, creating whimsical copy for Christmas ornaments, and she hosts the Rhode Island Meet & Greets for the NESCBWI. In her free time, Rachel writes strange and fantastical stories for teens. For more of her writings and ramblings, visit www.rachelmenard.com.

Born and raised in Boston, Massachusetts, **Errick Nunnally** served one tour in the Marine Corps before deciding art school was a safer pursuit. He enjoys art, comics, and genre novels. A designer by day, he earned a black belt in Krav Maga and Muay Thai kickboxing by night. His work has appeared in several anthologies and is probably best described as "dark pulp." It can be found in *Lamplight,*

Wicked Witches, The Final Summons, Protectors 2, the novel, *Blood For The Sun*, and the upcoming novel, *Lightning Wears A Red Cape* from ChiZine Publications. http://www.erricknunnally.us

---

Dave Pasquantonio is a board member at The Writers' Loft, a not-for-profit writing community in Sherborn, Mass., and a member of Grub Street and the Mystery Writers of America. A former instructional designer, technical writer, and corporate training manager, Dave is now a stay-at-home dad, a freelance writer, and a newspaper stringer. He misses office life, but listens to way more classic rock than he could in a cubicle. He writes fiction for adults and children, and he daydreams about noir films and baseball. He lives in Millis, Mass. with his wife and three kids. His website is at davepasquantonio.com.

Chris Philbrook is an Amazon best-selling author of Horror, Science Fiction, and urban fantasy novels. He has a young adult novel published under the pen name W.J. Orion as well. He resides in rural New Hampshire with his crazy dog, two amazing young daughters, and his amazing wife. One day, he hopes to sleep a full night, and wake up rested. Until then, he writes.

Suzanne Reynolds-Alpert writes science fiction, horror, dark fantasy, and the occasional poem. Her short fiction had been published in the anthologies *Killing It Softly, The Deep Dark Woods, and Luna Station Quarterly*. Her poetry has appeared in places such as the anthology *Wicked Witches*, Tales of the Zombie War, Strong

Verse, *The Wayfarer: A Journal of Contemplative Literature* and Eternal Haunted Summer. Her first chapbook of poetry, *Interview with the Faerie (Part One) and Other Poems of Darkness and Light* was published in 2013. Suzanne is a freelance editor, holds down a job in marketing, and is currently writing a novel and several short stories in between meeting the incessant demands of her feline overlords.

E.J. Stevens is the bestselling, award-winning author of the Ivy Granger Psychic Detective urban fantasy series, the Spirit Guide young adult series, the Hunters' Guild urban fantasy series, and the upcoming Whitechapel Paranormal Society Victorian Gothic horror series. She is known for filling pages with quirky characters, blood-sucking vampires, psychotic faeries, and snarky, kick-butt heroines. Her novels are available worldwide in multiple languages.

Connect with E.J. on Twitter @EJStevensAuthor. For more, including a list of her books, freebies, and upcoming events visitwww.EJStevensAuthor.com.

Morgan Sylvia is an Aquarius, a metalhead, a coffee addict, and a work in progress. A former obituarist, she is now a full-time free-lance writer. Her work has appeared in several anthologies, including Wicked Witches, Wicked Haunted, Northern Frights, Twice Upon An Apocalypse, Endless Apocalypse, and Haunted Houses. Her first horror novel, Abode, was released in 2017. She recently released another novel, Dawn, which is the first book of a fantasy trilogy. She is also the author of Whispers From The Apocalypse, a horror poetry collection, and As The Seas Turn Red, an ocean poetry collection. She lives in Maine, and actually enjoys the snow. Usually.

Steve Van Samson is the author of the vampires in Africa series "Predator World" which include the novels "The Bone Eater King" & "Marrow Dust". His writing tends to be on the pulpy side—intermingling genres like horror, dystopian with dark fantasy and adventure. An avid proponent of diversity in fiction, he believes character is king & that cliché should be avoided like the plague.When not tapping the keys on his Chromebook, he writes and records classic heavy metal, appears on as many podcasts as possible and watches entirely too many black and white monster films. Steve lives in Lancaster, Massachusetts with three amazing girls and one smallish dragon.

Made in United States
North Haven, CT
18 September 2022

24273991R00178